THE MAGIC IN THE RECEIVER

PAUL DILLON

MARK WILLIAMS INTERNATIONAL

DIGITAL PUBLISHING

ISBN: 978-1-908961-38-9

Published by Mark Williams international Digital Publishing.
http://www..mwidp.com

The Magic
in the Receiver

Paul Dillon

Dedicated to Dionysis Synodinos-Vallianos

—Fourteen years old at the time of the Kefalonian Earthquake

A man's work is nothing but this slow trek to discover, through the detours of his art, those two or three great and simple images in whose presence his heart first opened.

—Albert Camus

1

THE ISLAND OF KEFALONIA, WESTERN GREECE

He sat on a wooden bench, eyes closed, in the shade of an olive grove. I didn't know his name so thought of him simply as old man. Thyme scented the air, which remained strangely fresh, at odds with the suffocating mid-day sun. Intense though the heat was, it couldn't eclipse the sound cascading inside the canopy.

Singing ... I had no better description; the trees were singing ... their song familiar, a song of joy.

Puzzled by the sound's origin, I looked up, thinking perhaps birds, but saw none.

"Sit," said the old man. "Close your eyes and listen."

I sat beside him. After I got used to the rhythm and harmonics, he spoke again. His voice was soothing, musical, so very easy on the ear.

"They're cicadas," he said.

I had asked nothing.

Although I heard him clearly, I never stopped focusing on the sound.

"The males are calling the females," he continued. "Concentrate on the frequencies and step back in time, a time without birds, without animals, a time where nothing moves amongst silent trees and grasses. Eons pass, life finds movement and, with it, sound; a sound so primal that you still feel its music deep within you."

The old man's voice faded away but I continued to listen becoming ever more absorbed until the sound became a fountain, life's fountain, gushing up like a spring. For a moment, all nature's secrets were revealed, but even as the epiphany dawned so it dispersed. I retraced my thoughts, desperate to hold on to the exquisite knowledge but the harder I tried the faster it evaporated…

***

Ben's eyes opened to the whisper of intangible loss. Thin curtains drawn across the veranda took the sting out of the light. The heat ignored their feeble barricade. He stared at a fold in the drapes, where the sun's rays alternated shadow and brilliant fire through the louver doors. Focusing on the intense bands of sunlight kept him clinging to a trance-like state. Outside, cicadas called from the cypress trees; their chants forming the melody of some hypnotic August song.

He would not stir just yet. It would require an effort of will to release his gaze from the incandescent stripes. Eventually, his eyes withdrew, scanning the room for any object that might trigger a memory. A second bed, its green cover a flat and featureless meadow, stretched towards him. Only a bedside table held meaning; on it stood a bottle of water, a book, his mobile phone.

With scant regard for harmony, the clamor of squabbling crows drifted in from the garden.

Were they fighting or playing?

The question began Ben's ascent to consciousness and he raised his head to absorb the rest of the unfamiliar room.

A wardrobe with two narrow white doors stood next to a mirrored table, its glass top supported on a gunmetal frame. Nearby, a pair of jeans draped over an unopened suitcase.

Ben considered reaching for the water bottle; the first sip would formally awaken him. Resisting the urge to drink, his head rolled back on the pillow and he stared up at the ceiling, contented and serene. This disposition, almost numbing, had become his normal waking state for several years; he could not remember how long. He attributed this condition to his lack of purpose. This morning, as most others, there was no particular reason to hurry. He groped for his phone, checking the time; 10:05 meant little. Slowly, his brain activity reached critical mass; as the water wet his lips, Ben Anderson was loaded into consciousness.

Flip-flopped feet slapped the tiles outside his door, echoing along the corridor. Children shouted, their excited voices reminding him this was a hotel in the height of the Mediterranean summer. Ben rose, taking another gulp of water.

Drawing back the curtains, he opened the louver doors and stepped out. Clay tiles, warmed by the sun, felt comforting under his feet. The veranda overlooked a garden bordered by tall cypresses. Beyond the flame-shaped trees, hills of pine rose to meet a pristine sky. The garden would be a cool, pleasant place in the afternoon, once the sun disappeared behind the ridge.

He relaxed in a rattan chair, one of two, about a round white table and rolled the bottle back and forth, watching the sunlight reflect off the water. Something was more tangible this morning; he could not say exactly what: trees, insects, life, flowers, hills, himself, sun, sky, birds…

Two crows cawed and swooped down from the trees, bouncing as they landed on the smooth green lawn. He watched as they walked, like little people, past the sundial and under the cypresses. Nobody was in the garden to disturb them.

2

ARGOSTOLI, KEFALONIA
WEDNESDAY, AUGUST 12th, 1953

Nine-year-old Ioannis Katros sat on stone steps at the back of his grandmother's house looking out at a dry dusty garden. School had closed for the summer, a summer of unprecedented seismic activity. The sun crept towards its zenith in a cloudless sky, yet an ominous shadow threatened Ioannis's spirit. He wasn't alone with his fear; the whole of Argostoli was on edge. In rich and poor areas alike, neighbors talked, rumors spread, everywhere superstition held sway. Disaster, they said, lay right around the corner. Perhaps the doomsayers were right; the tremors were more frequent, more powerful this past week.

Ioannis's thoughts went back to yesterday, to an hour before dawn. The first earthquake brought down a section of ceiling in the bedroom he shared with his brother. The damage forced the family to move the boys to their grandmother's house. A second tremor, hours later, saw Ioannis running through the town, alone, searching for his brother, praying for his safety. Ioannis got his wish. There in the yard, Stamos played, without a care in the world.

10

The garden was small, unkempt, and enclosed by high walls. A lone pear tree rose above the weeds, its branches swept the rusty iron roof of an old stone outbuilding. Covered in vines, the ruin housed an ancient olive press, unused since the death of its owner a decade earlier. Now, only pigeons roosted there, flying in through a sun-bleached window, its paint and glass a faded memory. Under the window, fallen leaves and dead insects floated in a large wooden barrel, three-quarters full with winter rain.

Stamos played an improvised game. Placing sticks in the barrel, he climbed into the overhanging branches of the pear tree.

"Yanni, come and play," he called.

Ioannis didn't answer. From his perch on the steps, he watched his older brother throw stones in the water, causing the make-believe boats to lurch violently in the waves.

The garden was hot, oppressive, and filled with the sound of insects. Ioannis was on edge, too disturbed for play. He got up, walked over to the barrel and peered down at the floating decay. With a sense of disgust, he went back indoors.

It was cooler inside; Ioannis's gaze fell on his grandmother, hand-washing clothes in the old stone sink. A wooden cross protruded from the front pocket of her apron. The symbol reminded Ioannis of the upcoming festival in honor of the island's patron saint, Gerasimos.

Earlier this morning, the two boys had prayed with their grandmother at the small altar dedicated to the saint. Alarmed by recent events, the old woman called on Gerasimos for protection, lighting candles under his image. The boy could see the shrine now, in a darkened recess, across the room. A whiff of breeze caught the flames, casting shadows on the icon's ancient, gilded frame, upon the bearded figure in a hooded gown, his white scroll unfurled, a golden halo behind his head...

***

The old lady was wringing water from a heavy cotton dress when the earthquake struck, destroying the town of Argostoli. It was 11:24am.

Silence, infused with menace, descended like a fog, clinging to the last remnants of order. Then came the thunder; an ear-splitting crack, the sound of an entire island being lifted higher. Shock waves of unimaginable power hammered into the house. Ioannis's feet left the ground, a deafening roar blanked out his senses as he flew through the air. For a whole minute, the ground rampaged out of control, as if some mythological demon had but sixty seconds to shake every last person off the world. Tossed around like a plaything, Ioannis shielded his head with his arms and prayed.

The shaking stopped; the roar gave way to distant shouts, cries, and the sound of snapping timber. The rear of the house was a pile of debris. Grey sunlight, diffused with dust, rained down on Ioannis as he lay dazed on the rubble-strewn floor. There was pain in his leg, he couldn't move. He peered into the dust, straining his eyes until they hurt. Slowly, the impenetrable grey mist deepened, transforming into the dark, brackish water of the outhouse barrel. A drowning insect crawled onto a leaf to dry out in the sun. Ioannis passed out.

When he came to, the dust had settled revealing a new, disturbing world. Chunks of masonry covered the floor. He tried moving but could not. The sharp pain in his leg gave way to a numb throbbing that chilled him to the bone. Ioannis cried out for his mother.

His cries turned to whimpers, he lay paralyzed, choking with fear that he might never walk again. To Ioannis, paralysis was a horror beyond imagination. He lay still on the ground, listening to his own sobs, waiting for the mercy of sleep.

Drifting in and out of consciousness, time ceased to exist. When next he woke, the most intense pins and needles, hot and icy, stabbed and stung at his leg. He took heart, nothing pinned him down. Summoning his remaining strength, he turned away from the garden, where his eyes fell upon the Saint. The icon lay on the ground, at an angle, propped up against the broken altar. Ioannis prayed, as he had prayed yesterday, begging the saint that he might walk again. With the image of Saint Gerasimos seared into his brain, Ioannis passed out once more.

3

The monastery stood in the center of the island, on a wide plain surrounded by mountains. The road down was winding and steep; trees, mostly olive and pine, dotted the slopes. As the car snaked downward, the white buildings floated in and out of sight on the far side of the valley.

Elena sat in the back of the rental car, idly watching the scenery drift by. Her father, the driver, complained at the lack of power, as the vehicle struggled to haul its four occupants high into the mountains.

The journey's a pilgrimage for him, she reminded herself.

"I'm so glad you decided to stay. I thought you'd be dying to get back to Boston."

Elena turned away from the window and looked kindly at her cousin. Sophia was twenty-four, three years her junior. She spoke fluent English with barely a trace of her native accent. Last night, over dinner, she'd convinced Elena to extend her stay on the island.

Sophia lived with her grandparents, who owned a large villa in Argostoli, the island's capital. Elena had fallen under the spell of the house; her guest bedroom overlooked the family's olive orchard, which stretched down to the sea. She imagined a time, in her distant future, wanting nothing more than living in such a house, on such an island as this.

"Boston, you're kidding," said Elena. "Life's so much more relaxed here. I'm going to wake up every morning, open the curtains, look out over the olive grove and think I'm in heaven." She paused, "I'm still not sure what I'll do all day with you working and all."

"I told you, don't worry," said Sophia. "I can juggle my hours around for a week or two."

Pretty, with large brown eyes, Sophia worked at her grandfather's gallery in Argostoli. She had returned to the island only recently, having studied ceramics and art history at the University of Seattle. The studio, specializing in pottery, also exhibited the work of local painters.

Silence ensued; the car continued its winding descent. Elena's mother sat in the front passenger seat turning round repeatedly.

"Have you spotted the others yet? I hope your brother didn't get held up with the kids."

Elena ignored her question.

"They'll be right behind us." Her father spoke to no one in particular.

Close to the valley bottom, the first houses of a small community appeared. Less than a mile in length, the village was narrow, its buildings plain and modern. A few cafes and tavernas, crowded with tourists, stood out from an otherwise forgettable main street.

A group of restaurants, huddled together, marked the end of the township. Here, the road leveled out, the houses giving way to a wide avenue, bordered on either side, by hundreds of plane trees. Half a mile long, the majestic boulevard opened into a circular plaza at its mid-point, forming a stately approach to the monastery of Saint Gerasimos.

Cars, parked bumper to bumper, lined both sides of the avenue. Elena looked past them to a field littered with trucks and caravans

"What's going on over there?" she asked.

"It's a gypsy camp. They come every year for the festival." Sophia pointed over by the church. "See there? They've setup a mini-bazaar."

Tourists and locals thronged the area, spilling out into the street, forcing the car to inch its way along the last fifty yards. Elena lowered her window and leaned out. Heat rushed in, carrying with it the noise of the crowd. The air bristled with expectation. She looked up, straining to see the red-tiled dome that towered over the main roof of the church.

Sitting atop a series of wide stone steps, the massive white building obscured the older monastery compound. Elena thought it odd, how such an imposing structure could be built in the middle of nowhere.

Police, in navy polo shirts and baseball caps, marshaled the crowd behind temporary barriers, keeping the route of the procession clear. Above the steps, festival colors jostled for attention, banners and flags lined the promenade, where bandsmen waited in vivid tunics.

The car turned right at the crossroads, past the complex and into a dirt lot. As the vehicle drew to a halt, Elena laid a hand on her father's shoulder. He turned his head towards her, trying in vain to mask the unease in his heart.

Elena offered a reassuring smile. She understood what this day meant to him.

4

Elena sat at a large oak table under the shade of a cluster of pines. A clear blue sky promised another glorious Mediterranean day. From the east, over the Ainos Mountains, the sun filtered through the treetops casting patterns of light on the table. To the west, an olive orchard sloped down towards the glistening bay of Argostoli.

Across the table sat cousin Sophia, already dressed for work.

"How long do we have?" asked Elena.

"We should leave in about thirty minutes." Sophia refilled her glass with freshly squeezed orange juice, lifting the pitcher higher and higher as she poured.

Distracted by the noise of cicadas, Elena looked up into the veil of a blue-green archipelago and listened to their calls echo in the branches.

Aunt Nicia's voice, calling from the courtyard brought her attention back to the table.

"More coffee?"

"No, thanks," Elena replied. "Come and sit with us."

She couldn't get used to thinking of her aunt as Sophia's

grandmother. Nicia was standing between blue iron gates, under an archway at the rear of the house. On either side, two olean-der trees with silver bark stood ten feet high; their leaves bayonet shaped and covered with large red flowers.

"Don't move. I want to take a picture," called Elena.

Nicia stood, smiling.

"Okay, you can move now."

As Nicia walked towards the table, Elena stared at her aunt's image on the display. She flipped back through the recent photos; Nicia was in the last four shots.

"I'm jealous. You're in every picture I take, and you always look so happy. This one of you and Andreas is my favorite." She passed Nicia the camera.

"Was this yesterday? I don't remember you taking it. My memory isn't what is used to be."

Yesterday, here under the pines, Elena had spent a pleasant hour, listening to Nicia and Andreas reminisce about their life to-gether. It was a story she knew well but sharing it with them, by their peaceful orchard, had moved her almost to tears. Nicia was becoming an influence; that much was clear.

"Aren't you going to sit?" asked Elena.

"I was just thinking how lovely you two look together. It's nice to have you here." Nicia's simple and humble dignity echoed in her voice.

"Please, let me clear away the dishes," said Elena, deflecting the compliment.

The years had been kind to Nicia. Her hair, cut short, framed a face that could have belonged to a woman ten years younger. Thin, gold-rimmed glasses gave her a tender, distinguished look. Despite the early morning heat, she wore a cardigan over her scoop-necked summer dress.

Nicia sat. "I'm glad your father got home safely. How was the flight?"

"They had a delay in London—nothing major. He said he's missing you already," replied Elena.

"He said that?"

"Of course."

Sometimes it was hard to imagine that her father was Nicia's younger brother. Elena had always thought of her father as American and Nicia as Greek. Both were evacuated to the States after the earthquake but Nicia had returned a decade and a half later, married to Andreas, her childhood friend. Elena had many fond memories of Nicia; she'd been a regular visitor to their house in Boston.

"I can't believe it's been four days since the festival," said Sophia.

Before getting up, Sophia knocked back a last gulp of strong Greek coffee and grabbed her jacket from an adjacent chair. Even at this hour, the temperature had soared to eighty degrees. She draped the garment over her shoulder, letting Elena know it was time to go then walked off to the house.

Pushing back her seat, Elena paused before rising, giving her aunt an opportunity to speak. Nicia said nothing.

"Well, I should be going then. Are you sure you're okay with the dishes?"

"Don't worry. Go and enjoy yourself, you'll love Fiskardo, it is so beautiful."

Elena rose, put on a pair of sunglasses then helped Nicia to her feet. They walked back towards the house.

The magical courtyard, separating the villa from the olive grove, captivated Elena. Passing through the iron gates, she paused to admire the garden.

Bounded by the dwelling and three high walls, the area was a square of approximately sixty feet. The sidewalls, mostly overgrown with climbing plants, reduced in height via a series of curves until they met the rear boundary wall. Doors and windows bordered in white, with shutters and frames of a deep and glorious blue balanced the pastel shade of the pink house.

Elena's eyes darted around the scene, absorbing the colors; the ornaments, the flowers. Wall fountains, vines, vases, palms, geraniums … color abounded. Scarlet, flowering bougainvillea hung in baskets, climbing everywhere over the walls. Even the floor had luster. Earthenware pots, a hundred or more, both plain and decorated, big and small, sat on a deep patina of reddish-brown terracotta. Four diamond areas, each planted with flowering azaleas gave the space symmetry. In the center of the square, amid the riot of color, a wooden pergola held pride of place. Wisteria and vines grew up its stanchions, sprawling over the roof, providing shade to an enormous weather-beaten table.

Looking up at the house, Elena recognized her bedroom, from whose balcony she had sat reading in the early light of dawn. A swallow's nest clung to the eaves above the veranda doors.

"I've been hoping to see the swallows each morning. I haven't seen any," said Elena. "Did they leave?"

"Yes," replied Nicia. "About a week before you came. They arrive one moment and are gone the next. The older I get, the shorter they seem to stay."

The beauty of the courtyard touched Elena, prompting a question.

"You must be very happy here. Do you ever regret leaving America?"

"Not really. This is where I belong; this is my land, my people, my culture. Even though I left the island as a young girl, its memory stayed with me. How about you, could you be happy here?"

"Well, I'm going to say yes, standing in this courtyard but, really, Boston's my home—maybe when I'm older."

Sophia reappeared at the back door, clutching a portfolio case. She looked chic in a black suit with pencil skirt, hemmed just above the knee. "Come on, we've got to go," she said.

"Coming; let me get a bag from the room, I'll see you at the front." Elena hugged Nicia then followed Sophia into the house.

The car was running as she hurried through the front door. A leather bag hung from her right shoulder. Sliding into the BMW coupe brought little relief from the heat. The air conditioning was on full, the car had been in the shade, but the leather still felt warm against her legs. Sophia pushed a CD into the player. Reggae, thought Elena, turning up the volume. It's going to be a good day.

"So, who are these artists we're visiting?" asked Elena.

"Ah … Pasquali and Dimi," replied Sophia. "Like I said earlier, Pasquali's a recluse, I won't be able to take you to his studio, so I'll drop you off in Fiskardo after we see Dimi. You'll love it there. You should have an hour or two to look around before I pick you up."

The car made its way through the outskirts of Argostoli, heading towards the southeastern edge of the lagoon. Elena tried to imagine the strange artist, Pasquali, in his studio. It's an octagonal room at the top of a house. The walls and roof all glass. Strong light streams in from every angle, bouncing off the wooden floor; a moveable canopy provides shade. Pasquali wears a battered old fedora tilted at an angle, his beard reaches down to his white vest, stained with sweat. Looking more like a seedy criminal than artist, Pasquali paints his model. She's naked, plump with auburn hair, and chained to a wooden post. A fierce black dog looks menacingly on.

Elena stopped daydreaming. "Are you sure you're going to be okay on your own with Pasquali?"

"Yes, I told you, I'll be fine. Grandfather's known him for years and I've been there several times before. Besides, his wife's always in the house. Don't worry about me."

If anyone can take care of herself, it's Sophia, thought Elena.

Argostoli looked picturesque across the lagoon. The old stone Drapano Bridge, now closed to traffic, shone white in the sun. Elena had seen the town from this side of the lagoon four days earlier. That day, she'd been at the cemetery with her father.

Clinging to the curves of the corniche, the BMW climbed higher into the mountains.

"It's a magnificent drive to Fiskardo," said Sophia. "Cliff edge all the way."

Elena looked down at the turquoise sea far below. "You don't say."

"It's great if you're a passenger but mile after mile of hairpin bends tires me out. I'm glad I'm not driving alone."

"It's good to know I'm earning my keep."

"There are a couple of famous lookout points along the way. We'll stop and take some pictures. You brought your camera, right?" Sophia continued without waiting for a reply. "Oh yeah, when we get back, we're going to dinner with Nik, he promised to bring a friend along."

"Hmmm, I hope he's not expecting a blind date."

"Why? Worried your boyfriend will find out?" asked Sophia.

"Yeah, right … fine, I don't care, so bring him."

The conversation forced Elena to think about Greg, back home in Boston. There'd been a confrontation when she revealed her intention to stay on in Kefalonia. Confiding in Greg had been a mistake. If only she hadn't told him that Nicia would let her stay indefinitely, that Sophia had offered to help her find work that she enjoyed connecting to her cultural roots. He had taken everything the wrong way. Greg was serious about their relationship; she did not doubt he intended to marry her. Deep in her heart, Elena was still undecided.

Just as Sophia promised, the coast road was spectacular. On the driver's side, the crystal waters of the bay sparkled in the sunshine, hundreds of feet below. Across the channel, the mountainous Pali peninsula dissected sea and sky. Elena gazed out of the passenger window at the rugged hills; they seemed to tolerate nothing but scrub and pines. Every few miles, a stone ruin or abandoned farmhouse embellished the desolate beauty; each immortalizing some sorrowful tale.

Once more, her thoughts drifted back to Greg. She checked herself, vowing not to think of him again today, and started a new topic of conversation.

"I really love Nicia, she's so contented. It's a great story, how Andreas came to find her in America and how she waited for him. I wish I had that kind of conviction."

"Nothing so romantic is going to happen to us, that's for sure," said Sophia.

"After breakfast yesterday, the three of us sat talking about the earthquake and the evacuation. Listening to Nicia and Andreas tell their story, really affected me. It made me focus on the importance of family."

"I wish my mom would move back from Athens, but that's not going to happen. Grandma misses her."

"How is she? I don't think I've seen her in ten years."

"Still reporting, dreaming of becoming a famous writer. Every year she's going to take a break, come home and work on the masterpiece but it never happens. You're in a similar business though."

"If I haven't lost my job, but writing advertising copy isn't journalism. Mind you, if I stayed here long enough, even I'd get the inspiration to write that great novel. Lately, I've been thinking about a career change, photography maybe."

"Well you'll get plenty of practice today."

Bathed in light of an unworldly clarity, the dramatic Ionian view had a therapeutic effect on Elena. She watched Sophia take a drink of water. Her cousin looked tired; navigating the twisting, precipitous road required concentration.

Within half a mile, they reached the first stopping-off point. Sophia pulled the car over at a rest area overlooking the cliffs and opened her door. "Come on, bring your camera."

Mid-morning heat rushed into the car, engulfing Elena, calling into question the logic of going outside. Too late, Sophia was out, striding over to a low stone wall, overlooking the sea. Elena reached for her camera and followed.

"Myrtos Beach," said Sophia. "One of the most beautiful in Europe."

Elena looked down at the small curved bay far below. "Is that sand? It looks more like snow."

People, smaller than ants, lay on a mile-long strip of brilliant white. Kaleidoscopic shades of blue, green, and turquoise tinged the translucent waters of the crescent bay.

"I want to go down there ... right now," said Elena, clicking the camera shutter.

"Well, not today. Maybe you can get Nik's friend to take you tomorrow."

"Maybe," Elena smiled.

"It's not sand." Sophia answered the earlier question. "If you ever go down there, you'll be standing on small white pebbles. That's why the water has that gorgeous color ... Hey; let's ask these people to take our picture."

She approached a family of tourists, handing Elena's camera to an obliging teenaged boy. The girls sat on the wall with the white beach far below. Sophia put her arms round Elena's shoulder.

The boy handed the camera back to Sophia who passed it to Elena.

"What do you think?" asked Sophia.

"Two smoking-hot babes overlooking so-so beach," replied Elena, as she checked the image on the small display. "Let's go, before I convince myself to bring Nik's friend tomorrow."

They returned to the car in high spirits.

Sophia made another stop, at an overlook of the ruined castle at Assos. This time, she stayed in the car while Elena took pictures.

"It was built by the Venetians in the sixteenth century," Sophia called out.

Elena wondered what the castle had defended. From her vantage point, she could not see the village of Assos, nestled in a tiny cove far below. She took a single picture of the fort atop its rocky promontory and got back in the car.

"It's about ten more miles to Dimi's studio," said Sophia as they left the horseshoe-shaped lookout.

On the outskirts of Fiskardo, Elena became drowsy, hardly noticing the increased signs of habitation. Sophia braked sharply, turning off the main highway onto a narrow road heading into the hills.

At a bend in the lane, Sophia slowed the car to a crawl, opposite a group of pines. She turned right, through a gap in a rough-hewn stone wall, into a private driveway. Rising straight, for two hundred yards, the track cut through a small copse of cypress and pine trees. Elena lowered the window to smell the pines; the air was alive with the shrill sound of insects, singing in the summer heat.

The car drew to a halt where the drive dead-ended in a turning circle. Elena looked around for Dimi's villa. A tall limestone wall obscured the house; tree branches drooped over from within.

"This is it." Sophia got out, slipped on her jacket and reached for the portfolio case.

Elena followed her towards an archway, flanked on either side by large terracotta urns. From the pots, dwarf trees grew, like sentinels; their foliage trimmed into toadstool shapes. Daisies blossomed around the base of their slender, stick-like trunks. Inside the entranceway, wrought iron gates were fixed back in an open position and entwined with flowering red vines.

Elena looked up at a series of steps, cut from a pink-hued stone. Retaining walls of limestone followed the steps upwards.

To her left, cypress trees towered above the parapet. On the right, a terraced garden sloped up to the villa. From the entranceway, the steep incline concealed all but the clay tiles of the house roof. Terracotta vases, planted with flowering shrubs stood on each alternate stair. Elena stepped back a few paces to photograph the entryway. Sophia climbed on; now halfway to the top.

The two-storey house revealed its wonderful colors gradually. As Elena climbed, red roof gave way to pale cream stucco and deep purple windows with decorative wooden shutters. She followed her cousin along the side of the building. Large vases of trees and vines spilled their foliage and flowers against the wall.

Elena paused, fascinated by a strange doorway. Without calling to Sophia, she fiddled in her bag for the camera. As if an illusion, what appeared to be one door was, in fact, two, their combined width no more than three feet. Each was almost too narrow to be of practical use. She adjusted the lens, zooming in and out to best frame the shot.

It was the act of focusing that first attracted her to the texture, and complex color of the wood. She puzzled why the word 'purple' was now so inadequate. The old timber had a distressed patina that Elena sought to describe … in some areas, the paint is the color of grapes, in others, that of the dust that sometimes clouds their skins. Four small panes of glass, obscured by white lace curtains, were set in the top half of each door; the bottom had deep, raised panels. Dried flowers, oranges and browns, hung in bouquets, from each center-transom.

As Elena pressed the camera shutter for the third time, she became, momentarily, an artist behind her easel contemplating her painting. In this manner, she became aware of the dark, diagonal shadow that angled down across the wall and over the bottom of the doorway.

"What are you doing?"

Elena was startled out of her reverie by Sophia, who was

standing next to an olive-skinned, ruggedly handsome man in his fifties.

"Dimi, this is Elena, my cousin, from America. Elena, this is Dimi."

Deftly, but firmly, Dimi raised Elena's hand to his lips, kissing the back, throwing her off guard.

"Please to meet you Dimi," she said. "I was just admiring your door. Umm, have you ever painted it?"

Dimi did not answer her question. He pulled on a cigarette, the smoke wrapped around his tousled, dark-grey locks, refusing to disappear in the still and breathless air.

"I'm enchanted to meet you, Elena," said Dimi, letting go of her hand. He gazed straight into her eyes. "Your cousin is very beautiful, Sophia. Perhaps she is an artist also."

Neither girl answered.

"Shall we go inside?" asked Sophia. Without waiting for a reply, she walked off; Dimi followed. Elena had a moment to notice Dimi's broad back and powerful legs before he turned around to walk beside her.

"No I haven't painted the door. Perhaps you think it would make a nice composition."

He paused for a few seconds then the changed subject.

"I can see you are a very sensual woman."

Elena suppressed a laugh. She could sense an attraction to Dimi; indeed, his physical presence was intimidating, but his manner had suddenly become amusing. She thought ahead to the studio; Dimi would be wearing a silk dressing gown, smoking a cigarette, like a Hollywood actor from a black and white movie. In a debonair voice, he would say, "I'd like you to pose nude for me today. Would you mind terribly, darling?"

"I'm looking forward to seeing your work. Sophia tells me you paint still-life." Elena ignored Dimi's earlier remark. She could not remember whether Sophia had mentioned him having a wife.

At the rear of the house, they entered a courtyard. Tall cypress trees formed a boundary at either side. The property ended at a cliff with a view overlooking the bay and the nearby island of Ithaca. A low balustrade wall with spindles of classic design marked the cliff-edge.

"Let me show you the view, Elena," said Dimi, leading the way. The girls followed him across the neat, orderly grounds. Elena noted the contrast from the approach to the house, with its mass of pots and colorful plants to the formal, minimalist, space at the rear. The garden stretched forty or fifty yards from the house to the escarpment. A small grass border ran along the cypress trees at either side, abutting a wide avenue of limestone tiles, inlaid with red terracotta diamonds. In the center of the two pathways, a neatly trimmed lawn, about twenty yards wide, rolled out before a rectangular pond covered with water lilies. Between pond and cliff, the limestone flags formed a spacious patio furnished with tables and chairs in a style reminiscent of a Parisian Café. As they approached the wild hillside, the rhythm of cicadas grew louder, swept up by the ocean breeze. Multi-colored dragonflies, straying from the pond, hovered around the patio adjusting their flight in the wispy air.

"What do you think of the view, Elena?" asked Dimi, as they reached the drop.

Elena looked over the edge to the panorama below. Tree covered hills sloped down to Fiskardo; a cluster of red-brown roofs, surrounded by blue, white-speckled with boats. Maybe it was the height, or the angle of perspective, but to Elena, the large cruise ship anchored in the channel, even Ithaca itself, lacked dimension, substance, as though she viewed the vista with the eye of an artist.

"It's very pretty. Have you painted it?"

"Once. It was spring, the hillside was covered in wildflowers."

He gestured towards the house, pointing out his window on the upper floor. "The view is just as nice from my studio. Shall we?"

They walked back, passing an alfresco dining area before entering the house through a pair of purple doors, similar, but wider, than those Elena had photographed. Inside, the patterned limestone motif continued into a huge kitchen, blurring the line between inside and out.

Apologizing for the absence of his wife, Dimi offered the girls refreshments. "Alexia doesn't like to be disturbed when she is working. She will join us for lunch," he explained. "After we eat, Sophia can see her work."

Dimi poured three glasses of iced tea and led the girls from the kitchen into a long hallway. He carried on a conversation with Sophia as they walked along the corridor. Elena noticed several paintings hanging on the walls; she wondered if they were Dimi's work, but decided not to ask.

At the end of the hallway, a broad staircase with an ornate iron balustrade, swept up, in a one hundred and eighty degree curve to the upper floor.

"Here's Mikka," said Dimi.

Elena smiled as a tawny cat, sporting a leather collar, joined them on the wood-planked landing.

Dimi's studio was spacious; Elena judged it to run the full width of the house. The outside wall was constructed of sliding glass panels, each pane about one foot square. Several of the panels were open and led on to a wide veranda. Dimi went straight outside and invited the girls to sit at a mosaic-tiled table. The view from the patio was stunning, as Dimi promised. Mikka curled up on the limestone floor next to a potted plant.

An adjustable awning hung from the parapet above the glass wall. The studio looked out eastwards over Ithaca. The sun would be over the house during the hottest part of the day.

Sophia set her drink on the table. "Shall we take a look at your work, Dimi?"

"Elena would you care to join us, or stay and admire the view?" asked Dimi.

"We just drove an hour to get here, I'm seeing your work," she replied.

Somewhere overhead, the drone of a small aircraft, drowned out the rhythm of the garden.

Inside, an open ceiling exposed large roof timbers. Antique furniture lay dotted around the room; paintings lined the walls. Elena's eyes riveted on a blue velvet couch; a woolen blanket sprawled over its backrest. She imagined herself, naked, stretched out on the couch, the blanket draped over her knees and onto the floor. Dimi stood in front of a canvas, staring at her with a piercing glare. He would stride over to her, displeased with the pose, and rearrange the blanket on her legs. Still not satisfied, he continued to adjust her pose, moving her legs with his strong hands. She wondered if he would sit down on the couch and attempt to kiss her; and how she would respond.

Sophia called from the rear of the studio.

"Elena, come and check these out."

She walked over to join them, keeping Sophia between herself and Dimi. The two discussed a series of still life paintings; flowering plants, mostly orchids and vines. Although Elena had an untrained eye, she admired the way Dimi had used light and shadow to create an effect unlike anything photographic. Elena's mind went back to her aesthetic moment, behind the camera, at the side of the villa.

What percentage of people would walk past the purple doors and see nothing of interest? How did Dimi perceive the world? Did he take interest in everything? What did it mean to be an artist?

Lost in her thoughts, she shifted her gaze towards another area of wall. Here, the subjects were landscapes and buildings. She sauntered over to browse the canvases, feeling Dimi's silent presence behind her.

As she turned towards him, their eyes met. Totally assured of himself, he appeared to be daring her to hold his gaze. Sophia joined them and asked him a question, ending the contest of wills. Elena walked out to the veranda, still thinking about the couch.

Ten minutes later, with their business concluded, Sophia and Dimi re-emerged onto the veranda with several canvases rolled under their arms. At Dimi's suggestion, they returned to the kitchen, where a woman was removing dishes from the refrigerator.

"Elena, this is my wife, Alexia."

"Pleased to meet you." Elena offered her hand.

Elena guessed Alexia and her husband to be of similar age. Her grey hair, tied in a bun, still had a few streaks of black, adding tone. Coming straight from her studio, she was dressed in overalls. Petit gold earrings decorated her otherwise plain appearance.

"I hope you like vegetable dishes, Elena. I prepared some this morning."

"Love them," replied Elena. "Becoming a vegetarian would be easy in Greece."

"Shall we go outside?" Alexia led the party out to a long table, laid for four. Bowls of colorful dishes sat in the center, alongside carafes of red and white wine. Elena took advantage of the bright sunshine, putting on her sunglasses, as if to hide from Dimi.

"These are Greek meze—small appetizers." Alexia went from bowl to bowl announcing each dish. "Braised eggplant with tomato, dolmades, scordalia—which is a Greek potato and garlic dip, stuffed vegetables and spanakopita. Oh … and fresh bread from the village, please help yourself. There's red wine, white wine, water and ice tea."

Alexia passed the bowls around the table, Dimi poured wine.

As they dined, the hot sun, the breeze, the sounds and smells of the garden, the flavors of the meze intermingled, putting everyone in a pleasant frame of mind.

"Why don't you paint Elena?" Alexia turned to Dimi. "She would make a lovely model, she's so pretty, such beautiful legs."

Elena nearly choked on an olive and gasped, audibly, at the suggestion. Everyone at the table had surely noticed her surprise.

Dimi piled on the pressure. "What do you think, Elena?"

She took a moment to recover her poise. "I'm sure there are many more suitable models on the island."

Neither Dimi nor his wife pressed the matter further and the topic of conversation changed. For the next fifteen minutes, Dimi held center stage, reminiscing about the island, in the days before the tourists invaded.

Elena noticed her cousin glance at her watch for the third time. It was no surprise when Sophia shifted the conversation back to business.

"Lunch was wonderful; truly delicious. Perhaps we can look at your new pieces. It's getting late and I have another appointment…"

"Of course, we can go now, if you like," replied Alexia.

Dimi turned to Elena then back to Sophia. "You two go on to the studio, Elena will keep me company in the garden."

Without reply, Sophia followed Alexia into the house.

Being alone with Dimi caught Elena by surprise. She considered following her cousin but decided to stay put; Dimi would have scored a victory over her.

"Won't you have another glass of wine?" he asked.

Before she could reply, Dimi picked up a carafe and filled her glass.

"Let's go over to the patio," he suggested.

Topping up his own glass, Dimi got up, walked around the table and pulled back Elena's chair. As they crossed the garden, Dimi lit a cigarette and offered her the pack. She declined.

Iron and wicker chairs surrounded tables with marbled tops and cast iron bases. They sat, sipping wine. Elena watched the dragonflies flit above the lily pads, Dimi watched Elena.

"You say you are not an artist, Elena, but I can see you have an eye for beauty, for the mysterious. Perhaps you like photography then?"

Drowsy from the wine, she found his voice melodic.

"I'd like to take photography more seriously. I think the change in environment, the beauty of the island is having an effect on me. I have been here for nearly two weeks..." She hoped he wouldn't ask questions about her life in America.

"Will you be staying much longer? Many who visit never want to leave."

"No, I couldn't do that. I may stay another week but I have to get back."

"You have a boyfriend in America?"

"Well yes, but..."

Dimi didn't let Elena finish. "I can see that there is a conflict within you. Perhaps you are conditioned to a lifestyle that does not ... stop to smell the roses, as you say. Inside there is another Elena, trapped. Take off your sunglasses; let me see your eyes."

Like a shield, her glasses offered shelter from his magnetic gaze. Maybe it was the wine, but her fascination had grown to the point where she questioned her ability to resist should he pursue her.

Elena removed her sunglasses, placing them on the table next to her empty glass. Dimi looked into her eyes. She saw a deep kindness that surprised her.

"Perhaps the man you are looking for will remain hidden until you find your true self," he said. "Love is like a painting, Elena ... the lover is the subject, yes, but the artist takes that subject, injects himself, and creates..." He reverted to Greek. "How you say in English ... the painting, the love, it is just a reflection of your true self."

The spell of Dimi, the wine, the garden was suddenly broken as Sophia and Alexia reappeared. More time had elapsed than Elena had realized.

"It's late, we should be leaving," said Sophia.

Her cousin continued speaking to Dimi, explaining how she and Alexia had already loaded several pieces of ceramics into the car, together with his paintings. Elena was last to rise, she followed Sophia across the garden, to the side of the house. As they passed the narrow purple doors, Dimi turned to Elena.

"Ah, the doors—maybe I'll use them for my next painting. Perhaps, when you come again, I will present it to you."

"I'd like that."

They shook hands and said goodbye. At the bottom of the steps, Elena turned and waved. She looked straight at Dimi; he was looking at her too.

5

Alone and afraid, Ioannis lay on the stone floor for what seemed like hours. He had no way to mark the passing of time. Somewhere in the distance, shouts broke the silence.

He rubbed his leg just above the knee. A throbbing ache made him want to fade back into sleep. Close by, propped up against the debris, the icon of Saint Gerasimos appeared to watch over him. He closed his eyes.

***

January the seventh had been mild for a winter's day. A local clergyman paid a surprise visit...

"Ioannis," said his mother. "Sit up; Father Voutsinas is here for your Name Day."

She carried wine and cheese on a wooden tray, beckoning the monk into the parlor with a nod of her head. The man stooped under the doorway then sat in a high-backed chair, balancing the platter on his knees.

"I thank you kindly for the refreshment." He raised his glass, turned to Ioannis and offered the traditional Name Day greeting. "I wish you a long life."

"Thank you, Father."

Name Day was like a second birthday to Ioannis. He sat on a sofa, trying not to slouch, and remembered the dates his father had taught him. November eight is Name Day for boys called Stamos, January seven for Ioannis, Nicia is…

The monk leaned forward on his chair. "Where is your brother?"

Stamos had been standing near his mother, now they had both disappeared.

"He's playing in the garden," Ioannis found himself saying.

The house fell eerily silent. A candle burned behind the Holy Man, casting his shadow along the floor. This confused Ioannis; Father Voutsinas wore a black flat-topped headdress, the shadow belonged to someone in a hooded robe. He looked again. Sure enough, the tall round klobuk had a flat top.

The monk's grey beard flowed down the front of his cassock, almost touching an ornate gold cross, its chain thick and heavy. Father Voutsinas caught the boy staring at the cross and held it off his chest. "It's old … very old."

Gripped by a desire to touch the golden talisman, Ioannis rose but found standing difficult. He stumbled towards the monk, who grabbed his arm.

"Steady now. Your leg's a little numb from sitting such a long time. No need to worry."

Ioannis touched the cross, closing his hand tightly around it. The priest was right, he had pins and needles, nothing more.

"It belonged to Saint Gerasimos." Father Voutsinas took a sip of wine. "The Patron Saint of Kefalonia."

"Why do you have it?"

"That's a long story. First, I'm going to tell you about Saint Gerasimos. Would you like me to do that?"

"Yes, please." Ioannis knew all about the saint but the cross intrigued him. He itched to learn how it had come into the monk's possession.

"Well then, sit down, make yourself comfortable … and help yourself to those pastries over there."

Ioannis returned to the sofa, thinking it odd that he hadn't spotted them earlier. He examined the plain white plate and its tempting treats but didn't recognize his mother's baking.

Draining the last drop of wine, Father Voutsinas set his glass down. "Do you know where the Peloponnese is?"

Ioannis cleared his mouth of pastry. "Yes, everybody knows. It's part of Greece. My teacher says it's famous."

"Your teacher is correct. It's a large peninsula in the south of Greece, just across the sea from here. It's a wild and mountainous land, the birthplace of the Spartans, the Corinthians, the Mycenaeans and the Olympic games."

Wild and mountainous, the words evoked images of Spartans marching into battle. Ioannis wanted to hear more.

"Many hundreds of years ago, in 1506, a child was born in the village of Trikala," the Holy Man continued.

"Is that in the Peloponnese?"

"Yes, in the northeast. Dimitrios and Kallie Notaras named their son…"

"Saint Gerasimos?" Ioannis interrupted.

Father Voutsinas smiled. "Just Gerasimos, no one is born a saint … did you know the Notaras family had noble blood?" The monk didn't wait for a reply. "Legend says they were related to Emperor Constantine himself."

"I bet Saint Gerasimos had so much money, he didn't have to go to school?"

"Well you'd be wrong. He went to the finest schools in the whole of Greece."

***

The conversation meandered from shepherds to soldiers, emperors to goats; Father Voutsinas ended the yarn with the young Gerasimos getting lost in the mountains near Trikala and encountering wolves. Engrossed in the story, Ioannis forgot his surroundings and let his mind wander off to pine-clad hills. He dearly wanted to see a wolf; there were none in Kefalonia.

"Have you ever been through a terrifying ordeal?" asked the monk.

Ioannis shook his head.

"Well let's hope that never happens," said the Holy Man, raising his eyebrows. "After Gerasimos finished his education, he traveled far and wide."

"Did he go to Africa?"

"Well, he spent many years in Egypt, and Egypt is in Africa. He toured the Holy Land … was ordained a priest in Jerusalem, but a monastic life called. That's how he ended up at the Holy Mountain."

"Holy Mountain?"

"Mount Athos, I studied there too. It's far away … on the other side of Greece, further even than Thessaloniki. There must be twenty monasteries on the mountain, Ioannis. I hope you can visit one day. If there's one place Gerasimos loved—other than Kefalonia, of course—it was the Holy Mountain."

"What happened next?"

"After Mount Athos, he went to Crete then spent some time on Zante—I believe you once sailed there…"

Ioannis nodded, wondering how the monk knew about the time he'd gone with his father and Stamos to the nearby island.

"But only when Gerasimos came to Kefalonia, did he find his dream and stay forever."

Men shouted somewhere close by. Father Voutsinas appeared not to notice and pressed on with his story. "As I recall, Gerasimos came to Kefalonia in 1555. For the first five years he lived in a cave, not far from here."

"I've been there," said Ioannis. "It's in the hills above Lassi."

The monk paused, looked at the boy, and smiled. "Are you going to eat all the pastries?"

Only one melemakaronia remained, sitting in its white paper cup, tempting him. Ioannis put the plate back on the cushion.

"Gerasimos left the cave in 1560 and moved inland to Omala. Oh! How he loved the land he found there; he dug wells, worked the fields, planted trees, restored the church, founded a convent…"

Ioannis became sleepy; the monk's voice started to sound like a radio broadcast.

"Gerasimos dedicated the rest of his life to the valley. Even here, he lived as a hermit, in a cave which still exists underneath the monastery."

Ioannis looked through the open door into the kitchen. Where's mother? She's been gone a long time.

"Finally, as happens to us all, Gerasimos died in his beloved valley on August 15th, 1579. He was buried at the convent."

The candle behind the monk flickered wildly.

Mother must have opened a door, thought Ioannis.

"In accordance with Greek tradition, the body of Gerasimos was disinterred two years after his death. His bones were to be transferred to a permanent resting place."

Shouts rang out again, this time inside the house. "Hello, Hello. Is anybody here?"

Ioannis became scared; the candle went out plunging the room into darkness. Father Voutsinas continued, oblivious to the commotion.

"When they exhumed the body, a miracle had happened…"

Now, men were in the room, he could hear their voices.

One of them knelt beside the boy who reached out to the icon of the Saint.

"Who else was in the house when the earthquake happened?" asked the man.

"Grandmother," said Ioannis. "And Stamos; he's playing in the garden."

6

Water droplets on clay tiles formed a trail leading to the silver framed mirror. Ben stood facing his tanned, trim reflection; a white towel hung around his shoulders. Heat poured in through the open doors, evaporating the moisture on his skin, leaving a pleasant, tingling sensation. He put on a pair of cargo shorts and lay on the bed to cool off.

A novel sat on the bedside table, untouched since the night before. He fiddled with the frayed leather bookmark, inserted midpoint in the book. Flipping open to the marked page, he stared blankly at the text, unable to concentrate. In his mind, he retraced the events leading to his being here, at the Hotel Dionysus, in the small fishing port of Fiskardo.

Although he lived in Los Angeles, Ben preferred spending the summer at one of his parents' European residences. His father's wealth allowed the family to maintain a townhouse in London's fashionable Belgravia, a country estate in Surrey, and a chateau in the Loire valley. This year, he'd opted for the London residence. Two months earlier, a group of friends from Los Angeles invited him to join a cruise of the Greek Islands. The party of six planned

to charter a yacht in Corfu and spend ten days exploring the Ionian Islands. He had deliberated for weeks, eventually declining
the invitation in favor of a loose promise to rendezvous with the
boat at some point on the journey.

It was the vague nature of the arrangement that mattered.
Ben had become used to doing as he pleased. Committing to a
schedule, however pleasant, had no appeal.

Over the past week, he'd maintained regular contact with the
cruise organizer, tracking the yacht's progress. As he lay there, Ben
was unable to explain why he chose to meet his friends in Fiskardo, on the island of Kefalonia.

Buying a last-minute ticket, he'd taken a flight the previous
afternoon, arriving at the island's small airport in the heat of early
evening. Dusk had become night during the one-hour taxi ride
to the Hotel Dionysus. Without a concrete itinerary, Ben had reserved the room for two nights. He did not unpack.

The phone on his bedside table vibrated then beeped, announcing a new message. He reached over to read it.

"leaving sami harbor soon will be in fiskardo late afternoon
see u there e"

e, was Eric Miller, the cruise organizer, an American in his
early forties, and a successful biotech entrepreneur. They had
been friends for over a decade.

Ben replied.

"ok am here see u later."

The timing was perfect. He could explore the village, take a
leisurely lunch and meet up with the boat in the afternoon.

Ben studied the message again. Curious about the local ge-
ography, he picked up the visitor map he'd bought at the airport
and went onto the veranda. Outside, in the cypress-scented air,
he became conscious of the cicadas and wondered how the mind
makes oblivious their incessant sound.

He leaned against the balcony, letting the sun toast his back and began retracing last night's journey. From the airport, on the southwest coast, his finger followed the western coastline, through Argostoli, to the northern tip of the island.

The port of Sami lay on the eastern seaboard, fifteen miles south of Fiskardo. Just offshore, Ithaca Island stretched the entire distance from Sami to Fiskardo, separated by a narrow channel.

The voyage by sea would be spectacular, thought Ben.

Stepping out of the sunlight into the shaded room, he felt a twinge of regret, coincident with the change of light, that he would miss the experience.

Eager to explore the village, Ben prepared to leave. Rooting through the suitcase, he chose a T-shirt and spread it on the bed. As he smoothed out the creases, the texture of the fabric became rubberlike as his hand moved over a large print. He paused to admire the black and white graphic, a poster advertising a Japanese movie. A young man and woman lay asleep, perhaps dead, on the floor; their bodies forming a straight line, head to head, one yard apart. The ground, strewn with leaves, suggested a forest setting. Above the prone figures, three white lines of Japanese letters rose vertically, extending past the print and blending with the deep blue cotton.

Ben knew the image attracted attention. When asked about it, he always feigned ignorance in an attempt to cultivate an air of mystery. He pulled the T-shirt over his head, grabbed his mobile phone and rummaged in the suitcase for a point-and-shoot camera and his sunglasses.

***

In the narrow corridor, a middle-aged maid mopped the floor tiles, her cart piled high with clean towels and fresh linens. He smiled as he squeezed past. "Good morning."

Startled, the woman muttered something incomprehensible, though it sounded friendly enough. Ben was in good spirits, eager to explore; lacking a plan suited him fine.

Black and white marble formed a checkerboard pattern on the floor of the air-conditioned lobby; an oasis of cool before the furnace beyond. Outside, a few high clouds drifted over the sea in an otherwise blue sky. Ben flipped on his sunglasses, suppressing the blinding light.

Arriving in Fiskardo at night had robbed the village of its charm and color. Tired and weary, he'd taken a nightcap and gone to bed early; daylight revealed a pleasant surprise. Nestled in a small bay at the northern tip of the island, Fiskardo was the quintessential Mediterranean fishing harbor. Surrounded by pine and cypress hills, scores of white craft floated in shallow turquoise water. Like a verdant cloak scattered with sequins, brightly colored villas decorated the gentle slopes leading down to the quayside. Even the most jaded traveler might rejoice, gazing at the shimmering mirage of Ithaca Island across the narrow blue channel.

What had the taxi driver said last night?

The man could have been a tour guide the way he punctuated the journey with a tale for every place they passed. His ramblings drew little interest for the most part but two things stuck in Ben's mind; a mummified saint and the August earthquakes of 1953. That he should remember the earthquake was no surprise, the man's description was vivid, telling of hundreds dying, thousands evacuated, the entire island lifted up sixty centimeters. Later, in the hotel room, Ben had checked online; Kefalonia was on a major tectonic fault, where the European and Aegean plates collide. The driver hadn't exaggerated, the earthquake had leveled almost every building, erasing centuries of culture and history. Fate had seen Fiskardo escape, preserving a trace of the islands' past.

The village was concentrated on the west side of the bay, its architecture classic Venetian. Pastel painted houses, their walls festooned with flowers, lined the quayside. At the water's edge, cafes and tavernas served guests under shaded cabanas. Here was a peaceful place, where waves lapped against the quay … gently, like leaves rustling on a tree.

Ben stopped at a cafe for coffee and a small bowl of fruit before continuing to explore.

At the central plaza, the promenade became an artist's canvas. Here, a blue gable, lush with red and pink blossoms, abutted an orange building with a clay-tiled roof. He paused to admire a two-storey house, harmonious, with its ochre walls and pale green woodwork. Three giant vases of the most vivid-red stood against the pastel masonry creating a sublime contrast. Thick, gnarled trunks grew from the urns, a meter high, before bursting into foliage and flowers. The flowering vines conspired to cover just enough of the ochre wall for Ben to imagine an artistic gardener meticulously pruning to keep the composition in check.

He photographed the building in classic landscape, throwing in a few unusual angles for good measure. He checked the images, thinking of the artistic gardener, hoping to make him proud. One of the shots, at least, showed promise.

Ben was happy to linger, content to be alone. No one would urge him to stop taking pictures or hurry him to another destination. Every action would be for his own pleasure and in his own time.

He sat on one of the benches at the water's edge and gazed out over the harbor. A mild breeze blew off the bay, ruffling his hair. He may have stayed five minutes or half an hour, he could not say. Eventually, he left the bench and turned to face the village. Several narrow streets, crowded with tourists, led off from the main promenade. He chose one at random, mingling with the crowds, briefly sharing in their lives. Gradually, the shops gave way to houses and the street became quiet.

At a crossroad, another vase caught his attention. Burnished and intensely blue, it stood one meter high, on a platform, outside a rose-colored villa. An iron rail bordered the plinth. Out of the container grew a bougainvillea in full bloom, its mass of purple blossom splashed against the wall. The blue of the house door matched the vase, its ceramic handle painted in a floral pattern. Further down the street, more bougainvillea-clad cottages funneled his vision, leading to a narrow view of the harbor. Ben focused his camera lens on the urn and its flowers, hoping the distant bay would make a pleasing composition. He moved back a few paces, checking the photograph in the viewer. Satisfied with the shot, he was surprised as the door edged open and a small boy emerged. The child was dressed curiously, wearing a flat cloth cap and raggedy clothes; he stared at Ben who made a gesture so as to take his picture. The boy gave a smile, confirming his consent. Ben returned the smile, snapping an image before retracing his steps back to the promenade.

7

August 8, 1953 fell on a Saturday, another day in the high eighties. Eleven-year-old Nicia Katros sat with her friend on the harbor wall, staring out over the lagoon.

A church bell rang out, announcing the hour. Nicia tossed a pebble into the air, watching it drop into the sea with a satisfying splash. "I win ... again."

"I didn't see the last one," complained Larissa Matsakis. "Besides I'm still winning."

The two girls had walked the length of the eastern Fanari Peninsula, along the Argostoli waterfront, looking for loggerhead turtles; a common sight at this time of year.

Nicia pulled a piece of chalk from her pocket and began drawing on the stone floor. "I don't think so. Look." She sketched out the long cigar shape of Argostoli bay, then the narrow Fanari peninsula jutting into it. Getting her bearings, she looked to her right, to the south, where the old stone bridge crossed the lagoon to the mainland.

"Here's Drapano Bridge." Nicia drew a crooked line across the inlet. "A cross for me and a circle for you." She marked the spot where each girl had spotted a turtle. She went on to draw the rest of their neighborhood topology, the port, the northern tip of Fanari, the lighthouse on northwestern edge opposite the much larger Pali Peninsula. She chalked more sightings.

"Count them. Did I miss any?"

"I can't remember," said Larissa. "But I know I'm winning."

Half a mile to the north, the Argostoli-Lixouri ferry sounded its horn and began the twenty-five minute crossing of the bay.

Nicia tugged her friend's dress. "Come on. The ferry's leaving. It's time to go. I've got the tally on a map in my room; we can count the score later."

Before they had walked a hundred yards, Nicia called out, excited. "Another. Over there."

The reddish-brown shell of an enormous turtle surfaced near the seawall. More than a meter long, the creature poked its head out of the water, opening its nostrils to draw breath.

"It's the biggest one yet," said Larissa.

The turtle's massive flippers, like sea wings, moved with a slow grace, propelling it forward as though gliding through air. The girls followed its nonchalant journey along the quay, under a fishing boat, where it surfaced again, filled its lungs then plunged into the depths.

At the moment of descent, a tingle ran down Nicia's spine, as if she, herself, were submerging, opening her eyes underwater, holding her breath to disappear into an unknown world. She wanted to follow.

"I thought you had to get back early," said Larissa.

"I do, let's go."

Nicia lived in a small two-story house close to the Argostoli ferry terminal. The neighborhood was poor. This didn't bother Nicia. Her father often told her, "In Argostoli there are rich people, poor people and desperately poor people. We are lucky."

The family owned a smallholding on the outskirts of town,

which had passed down to the eldest son for generations. The farm was little more than a small orchard of pear and olive trees and an adjacent half-acre field planted with vines, tomatoes, and eggplants.

As the girls turned into their street, Nicia schemed. Her brothers were building a tree house in the old oak behind father's barn. Ioannis had talked of nothing else for the last few days. From what he'd told her, Nicia formed a gingerbread image of their handiwork, based, in part, on a picture she had once seen in a children's book. Tonight, together with Larissa's older brother, the boys planned to sleep in the den for the first time. Nicia was jealous.

"Mom's taking me to the farm. We're delivering food to the boys."

"Can I come?" asked Larissa.

"No. Andreas is there. Who will look after your mom?"

The Matsakis' lived next door to Nicia; they operated a general store selling all manner of goods, including produce grown on the Katros allotment. Mrs. Matsakis suffered from stomach problems and was often too sick to mind the shop. At such times, Nicia's mother helped out; the two families were close.

In truth, Nicia wasn't sure what arrangements had been made. Her older sister, Nessa, usually worked at home, lacemaking, but sometimes assisted Mrs. Matsakis in the store. Secretly, Nicia wanted to sleep in the tree den and hoped to convince her mother to agree. Having Larissa along would spoil the plan.

Nicia said goodbye to her friend and entered the house. On the other side of the kitchen door, she heard her father's voice.

"What are you going to do, woman, climb the tree? I've checked the thing myself; it's safe. The boys have done a good job; they won't come to any harm."

Her mother was opposed to Ioannis spending the night on the farm, but reluctantly agreed, on condition she inspect the tree house. Nicia opened the door making as little sound as possible.

"I'm not going to climb the tree; I just want to see how high it is. I'm going over there with Nicia before it gets dark. I still think, with the recent tremors and all…"

A wry smile and a shake of her father's head ended the discussion on an amiable note.

***

With the afternoon sun far to the west, Nicia and her mother set off through town carrying a bag of food.

Even at her young age, Nicia's was aware of a connection to Andreas Matsakis. Handsome, and one of the most popular boys in school, Andreas didn't tease her like the others. Nicia treasured the protection she enjoyed from being in the favor of Andreas. Today, she was pleased to be bringing his supper.

The narrow dirt path leading to the allotment wound through the pear and olive orchards. This was Nicia's favorite part of the farm. She loved how the pear trees grew v-shaped trunks, often quite close to the ground. Sometimes she'd scramble up a tree and stand in the fork, an arm around each bough, doing nothing, just watching the world and listening to the cicadas in the branches. Most everything about nature fascinated Nicia; even touching the thick rugged bark of the pear trees filled her with a sense of delight.

"Can I sleep in the tree house tonight?" Nicia chose this moment to ask. She imagined how it would feel to open the door in the dead of night, and sit, motionless, high in the branches, listening to the crickets and the owls.

"No." Her mother's answer was empathic. "Girls don't sleep in tree houses."

"But why?"

"They just don't. Besides, the boys won't want you around. Don't ask again."

'The boys won't want you around.' The words echoed in

Nicia's head and they hurt. Ioannis wouldn't have said that, they were too close. He was always the first to leap to her defense when Nessa teased her. Perhaps Stamos or Andreas had spoken to mother but it was hard to imagine. Just the thought of not being wanted blunted her desire to sleep in the tree house. If only her mother hadn't spoken.

The lone oak grew behind the stone barn. From the path, only the higher branches were visible above the clay-tiled roof; there was no sign of the tree house.

Nicia's mother breathed a sigh of relief, "Thank goodness it's not too high."

Still smarting from the hurtful words, Nicia ran on ahead to catch her first glimpse of the den.

Andreas knelt on the flat roof, leaning over the side with a paintbrush in his hand. He heard Nicia's approach and motioned her to climb; she looked pensive.

"Come on," he teased. "A baby could do it. Just use the nails as steps."

Nicia assessed the difficulty. The boys had hammered thick iron nails into the trunk, every couple of feet, until a gently sloping bough made the climb easy. She wondered if the tree felt pain when the nails pieced its bark.

"Nicia," her mother yelled.

The shout alerted Ioannis, who opened the tree house door; Nicia was halfway up the trunk.

"Get down," her mother called.

Nicia didn't stop. With the agility of a cat, she reached the sloping bough, balancing along, until Ioannis grabbed her hand and pulled her through the door. The young girl looked down at her mother who swung the bag of food on her wrist.

"It's safe, mom," said Nicia with a smile.

In reality, the tree house wasn't more than twelve feet off the ground. Nicia's mother relaxed and sat on the stone steps outside the barn door.

"Where's Stamos?" she shouted.

A voice called from inside the stone building.

"In here, Mom."

"I've brought your supper. Come and get it, we have to get back. Nicia, come on, please."

Like a gymnast, Andreas swung from the roof and through the tree house door. Ioannis and Nicia frolicked on the pillows and blankets scattered around the wooden floor. Nicia wished she could stay with the boys; her mother called again. It was time to go.

8

Ben tired of exploring; the yacht was still a couple of hours away. He decided to return to the hotel, take his book down to the cypress garden, and read. Besides, he needed the mosquito spray from his suitcase. On his last visit to Greece, he'd come back covered in bites.

With less than thirty rooms, the Hotel Dionysius had a cozy feel, reminiscent of a large house. It sat beneath the hills, a short walk from the quayside.

Back in the lobby, his friendly maid mopped the checkerboard floor. Recognizing him, she took a moment to lean against her mop and smile. With a wave, he hurried past, en route to the stairs.

Ben looked down from his balcony at the green expanse below, a peaceful hour beckoned. With mosquito spray still wet on his legs, he grabbed the book and headed down. Standing at the entrance to the garden, he soaked up its moody atmosphere. Even with the midday sun directly overhead, shadows crept out from under the trees. Somewhere in the cypresses, crows rioted again.

A canopy, covered in vines, extended from the hotel and over the rear dining area, providing shade to a wooden bench. Ben sat and photographed the scene. The garden's charm was more than visual; he switched over to video mode, capturing the sounds. Empty of people, the crow and cicada orchestra played only for him.

The space had a symmetrical design. A gravel path ran down the center, between two low walls, which tapered in the distance. At the halfway point, on each side, iron gates opened onto a lawn, carefully manicured, and dotted with ancient dwarf pines. The symmetry drew the eye towards a stone sundial and beyond, to a ruin, hidden in the trees.

Curious, Ben set off down the gravel path, glanced at the sundial, and stood, staring at a folly, overgrown with flowering vines. The whimsical structure, a faux wall and roof, suggested an abandoned cottage or farmhouse. Wooden shutters covered non-existent windows, their paint cracked and faded. Barely visible through the leaves, an old rusted iron gate led nowhere. At the top of the wall, about ten feet high, clay roof tiles sloped back until hidden in the cypresses.

Two trees grew close to the sundial, overhanging the folly. Loaded down with red blossoms, their branches arched over the rusty gate, coalescing with the purple flowers below. One of the crows looked down from the roof as if to enquire of his presence in the garden. Ben acknowledged the bird, as he would a fellow guest then sat on a bench to read.

Where was he up to?—Van Norden was re-telling Carl's fictitious story of his amorous encounter with the wealthy Irene.

Perhaps it was the raucous birds but Ben couldn't concentrate. The book dropped to the bench and he let the garden enter his mind. It had summoned him since waking, maybe even as he slept. Now, it had taken on a persona, questioning him, demanding an explanation of his presence, probing into his solitary, aimless life.

Ben rarely felt the need to justify his man-of-leisure existence. Last year, at a party, some woman had called him a dilettante and that had riled him—it wasn't even true. He thought about the word again, with distaste; a dilettante, a dirty, stinking dilettante.

In truth, Ben had never been troubled by the lack of an occupation. He'd toyed around in his father's businesses, vaguely hoping to find direction, expecting to take over the reins at some point in the distant future. It was only after the death of his fiancée that he'd lost interest and taken a long leave of absence. His father, always supportive, set up a trust fund allowing him to live a comfortable, if not extravagant, life.

Soul-searching seemed natural in this empty, peaceful place; it deepened his affinity with the garden.

After Maria's death, he moved to Los Angeles; LA soothed the pain caused by her loss. He knew it was psychological but, somehow, he convinced himself that the sun, the low humidity, provided a barrier from grief. He only had to stay there to be free from sorrow. In this way, time healed his wounds and he found the routine of his life. Maria had died, at the age of twenty-one, in a pointless traffic accident ... the girl wasn't even driving. She was his second love; the first had ended in heartache too, but not of such epic proportions. Perhaps, even now, the loss still affected him. Hadn't it only been a few months earlier that some melancholy song, a memento from their past, had briefly revived the devastation following her death? Now, fifteen years later, here in the garden, he willed the sadness back. He would never see Maria again—ever. No amount of money, not his fathers', or the combined wealth of the world could make any difference. Even if it were possible to clone her, it would not be Maria. No technology, on any drawing board, could replicate the trillions of neurons firing in precisely the same order, for twenty-one years, making her 'his Maria'. She was gone forever.

A loud commotion in the trees jolted him back to reality. He thanked the birds.

He was just proving a point to himself. He was over Maria,

could think about her anytime, revive the pain then dismiss it at will. Dwelling on the conquest of emotion led him to consider his relationships since Maria. Several had promise; all had faded into oblivion. He could trace their decline back to trivial incidents. Julia, for example, she had given him a photo of herself; he assumed she took a certain pride in the picture. Even though he found her attractive, the photograph somehow repulsed him to such an extent that he went from the precipice of love to abandoning the relationship shortly after. He had come to suspect that some love-safety-valve would forever trigger in his subconscious, warding off future pain.

Voices drifted over the lawn. An elderly couple strolled, arm-in-arm, towards the sundial. Their presence disturbed him; he did not want to share his peaceful oasis. Shadows deepened, down at the bench, by the folly. Later, the garden would become dark, green and gloomy. He wanted to be there when it did.

9

The campfire smoldered inside a ring of stones on the barren ground behind the Katros barn. Once a roaring blaze, it had burnt down to a flickering glow. Ioannis poked in the embers with a stick sending plumes of smoke into his face. He leapt back, eyes stinging. Stamos and Andreas Matsakis watched his antics with amusement. The moon was in the final day of the last quarter, faintly illuminating the black night.

"Stop poking around in the fire, they're not done yet," said Stamos for the second time.

Ioannis let his stick drop and rubbed his watering eyes. The potatoes had been roasting an awful long time. He was ravenous.

As though reading his mind, Stamos aloft held a basket covered with a red-checkered wrapping. He untied the cloth, whipping it off like a magician before revealing the snacks inside. A surprise bonus, the extra food supplemented the rations they'd secretly hoarded over the past few days. Stamos began dividing out equal shares.

"Wait until the skins are black, they taste better." Andreas passed along a chunk of bread and some pastries from their new larder.

Staying awake late into the night had left Ioannis in an excitable state. He paced around the fire. The urge to grab a stick and poke the embers was like a nagging itch.

"We got lemonade," Stamos shouted. He'd stashed a bottle of his mother's homemade lemonade next to a pile of logs, behind his seat. He held the bottle above his head, waving it around. Ioannis nearly tripped over Andreas's leg as he rushed across to claim a swig of his favorite drink.

The boys snacked on bread, pastries and hard-boiled eggs. An owl called from the orchard, prompting a suggestion from Andreas.

"How about a ghost story?"

Ioannis wished Andreas hadn't spoken. At home, he might have enjoyed a scary tale but tonight, outside in the dark, he wasn't so sure.

"I know one," said Stamos. "Let's get the potatoes out first; they should be done now."

Finally … those words were like a bell, signaling the end of school. Ioannis sprang to his feet, grabbing his stick. He thrust it into the embers, maneuvering his potato to the edge of the fire, only to see it wedge between the stones. His efforts merely served to puncture the blackened skin, creating a long white scar. Frustrated, he reached in with his hand, burning his fingers on the hot bricks.

"Here, use this." Andreas held up a knife with a carved bone handle. A black and charred potato sat impaled on its tip. He slid his supper onto a metal plate, which balanced on his knees and passed the blade to Ioannis.

"This is a true story," began Stamos. "One night, on a farm just like this." He waved his hand in the direction of the outbuilding. "A vampire lay buried in a crypt, behind a wall, in an old stone barn. Every month, at the start of a new moon, the vampire pushes up the creaking lid of his coffin and opens his coal black eyes."

Ioannis stabbed the knife into his potato, lifting it out of the fire. He knew he wasn't going to enjoy this story. The very idea that a vampire could live in their barn was unbearable. He thought about putting his hands over his ears or escaping to the tree house.

Andreas let out a yelp. Ioannis took heart from the sound, believing the older boy shared his fright. The empathy was short lived; Andreas had burnt his lips on the hot potato.

Much to Ioannis's relief, Stamos fell quiet, focusing his attention on supper. If Ioannis thought his brother had forgotten the story, he was mistaken. Two minutes later Stamos continued.

"When he leaves the crypt, the vampire crawls on his belly through a narrow tunnel under the wall and emerges, hissing, and hungry for the blood of young boys."

Ioannis could hardly contain himself; he didn't want to hear another word. Only concern for what his brother might think stopped him escaping to the tree house.

Untroubled by the vampire, Andreas sprinkled salt on his potato.

"One winter's night, a young boy got lost and strayed into the barn to shelter from the rain. The vampire opened his eyes. Even in his coffin, he could smell fresh blood close by."

Ioannis tried not to listen. He thought about school, about the jars of candy in the Matsakis' store, about Nicia climbing into the tree house…

"The full moon was bright, it shone through a hole in the roof, lighting up the entrance to the crypt. The boy moved closer to the opening and bent down. Something glistened in the darkness, perhaps silver or gold. Believing the moonlight pointed to hidden treasure, he squeezed into the narrow tunnel…"

"What was that, a bat?" Andreas jumped up, pretending to fend off an imaginary winged creature.

Stamos laughed then continued. "The crawlspace was only

five feet long and the lad wasted no time scampering through into a dark cellar that stank of damp earth. All of a sudden, the coffin lid creaked. The boy screamed as an inky black shape, much darker than the dimly lit room, rose up from nowhere. He dashed into the tunnel, crawling on his belly as fast he could. The vampire grabbed his foot just as the boy reemerged into the barn…"

Ioannis could stand no more. "What rubbish! There's no such thing as vampires."

He hurled his last chunk of potato into the fire; sparks showered into the air like a swarm of fireflies. Without another word, he marched over to the oak, listening intently for any sounds in the darkness.

The two older boys smiled at each other.

"Save him some lemonade," said Stamos.

Ioannis shinned up the last branch and inched open the tree house door; the hinge creaked ominously. A candle glimmered atop a wooden crate, illuminating his hands as they clasped the jamb. Too scared to enter, his imagination ran wild. A black cape lay strewn across the floor, waiting for him; he just knew it. If he dared look, the cloak would rise up, inflating with horrifying speed until it towered over him, dragging him inside. He covered his eyes then took a deep breath, stealing enough courage to peek through his fingers. To his relief, the candlelight bathed the interior in a comforting glow. He scurried in, snatching a comic off the blanket-strewn boards.

Reading helped take his mind off the undead but made him drowsy. Soon, his eyelids closed and he fell into a fitful slumber.

***

The tree house was too small for three boys to sleep with any degree of comfort. Ioannis woke often during the night. At times, Stamos squashed him or his blanket would shift underneath, exposing the bare wooden planks which hurt his sides and chafed his knees. The night dragged on forever.

Dawn eventually broke. Nearby, roosters crowed, lifting him out of an uneasy dream. Parched, he groped around for the lemonade, finding it near the door. Despite its warmth, the tangy drink quenched his thirst. Ioannis thanked Stamos for saving him a share.

Inside the tree house, the stuffy air reeked of wood smoke. Ioannis sniffed the sleeve of his shirt and turned his head away in disgust. Stamos and Andreas slept soundly. He opened the door, causing the candle to flicker, and crept into the branches to see a glorious sunrise, above the mainland hills.

As the interval between cockcrows lengthened, he grew tired and climbed back inside, snuggling into the blankets next to his brother. He fell fast asleep.

***

In the final years of his life, Ioannis would remember this scene, sat in the boughs of his father's oak tree, listening to the crows and the roosters greet the sun as a cardinal moment, a moment that embodied his childhood, his island, his loss; a memory fundamental to the kernel of his being.

***

Just after nine, a 6.0 earthquake struck; the first of three that would bring Kefalonia to its knees. The oak shook with a savage force, throwing Ioannis against the wall; Andreas crashed into him. The wooden structure folded in on itself causing the roof to drop, almost crushing the boys inside. Nails, fastening the floor joist to the tree, screeched as they popped out; the den pitched precariously on the branch.

Stamos reacted first, squeezing his way through a gap that was once the door. By sheer force, he wriggled free and managed to get a foothold on the bough. He shouted for Ioannis to get out; collapse was imminent.

The tree house creaked and groaned. With a shudder, it tilted ever more dangerously. Andreas stayed calm, propping up the roof with his back and pushing Ioannis through the mangled door. Stamos reached in, grabbing him under the arms. With one almighty tug, he yanked Ioannis free. It was not a moment too soon. Seconds later, the den crashed to the ground. Andreas was still inside.

With his brother safe, Stamos bounded down the trunk, scraping his hands on the iron nails in the dash to reach his friend.

Fate would be kind this day. Cocooned in the wooden boards, the fall to earth left Andreas unharmed. He emerged from the wreckage before Stamos reached the ground. Only a few bruises would provide proof of his ordeal. The two boys started laughing, exhilarated by their brush with danger.

"Stamos, come and look," shouted Ioannis.

Ioannis had climbed down after his brother. He stood over by the stone barn where a large crack had appeared in the wall. Andreas shoved at the door but it remained jammed shut.

With an almost telepathic understanding, the boys realized the implications for the town. Without a word, they raced off down the dirt lane heading for home. Ioannis followed, struggling to keep up. The quake of the tree house morning began series of events that would define the rest of his life.

10

Getting a table by the water's edge proved easier than Ben expected. A gentle breeze rolled off the bay and under the canopy, making an ideal spot to idle away the afternoon. Below his feet, rippling waves created patterns of sunlight on the shallow, stony bottom. Small black fish darted around in the translucent water, scavenging for bread tossed in by the diners.

Eight tables covered in crisp, turquoise cloth enjoyed the shade under the cabana; only two were occupied. Ben grabbed one of the striped cushions off his rattan loveseat and stuffed it behind his back. He started people watching.

Across the public boardwalk, sandwiched between the restaurants, a souvenir shop did brisk business. Most of the pedestrian traffic turned back towards the main square after reaching the gift store. Further on, the harbor walls sloped down to a small gravel beach, marking the end of the village.

Several minutes elapsed before a man came to take an order. From his demeanor, Ben guessed him to be the owner.

"Will you be dining alone?"

Ben nodded and the man handed him a menu with a red

leather cover.

"Something to drink?"

"I'll have a Mythos." Ben was so thirsty he could already feel the condensation on the cold green bottle, wetting his fingertips.

"We have Mythos, but I prefer Alfa beer. Have you tried it?"

Ben wasn't expecting service with a personality. It reminded him of the time he passed through Alabama and stopped off at a roadside diner. His waitress sat next to him at his booth and chatted for ten minutes before taking an order. He warmed to the man, accepting his recommendation.

"Okay, Alfa it is; a large one please."

The man smiled and walked across the esplanade to the taverna.

Sitting with his back to the main square, Ben faced a small beach. From where he sat, the sand appeared to be grit or gravel of a dirty brown color; the beach was empty. A few yards to his right, two outboard engines, hoisted out of the water, loomed over the stern of a boat named Magdalena. He had an uninterrupted view of this end of the shallow bay.

Watching the marina reminded Ben of the yacht. He wasn't sure how long the journey from Sami would take or whether Eric would stay out in the channel, fishing.

The owner reappeared carrying a tray. He set a basket of bread on the table before pouring a measure of beer into a glass, holding it up to the light, examining the color. Ben half-expected him to take a sip and probably wouldn't have cared. The man placed the drink on a paper mat, folded his arms and waited. Ben felt obliged to treat the beer with the same respect as his host, mimicking him before savoring the cold fresh taste.

"How is it?"

"Perfect," replied Ben. Suddenly, and without thinking, he added. "I'll never order Mythos again."

As the man left, Ben flipped open the menu, squinting to read the scripted font.

A woman shouted to her child, in the doorway of the souvenir shop, directly opposite Ben's table. She ushered the boy away from a rack of belts, stooping to retrieve one off the floor.

It was unclear to Ben, whether the store belonged to the restaurant. Outside, under a yellow canopy, a constant procession of people stopped to examine the displays of postcards, T-shirts, hats and caps. Ben's attention alternated from people watching on his left, to the bay on his right.

On the far side of the harbor, three fishing boats lay anchored in front of an official-looking white building that stood, conspicuous, against a hillside of pine and shrubs. Between the office and the gravel beach, a handful of cars, parked on a dirt lot, vied for shade under scrawny trees. Turning his head to the right, a cruise ship loomed in the distance over the top of the twin-engined Magdalena.

"Ready for another beer?" The owner reappeared as Ben looked over his shoulder at the cruise ship.

"Not just yet," replied Ben, who looked across the esplanade and smiled. "Nice restaurant. Are you the owner?"

"Yes, I'm Spiro. Where are you from?"

"Los Angeles. I'm meeting up with some friends."

Spiro had visited cousins in California three summers ago, providing a topic for further conversation. In a leisurely manner, the host returned to his duty and asked whether Ben was ready to order.

"I'll have the shrimp saganaki—and I'll get a bottle of water, please."

Spiro scribbled on a pad and left.

Ben sipped his beer, watching the lazy harbor scene. Over on the gravelly beach, a fat, hairy-chested man ambled towards the waters' edge. From the shade of a stunted palm, a scruffy dog got up and followed him to the shore. The mutt barked at two kayaks, which turned around before their hulls scraped the shallow bottom. Ben started to feel drowsy.

A waiter, balancing a tray with a practiced hand, arrived and set the shrimp dish on a woven placemat in front of Ben.

"Be careful, the plate is very hot."

Ben thanked the man, who opened a bottle of mineral water, pouring the fizzing liquid into a tall glass.

The saganaki came served in a cast-iron skillet. Ben placed his finger on the metal for a split-second, just to sense the searing heat. Four large shrimp, unpeeled, lay sizzling in the juice of tomatoes, garlic, and olive oil. Feta cheese pieces melted on the surface, relinquishing their flavor to the dish. Ben dipped a piece of crusty bread into the sauce and began to dine. He ate slowly, extracting the shrimp from their shells with a sharp, serrated knife.

***

As he pushed the plate into the center of the table, he looked up. That was when he saw her. The color of her dress, olive, struck him first, even before his eyes traced the fabric around the contours of her body…

A boat named Magdalena, an iron skillet, a turquoise tablecloth … such trivialities are background noise, forgotten, even as they are seen. However, these images belonged to a pivotal event, one with the power to stamp sight and sound into memory; a memory ever to be associated with the place that first brought him acquainted with the girl in the olive dress.

She appeared, seemingly out of nowhere, standing as though in a daze in front of the souvenir shop. Paying no attention to the merchandise, something clearly troubled her. Fascinated by the girl's strange behavior, Ben's preoccupation was such as to distort his perception of time.

Her dress was knitted, with a crew neckline. By some trick of the mind, Ben was struck by the odd notion that the olive color was an illusion, a combination of black, gold and dark green threads. Its hem was short, revealing legs; perfectly formed, as though designed exclusively for him. She remained motionless, rooted to the spot—it must have been two minutes now.

In her twenties, about five-feet-nine, she was standing less than ten yards from his table. He looked at her profile; a small brown shoulder bag hung down to her waist. The girl's hand rested on top of the bag, holding the strap, which placed her arm to the side, allowing Ben an unrestricted view of the shape of her breasts.

She knows I'm looking at her.

It was Ben's opinion that women possess an innate ability to detect observation, no matter how the onlooker disguised his attentions. Still the girl did not move. She continued to stare at the gravel beach, perhaps deciding whether to head in that direction or go back and become a mystery to him. He wanted her to stay, to turn round and face him.

In the seconds before she moved, Ben studied her one more time; her face, her hair, the dark glasses. A brunette with highlights, she wore her hair straight, just above the shoulders. She had the look of a Mediterranean, perhaps Greek or Italian; he really couldn't say. There was something about the shape of her nose that made her face extraordinarily perfect, embedding itself into his subconscious. It did not matter that he had only seen her in profile; unless there was some terrible defect yet to shock him, he was already hooked.

The girl walked away towards the beach, almost colliding with Spiro who headed for Ben's table.

"How was the shrimp saganaki?" he asked.

Ben's eyes followed the escaping girl. Like a bird, wounded and unable to fly, she clearly did not know where she was going.

Spiro spoke again. "Would you like another beer, a coffee maybe?"

Ben bounced back and forth between his reverie and the conversation, finally landing back at the owners' original question.

"The saganaki was excellent, really delicious."

Switching his glance back to the disappearing girl, he took a long drink of mineral water before ordering. He spoke on auto-pilot.

"I'll have a cappuccino."

Spiro, assuming Ben didn't want to chat, picked up the iron skillet and went back to the taverna. By the time Spiro reached the restaurant, the girl had passed the palm tree with the scruffy dog and was approaching the last building in the village. As Ben saw it, she had two options: either turn around at the car park and come back or continue around the bay to the fishing boat dock. He thought the latter option unlikely; he hadn't seen anyone on the opposite shore.

Suddenly Ben became thirsty and gulped down the remaining water. The girl reached the parking lot, he wouldn't have long to wait. She turned around and faced him. From this distance, Ben couldn't make out her expression but her body language suggested she would walk no further. She looked to her right, walking closer to the sea, eventually sitting on one of the large rocks lining the opposite shore. He felt sure she would come back his way.

Her choice, to sit on the rock, allowed Ben a respite from second-guessing her movements, freeing him to contemplate his move when she walked back to the restaurant and past his table. He would have to say something; nothing was ever so preordained. As he waited for the moment to intercept her, he fantasized about an amorous island adventure.

Maybe she could join him on the yacht; he could spend the week with her, and then head back to London. Seven days would be enough; after all, long-term relationships didn't work for him. Perhaps what he needed was a pet, a female human pet. One he could love, as he would love a cat, a dog or a caged bird; a pet that he could leave with friends when he went on vacation, one he could take out of the house at his whim.

Still the girl didn't move.

"Do you need anything else?" Spiro placed a cappuccino on the table and waited. Ben looked over to the rocks two hundred yards away. The girl had already started her walk back to the harbor.

"I'm okay for the moment," said Ben.

He hoped he would not need the bill just yet.

11

Even though Sophia had left the windows open, the air inside the car was hot and sticky. Elena turned the air-conditioning to the highest setting as they made their way down the mountain towards Fiskardo.

"What did you think of Dimi?" asked Sophia.

"I like him," said Elena. "I wasn't sure at first." Mixed emotions welled up; attraction, a touch of disappointment never to become his model, regret even. "I think he's a nice person." She changed the subject. "I dread to think what Pasquali is like. Are you armed?"

The girls laughed as they reached the outskirts of town.

Sophia turned into a steep narrow road leading to the harbor and pulled the car to a halt.

"I'll drop you off here. Vehicles are not allowed after this point," said Sophia. "Just turn left and you'll be at the waterfront. Be good, and have a great time, I'll be back in a couple of hours— if Pasquali doesn't get me, that is."

Elena waved her cousin goodbye and walked down the narrow lane, turning around one time to watch the car pull onto the main highway.

She caught her first glimpse of the harbor through the garden of a small house. Tall masts poked up, like thin white trees over the flowering shrubs, inspiring her to take a photograph. Further along the street, she stopped at a gift shop, attracted by hats hanging from metal stands under the canopy. To pass time, she modeled a sombrero and cream fedora in a mirror sitting atop the rack.

Sophia won't be back for at least two hours, thought Elena. Without a plan, she decided to find a cafe, relax, and read for a while.

The harbor was close, less than two hundred yards from the gift store. Elena sat on a wooden bench, by the quayside, admiring the flotilla in the bay. Tavernas, housed in pastel painted buildings, competed for her attention with their extravagant, flower-covered walls. She chose a beige gable-fronted cafe.

Dark green shutters decorated the attic and upper-storey windows. Outside, a small blackboard, set in a wooden frame, stood tent-style on the boardwalk. Colored chalks, a different one for each word, spelled out:

"Breakfast, Coffee, Sandwich, Omelets, Tost, Ice Cream."

Elena smiled at the misspellings, thinking it quant.

A green awning with a patterned fringe hung beneath the upper-floor windows, providing glorious shade for half-a-dozen tables in the cozy space below. Masses of flowers covered the walls, resting on the canopy, suggesting its collapse. At least three different species of vines spurted pink, red, and purple blooms across the entire width of the building.

She sat under the awning at a table-for-two and dug out her book, flipping it over to read the back cover.

"The Ten Thousand Things is a novel of shimmering strangeness—the story of Felicia, who returns with her baby son from Holland to the Spice Islands of Indonesia ... a book that is at once a lament and an ecstatic ode to nature and life."

The paperback had been sitting on top of a pile of sweaters at a local yard sale back in Boston. Its title intrigued her, she was vaguely aware of a tenet from Taoism or Zen with the same name. Karma, Zen … this was her latest promise for contentment; fifty cents was a fair price to pay.

A waitress, delivering breakfast to a quayside table, spotted Elena and came over.

"A regular coffee," said Elena. "What desserts do you have?"

The woman pulled a menu from her pocket, handed it to Elena and waited, without saying a word.

"I'll have the tiramisu," said Elena.

The waitress took the order, rather off-handedly in Elena's opinion, and went back inside the cafe.

What was that about? Elena shrugged, returned to her book, and began to read. Half way down the first page, her phone rang. She rummaged in her bag, curious who could be calling; it had to be Sophia.

Greg Buchanan's name showed on the caller ID. Elena pressed the talk button.

"Hi Greg, is there something wrong? It's early there, isn't it?"

"I didn't sleep much last night, I've been thinking about you. How've you been?" Greg's tone made the question rhetorical.

"Fine."

Elena gave a two-minute recount of her day; the scenic drive with Sophia, the visit to Dimi's studio. She lost concentration at the thought of Dimi; the two of them alone, sitting on the balcony, overlooking the harbor.

"It sounds like you're having a great time, honey." Greg's sarcastic tone confirmed his lack of interest in her morning.

She pictured him, tapping his fingers on the dashboard, stuck in traffic on the 93 freeway.

"Have you booked your flight home yet?" he pressed.

The waitress arrived with the coffee and dessert; she glared at Elena, chastising her for holding a telephone conversation in her cafe.

Elena multi-tasked her frustrations between the rude woman and the pestering boyfriend.

The unfortunate timing of the waitress' arrival coincided with Greg's uncomfortable question. Her brief pause, to acknowledge the server, must have appeared as a stalling tactic to Greg, launching him on the offensive.

"Well, aren't you going to answer?" His voice was beginning to grate.

She was in no mood for a repeat of their earlier argument. "No, I haven't booked my flight home."

"I think we need to sort this out."

"Hold on a minute," she said.

The conversation was becoming too intense, too personal for the surroundings. Elena walked off the patio towards the nearest isolated spot over by the quay wall. Instinctively, she picked up her book and bag. The delay added to Greg's frustration.

She tried to explain, as she had a few days earlier, that she was just taking an extended break; nothing had gone wrong with their relationship. She did not say that she needed some time to herself; that something was missing from her life; that the island was affecting her; that she had begun to think of not returning.

Greg was using his attorney-voice, pontificating, pointing out the obvious course of action to the stupid client. She hated that.

An elderly man walked up and stood next to her, looking out over the bay. Begrudgingly, she moved ten or fifteen yards further away from the cafe, until she found another private spot.

Greg was on the warpath, wanting answers. Elena knew him too well; she guessed he'd slept little last night, churning things over in his head, frantically trying to second-guess her motives. One minute blaming her, the next, making excuses on her behalf for what he perceived as her unacceptable behavior. In her mind, the confrontational Greg had won the latest round; today he was being a man, taking control. Any moment she was expecting the question; "Had she met someone else?"

"Listen, Elena, I'm going to buy you a ticket home. I want you to tell Sophia, that you're going back to Boston next week."

Elena seethed with resentment. "I have a ticket. I just need to call the airline and give them a new departure date. It's a hundred dollar fee. No worries."

"If that's the case, you must have given them a date when you cancelled the return flight," said Greg

She sensed his attorney-mind springing into action and wandered further along the quay, as if to escape the conversation.

"What date was that?" he continued. "Exactly how long are you planning to stay? What the hell's going on?"

"Greg, I don't want to discuss this right now."

"How long?" insisted Greg

"I don't remember."

"You don't remember?" Greg was shouting now.

"I've got to go. I'm not going to spend all day arguing with you. I'll call you later, okay?"

"No, don't hang up. Let's talk about this. Are you planning on staying there permanently?"

"I'll call you later, bye," Elena hung up and walked away, confused and angry.

A hand tapped on her shoulder.

"Excuse me. Excuse me. Nine Euros, you pay now, nine Euros."

Elena turned around. The waitress from the cafe stood in front of her, waving the unpaid bill.

"Dammit, I forgot, I'm sorry," said Elena.

Recovering her composure, she fumbled for some cash and pulled a twenty Euro note from her purse.

The waitress examined the bill, holding it up to the light, inflicting further insult.

"You come back to restaurant for change," she ordered.

"It's okay, keep it. Have a nice day." Elena vacillated between giving up the extravagant tip and not having to deal with the woman a second longer.

The waitress relented, offering a begrudging "Thank you" before her parting shot. "You dropped your book." She pointed at the pavement and turned around.

Elena scowled at the waitress's back, who strutted off along the boardwalk. As Elena's indignation subsided, she looked down. Sure enough, the paperback lay there; funny how she had not noticed dropping it. She stooped, pausing, as she became aware of three large vases of a brilliant red color, a few feet away. Thick, gnarled trunks grew from the pots and up the ochre colored walls of the building, before bursting into foliage and flowers.

Gorgeous, thought Elena as she picked up the book.

With no clear purpose, she walked in the opposite direction to the cafe. Before she had gone fifty yards, her phone chirped the ringtone for a text message. She stopped. It had to be Greg. Standing in front of a souvenir shop, she took stock of her surroundings; a little beach ahead, restaurant tables to her right. Torn between reading the message and wanting nothing more to do with Greg, she deliberated. It was still early; Sophia would be at least another hour away.

She stayed rooted to the spot. A minute went by, maybe more; she didn't care. Going back in the direction of the cafe held no appeal; ahead, the village ended. Greg's message nagged at her; she wanted to read and ignore it in equal measures.

Finally, she decided to head towards the beach; more out of the necessity to make a decision than with any purpose in mind. Vaguely sensing a man watching her, she walked away without looking in his direction.

Unable to find a bench, she stood at the waters' edge, taking deep breaths of ozone-rich air. The bay spread out before her, calm like a lake; a cruise ship, at the entrance to the harbor, dominated her view. She sat on a smooth flat rock, letting the peaceful setting wash her tension away.

Composed once more, she reached for her phone and stared at the message. It was from Greg. "Sorry I got angry I didn't mean what I said miss you please come home soon love greg"

"We both need to calm down will call you later," she replied.

Here, gazing out over the tranquil harbor, the possibility of a lifestyle change crystalized in Elena's mind. She realized how easy it had been, accepting Sophia's invitation to stay. How she'd fallen under the influence of Nicia and her idyllic world. The more Elena pondered the logistics of relocating to Kefalonia, the more feasible it became. She was part Greek, could get papers; could live with Aunt Nicia. People did crazy things, like move to a Greek island. Why couldn't she?

She felt more alive, more sensual here.

What was it Dimi had said … 'Love is like a painting…'

Greg didn't fit into this picture; he belonged to another world. In that world, she loved him, could see a future together. She had been fine before leaving Boston or so she'd thought…

Now was not the time for decisions, Elena resolved to enjoy herself, put thoughts of Greg aside. She would make her choice when ready; perhaps she would visit Dimi again.

In better spirits, she got up and headed back to the plaza.

12

Ben's eyes fixed on the approaching girl. The olive colored dress with the shapely legs was less than a minute away. He had somehow convinced himself that she would be expecting his advances, that an affair was a fait accompli; he had not rehearsed what to say. He gauged the distance and velocity that would intercept her at the closest point to his table before getting to his feet.

"Hi," he said. "I saw you standing here earlier. You looked lost." Ben paused, aware that the girl might not understand English. "Is everything okay?" His voice lacked its usual confidence.

Elena vaguely remembered someone watching her and guessed this was the man.

"Yes, I'm fine. Thank you for asking."

The strange black and white image on his T-shirt intrigued her. What was that? Are those people asleep?

He continued to block her path. "I'm waiting for some friends; I thought you might be doing the same."

"I am, actually—my cousin. She may be another hour. What time is it?"

She asked herself the question, more so than him and checked her watch. His eyes never left her face.

As he stood in front of her, Ben realized he was sexually aroused. It was hard to believe. He was a grown man, not a teenager; he was merely talking to her. The sensation both excited and intrigued him. Despite the improbability of her noticing his erection, he became anxious to sit back down. Turning around, he pointed at the table, putting his hands around his waist in a conscious attempt to hide his condition.

"I'm having a drink, watching the world go by," he said. "You're welcome to join me."

"Okay, sounds like a good idea."

He slid back the rattan loveseat, allowing her to squeeze in.

"I'm Ben, by the way."

"Elena."

"Would you like a cocktail?" He passed her the menu. "I've eaten already."

While she browsed the drinks list, he weighed the odds that she'd order then go to the restroom and check her appearance.

"I'll have a glass of white wine. This one looks interesting." She pointed to the moscofilero varietal. "Excuse me. I have to go to the bathroom."

A waiter, serving the nearby table, looked up as Elena rose. Ben attracted the man's attention, all the while keeping his eyes on Elena, following her until she disappeared inside the taverna.

Her absence allowed Ben chance to take stock of the situation. Sparks were flying for him but what about her. His disadvantage was obvious; she had just bumped into him, whereas he had focused solely on her for the last ten minutes. For all he knew, that intense concentration could have ignited some primal urge. Perhaps the unusual color of her figure-hugging dress had acted as a supernormal stimulus, causing his erection. He checked himself for being neurotic.

The waiter came over. Ben asked for the wine and a small Alfa beer. He didn't want the beer, but the girl might be more at ease if she wasn't drinking alone.

She was taking her time. Ben filled in the moments with more speculation. Why was he attracted to this particular girl? Yes, she was good looking but, in truth, nothing more than countless others he saw daily in Los Angeles or the West End of London. Wasn't it only last week he'd lunched with a friend; their idle talk spawning a theory; what was it again? Seeing a constant procession of new, attractive women every day, anesthetizes you from ever singling one out for special attention. So with this girl, it had to be the surroundings, the island, affecting him.

If she is willing, this could get interesting.

The waiter brought the drinks as Elena came out of the restaurant. Ben stood as she reseated.

"So, tell me what you are doing in Fiskardo. It's charming, don't you think?" he asked.

"Yes, it is. I'm staying at my aunt's house in Argostoli. That's where my cousin lives—the girl I'm waiting for. I've been here for a couple of weeks or more."

He understood from her accent that she was American. "Are your aunt and cousin Americans?"

"No they're Greek, so is my father, but he moved to the States as a child. I suppose, I'm Greek-American. How about you; where's that accent from?"

"I was born in Paris, grew up in London, now I live in Los Angeles."

"Well, you'll be used to the sunshine, then."

"You know, it's different here. Southern California's technically semi-desert, the evenings are cool and the humidity low. You don't get the magical, warm and humid nights we get here in Greece; you can almost cut the atmosphere. I miss that, the dinners outside under the vines..." He left the sentence unfinished.

"I know what you mean, that's one of the reasons I've stayed longer than planned. I don't want to go back yet." She paused then said simply. "I've become enchanted."

Things were going well. He must keep her entertained and get her onto the boat.

"How's the wine?"

"Fine."

Both of them wore sunglasses and he wanted to make eye contact. They were in the shade, under the canopy; he'd start by removing his glasses, perhaps she'd follow suit.

Where is the yacht? He hoped it would arrive before the girl's cousin. Checking the time, he circled back to her earlier remark: 'I've become enchanted.'

That would be his best ploy, get her to talk about herself; something abstract, intimate, make her describe the enchantment.

An idea sprang to mind. "Did you bring a camera?" He continued before she could answer. "There are so many things here to photograph; the hills, the boats, buildings; hell, even just doors and window frames. I only got in last night but I'm hooked on the place already."

Mentioning camera and door in the same breath had Elena thinking of Dimi and the purple door. "Yes to both questions. I have a camera and you're right."

She warmed to the conversation, eager to accept his company; an easy distraction from the stress caused by Greg.

Ben took the camera from his pocket and placed his sunglasses in the table.

"I took a few pictures today, I like one or two of them; what do you think?"

He cycled through the images, stopping at the ochre building with the bright red vases and passed the camera to Elena.

If her sunglasses are polarized, she won't be able to see the pictures and will have to take them off.

They were not.

"Hey, I recognize this..." She pointed down the street, to where she'd dropped her book. The picture brought back her emotions at that moment; anger, embarrassment, admiration for the beauty of the building, a hint of pity for Greg.

"These are nice. I love all the contrasting colors they use on the buildings." Her voice conveyed a charming sincerity.

Suddenly, her expression changed to one of surprise.

"No way. This looks like my father in an old black and white photograph ... it's the only picture of him as a child, before he left the island."

She handed back the camera. Ben couldn't believe his luck, the photo of the boy, who had appeared at the blue door, resembled her father. He hoped she subscribed to the 'everything happens for a reason' philosophy.

"That's strange. I take half a dozen pictures, you recognize one and another reminds you of your father."

"I know."

"Do you mind?" He pointed the lens at her.

Elena smiled, holding the smile, as he pressed the shutter.

"You're really pretty. How about one without the glasses? Let me see those eyes."

Elena obliged and he snapped another, handing her the camera before she could retrieve the sunglasses.

"Are you a photographer?" she asked.

"No, but I like taking pictures. If a subject's worth photographing, it's probably something you want to remember. I think photography helps you collect more memories. You know ... like that building with the red vases; we could've walked right past, but now, we'll both remember it—all because I took a picture. I try to be aware that I'm looking at something, or someone, or some moment that is about to become a memory. I like to capture that moment. Take today, for instance, there's a garden at my hotel, I call it the cypress garden. It's nothing special but it holds some intangible attraction for me; I just know I'll never forget it. When you think about it, the only experiences that matter are those we remember."

'The only experiences that matter are those we remember.' Elena had heard something similar, four days ago. That day she'd been in a cemetery.

"I've never thought of it like that before. You're right; if an experience mattered, we would remember it. Actually, that's kind of sad because we spend most of our time in routine that gets forgotten."

She took a closer look at Ben; the things he said resonated with her. She decided he was quite attractive, mid to late thirties, she liked his hairstyle; dark brown, medium length with long layers, slicked backwards. She was drawn to his eyes.

"You have the most beautiful eyes … like they're sparkling."

Her comment took him by surprise. He managed a semi-humorous reply.

"It depends what they're looking at."

He held her gaze.

Only a drop of wine remained in Elena's glass. Ben poured a small measure of beer into his, leaving the rest in the bottle; she probably doesn't realize I'm not drinking.

"Would you like another?" he asked.

"Not just yet." She kept open the possibility of staying a while longer.

Ben switched the conversation back to the island. He thought it likely she'd be comparing life on vacation to the routine of home. This was something he did too.

"So, I've only been here a day, you're already acclimatized. What fascinates you about the Kefalonia?"

Elena spoke about her Aunt's house, the courtyard, the al fresco family dining, the way the place made her feel more alive, more aware of herself.

Everything was going to plan; all he needed now was the yacht. He recalled the harbor from last night, from the taxi window, how the water danced with colored light. Such settings were the stuff of romance. He widened his ambitions to keeping her on board for the sunset.

"Did I tell you my friends were arriving in a yacht?"

"Oooo, Mr. Fancy Pants."

"I'm expecting them any time now. There's sure to be a party on board. Will you be able to join us? I'd like that. The harbor is very pretty at night."

He anticipated a favorable reply.

"Okay … but only until my cousin arrives. We live in Argostoli, it's an hours' drive through the mountains. We'll have to leave at least an hour before sunset."

Disappointment cast its shadow; he'd overlooked the journey back to Argostoli. Elena, too, suddenly awakened to the possibility that she might squander an evening; the type of which she'd hoped for when prolonging her stay. They both schemed; he: how to convince her to stay; she: how to convince Sophia.

Elena thought back to the coincidental pictures, to the change in her mood since Greg's call.

Everything happens for a reason, she told herself.

Ben's phone rang. The caller ID showed 'Eric Miller'

"Excuse me," he said.

She watched him stand, stride over to the boardwalk, orienting himself with the yachts' location as he took directions from the caller.

"He really wasn't bad looking. I hope Sophia is late."

Ben caught the waiter's attention, signaling for the check. He hung up and rejoined Elena. They chatted about the boat, wasting the moments as the waiter processed his credit card. Finally, he signed the slip, stood up and held out his hand, helping Elena slide out of the loveseat. Her legs, now legendary in status, filled his mind.

If only she had a coat. Now would be the perfect time to help her into it, to put his hands on her shoulders.

He smiled.

"Shall we go?"

13

Elena stood on the dusty ground outside the Church of Saint Gerasimos, her hand stretched into the car, helping Sophia out into the fiery heat. A gypsy boy, no older than ten, leaned against the trunk of a nearby tree, watching them from under its shade. Elena looked up and spotted the boy who stared back, unflinching. She smiled; the boy didn't reciprocate, and she broke free of his gaze.

"Sophia, can you pass my hat? It's on the back shelf," said Elena.

Yesterday, she had bought a black hat, the type suitable for a solemn occasion. Judging by the crowd, she needn't have bothered, though it might come in handy during the procession. She glanced at her mother, who was tying a black scarf around her head.

"Look at us; anyone would think we're heading for a funeral and Sophia's off on a date."

"Told you so," said Sophia.

"At least Dad got it right."

Wearing a white, open-necked shirt, her father locked up the vehicle. Never a man of many words, he'd become increasingly distant as they neared the monastery. For a brief moment, he was not her father but a stranger, standing in front of a stark white church, awaiting an audience with the Patron Saint of Kefalonia.

Cars, parked in chaotic fashion, covered the hard stony ground. Despite the fierce heat, nobody made a move. It was as though an unspoken agreement existed; to wait for her father's signal. He glanced at his watch then dropped the car keys into his trouser pocket.

"Can you check on Stephan?" he said.

Elena pulled out her phone, dialed her brother's number then set off through the maze of vehicles towards the church. The sun burned hot on her face; she raised her hat and looked for shade.

"Let's meet them under the portico at the front of the church," she suggested.

Her father nodded.

"He's less than five minutes away, right behind Aunt Nicia." Elena hung up the phone and glanced back towards the car, looking for the gypsy boy. He had vanished.

The family walked in silence. A choral chant increased in volume as they approached the welcoming shade of the north-side portico. Worshippers, waiting in line, began filing into the church. Elena stepped away from the others and walked around to the eastern side. She looked down a wide avenue, paved with limestone that ran parallel with the side of the church. In less than an hour, the promenade would become the route of a procession, carrying the mummified body of Saint Gerasimos from the church, past the old monastery, to a place held special during his life.

Elena fought her way against a tide of people to rejoin her family. Still, the others had not arrived. Nobody spoke. Perhaps like her, the music captivated them. Never before, had Elena been moved by church music. Haunting and joyous, sad, yet beautiful, it seemed to embody the essence of this auspicious personal occasion.

"That's Andreas's car." Her mother pointed at a white Mercedes. The vehicle slowed to a crawl at the end of the tree-lined drive, turning right to disappear behind the crowds.

"Stephan should be right behind. Did you see his car?" Her mother adjusted her headscarf as she spoke.

"It was behind the Mercedes," said Sophia. "Everyone's here."

An old woman hobbled past; a cane in one hand, a young man on the other. The old lady was a reminder that today was a day for miracles. Many of the congregation would lie, inline, face-up on the ground, waiting for the body of the saint to pass over them. Her father intended to be one of them.

"What kept you?" Veronica Katros greeted her son, as he strolled up to the portico.

Stephan held the hand of his youngest boy. "You know what it's like with kids."

Only yesterday, Aunt Nicia had pointed out the similarity in the age of Stephan's boys to Ioannis and his brother at the time of the great earthquake. The family planned to have them accompany their grandfather in the procession.

"When can we hear the band?" The youngest boy pointed over by the promenade, where two brass bands waited for the order to march.

The church was filling up fast; the family barely had time to greet one another before heading for the entrance. Three earthquake survivors led the way: Ioannis, Nicia and Andreas. The moment was finally at hand. Elena watched her father close his eyes before entering the church. The next hour was going to be emotional for him; she did not know whether joy or sadness would prevail.

14

At sixty foot, the ten-berth motor yacht, Lamia IV, dwarfed the neighboring boats. Moored by the main plaza, it lay less than two hundred yards from where Ben and Elena had met an hour earlier. As they walked past the ochre colored building, Elena ran her fingers along the glazed surface of one of the red vases and smiled. She hadn't told Ben about the confrontation with the waitress. A short distance further, they turned onto a concrete jetty that extended out into the bay.

"Eric said to head for the biggest boat," said Ben.

"How many people are onboard?" she asked.

"Six. Oh, and Eric's son—seven. I should have joined the cruise earlier but I was tied up in London."

"Then we wouldn't have met."

"That's right. Corfu, Paxi, Lefkada, I gave those islands a miss. Something told me to come straight to Kefalonia."

"So this is the last island on the trip? You left it late."

"There's still Zante. I think the plan is to sail to Argostoli in the morning then Zante before dark; it's pretty close. They'll drop the boat off there and fly back to the States."

A voice called above their heads. "Hey, Ben."

Ben stopped, gave a mock-salute to his friend then stepped onto the gangway, stretching out his hand for Elena.

"Eric, good to see you." Ben shook his friend's hand at the bottom of the stairs.

"Glad you could make it. Joe's up top, the girls have gone into the village." Eric looked at Elena. "You didn't say you were bringing a guest."

"Oh, this is Elena. We just met. Elena, this is my good friend, Eric."

In his early forties, and heavily tanned from a week in the sun, Eric stood six foot three in his flip-flopped feet.

"Welcome aboard, Elena. Why don't I give you the tour?"

Stepping into the main cabin reminded Ben of his father's yacht; sumptuous, with white leather seating and mahogany woodwork. An action movie played on a large-screen TV at the far end of the salon; its sound muted.

"Nice, eh? There are plenty of spots to hang out and enjoy a cocktail; here, the flybridge or the lounge area on the foredeck," said Eric. "I'll make up some drinks after I've shown you around."

"Flybridge, foredeck," Ben turned to Elena. "I forgot to pack my nautical phrase book."

"You'll get used to it." Eric smiled. "This is the galley—kitchen to you."

"You cooking tonight?"

"Not on this trip."

"Eric's quite a cook," Ben explained.

"Here's the cockpit, where all the technical stuff happens." Eric pointed at the instrument panel in front of the wrap-around windshield.

"Is it German?" Ben sat down and played with the helm.

"French; we wanted something bigger but this was the largest bareboat we could find."

"It doesn't look bare to me," said Ben.

"As I think you well know, a bareboat is a charter boat without a skipper. All the ones seventy feet and up had a crew and you know how I like to be in charge."

Further aft, under the windshield, three steps led down to the staterooms. Ben's feet sank into the plush white carpet that brushed up against the polished mahogany walls.

Eric opened the portside cabin door.

"Joe and Clotilde," he said, allowing a few seconds for his guests to glance inside before closing the door. There was an identical bedroom on the starboard side.

"Alan's sleeping in the skipper's cabin, under the stern," he went on.

"Alan is Eric's son," explained Ben. "How old is he now?"

"Ten."

"Main bathroom ... shower room's opposite. And finally ... the master's suite."

"Yours perhaps?" Ben stepped aside, letting Elena enter first.

It was hard not to be impressed. The stateroom had a king sized bed, closet space, mirrored wall and its own en-suite bathroom.

"So, what do you think?" asked Eric.

"Time for cocktails is what I think," said Ben. He turned to Elena. "Do you like mojitos? Eric makes the best in all of Southern California."

"Are you kidding? I love mojitos."

Back in the main cabin, Ben stood, leaning against the small bar area, watching the maestro work on the drinks. "You're having one, right?"

His friend grimaced at the redundant question.

As Eric mashed mint and lime juice into a Collins glass, Ben's thoughts returned to scheming and Elena.

"So Eric, what's the plan for tonight? I'm hoping the lovely

Elena will be joining us for the evening."

"Dunno, the only plan is, we have no plan. The girls will probably want to eat at a restaurant later; or we could have food delivered. I'm easy."

He handed the mojitos to Ben, who passed one to Elena.

"Cheers."

They chinked glasses.

"Let's go up top," suggested Eric.

Outside on the stern deck, Ben headed for the stairs.

"Not those," said Eric. "They lead to the aft lounge."

He started to climb a much steeper flight. Half way up, he stopped and looked back. "Be careful Elena, they're very steep."

Ben insisted she go before him, his chivalry brought his face its first brush against the silk of her legs.

Stark whiteness dazzled Ben as he poked his head through the trap door and got his first glimpse of the flybridge. The floor, the seats, the table; nothing of color existed. He flipped on his sunglasses and took stock of the view.

The upper deck was about twelve feet from the water, an excellent vantage point for observing the village street life. Ben noticed the second cockpit; the thought of steering the craft under a starlit sky flashed through his mind. Close to the trap door, a circular table sat in the center of wrap-around seating; a retractable canopy provided shade.

"Joe." Ben raised his glass to a thickset man who leaned against the guardrail. By way of acknowledgment, the man lifted his beer bottle a foot off the rail and let it drop down again.

"So, you only got here last night and you met a girl already?" growled Joe.

In his mid-forties, Joe Marchetti was of Italian descent and fiercely proud of it. He had a grouchy manner, but possessed a sense of humor with a razor sharp wit. Joe liked to poke fun at people and Ben was often the butt of his jibes.

"Joe, meet Elena." Ben's wry smile let Elena know Joe's remark was playful.

They both said 'Hi' at exactly the same time.

"So where's the new French girlfriend?" asked Ben. "I'm dying to meet her."

"She left him already. Gone looking for younger guys," chipped in Eric.

"Guys?" said Ben.

"She told me she'd have more fun with two twenty-five year olds than with a fifty year old."

"Fifty, who the hell's fifty," said Joe.

"Is the old Italian charm starting to wear off, then?" said Ben.

"Are you Italian, Joe?" asked Elena.

Ben replied on his behalf.

"No, he's American, from New Jersey. For some unknown reason, he just likes to think he's Italian."

Joe let Ben finish.

"I was born in New Jersey. Both my parents are Italian."

That was the about the limit of Joe's sincerity. He reverted to type, turning his attention to Elena. "Where are your girlfriends? Call them up; we can all go out for a moonlight cruise."

"You're out of luck, Joe. They're in Argostoli and it's an hours' drive from here. My cousin Sophia will be here soon though…"

"Sophia … there you go, Joe," said Eric.

"Joe's always babbling on about Sophia Loren," Ben explained. He tried mimicking Joe's accent, adding a whiny tone, "The most beautiful woman of all time."

"My Sophia is pretty too, but she won't be able to stay for your midnight cruise," said Elena.

"That's a pity. And even more of a pity that you hooked up with this guy." Joe nodded at Ben.

In need of a wisecrack, Ben was beginning to flounder; he was no match for the Jersey boy. Clutching at straws, something popped into his head.

"Hey Joe, you just reminded me of an article I read on the flight over."

"Yeah, what was that?"

"Some university research group conducted a worldwide study of women's sex lives…"

"You reading women's magazines, now?"

"It was a science publication."

"And?" said Joe

"So each time the women had sex, the researchers had them record how long it lasted."

"Sounds like a woman's mag to me," said Joe.

"Get this … contrary to popular belief; the Italians didn't perform too well. Apparently, Northern European men outperformed the Southern Europeans by a factor of thirty percent."

Joe let out a gasp. It wasn't surprise or laughter, but a strange mannerism of his. "Bullshit, go screw yourself."

"No, honestly, I'm serious. In fact, Englishmen came out on top." Ben paused to allow his audience to get the pun. "Followed by the Americans." He was making it up as he went along.

"Who conducted the survey then, the BBC?" snapped Joe.

"I'll find the article on the Internet, and send it to you. In the meantime, try searching online for Italian Sex Rapido."

"What's a bonehead like you doing with a science magazine anyway?" Joe turned to Elena. "Ben can only manage really small books like The History of Great English Lovers."

"This guy's too good," said Ben. "I just can't compete with him."

"You are both funny," she replied.

The banter paused. Sparring with Joe wasn't easy. Still, he'd come away unscathed; was in good spirits and the mojito tasted good.

Elena's phone beeped with a text message. She reached into

her bag, retrieving the handset and turned to Ben. "It's Sophia. I need to call her."

"You're going to be staying, aren't you? You can't leave yet." His question, couched in a playful tone, masked his concern that Elena might be unable to persuade her cousin on board. "Tell her she's invited to a party on a yacht."

Elena got up, descended the steps, and stepped off the boat. Ben watched anxiously as she walked down the jetty with the telephone to her ear. He strained to hear her voice but could not.

"You dog, you," said Eric.

"What?" Ben forced a smile. The guy talk had started, right on cue, the minute Elena moved out of earshot; Joe would surely say something next. Typically, Ben didn't engage in the kind of lewd banter that was about to ensue. He preferred to keep low key and feign amusement. He kept his focus on Elena; she was outside one of the restaurants, seventy yards away.

"Look! He can't keep his eyes off her. What are you, desperate or something? The guy's tongue's hanging out." Joe was beside himself with glee.

"She probably has to go back to Argostoli with her cousin." Ben refused to take the bait.

Depressing thoughts began to cross his mind. She might just carry on walking and not come back. He didn't have her number. Her cousin might insist she leave right away; she may have no choice. He would not be able to find her again.

Being more anxious than the situation warranted concerned him. She was triggering unusual emotions.

Elena turned into a side street, disappearing from view.

"Ha, she's left you," said Joe. "So much for the great English …French lover—whatever the hell you are; she's gone off to find an Italian."

Repeatedly checking the time, made the minutes pass slowly. He kept calm, thinking logically. The girl was unlikely to walk off without saying goodbye, without so much as a wave. It was possible; perhaps there was an emergency. The obvious explanation; she was having difficulty persuading her cousin to come to the boat. He braced himself for further delay.

"Nobody can predict what a woman will do. Hey, I only just met her." Ben's reply was weak; he was unable to concentrate enough to continue the repartee.

Something in Ben's tone must have dampened his friends' enthusiasm for the topic. Their thoughts moved on; his did not.

"I'll call the girls, see where they're at," said Eric.

More than ten minutes elapsed with no sign of Elena. Ben debated the merits of looking for her, deciding against it. He would look a fool chasing after her and he could hardly make an excuse like he'd left something at the hotel.

"They're having coffee and ice-cream on the promenade," said Eric. "They'll be back in a few minutes."

Relief came only after Elena and another girl emerged from a side street, heading towards the boat. He looked away, reengaging in the conversation; he would feign nonchalance should one of his friends spot them. Now that she was back, he analyzed the swing in his emotions: disappointment, lest she not return, followed by joy. He resolved to stop being so ridiculous about a girl he had only just met.

From his vantage point on the guardrail, Joe spotted them first. "Looks like your girlfriend's back—she's so-so but her cousin's not bad."

"I'll get them a cocktail," said Ben, heading for the stairway.

"Wow, pussy-whipped already," barked Joe.

As Ben descended the stairs, Sophia and Elena reached the gangway. "Hey, you're back. I thought you'd left me."

He waited until they were on board before turning to the stranger. "This must be Sophia, the most beautiful woman in the world."

She looked puzzled. Elena explained the remark.

"I'm a little overdressed, I've been working today," said Sophia.

Ben took this to mean overdressed for a party, tonight's party. "No worries. Let me get you a drink, what would you like? How about a margarita? These guys FedExed cases of tequila to the charter company."

"Okay, but not a strong one. I have to drive back to Argostoli soon."

"Another mojito, Elena?"

She nodded.

***

The excited shouts of a child heralded the return of the women. They paused at the sight of strangers. Recognizing Ben, the young boy rushed onto the boat and into the main cabin.

"Hey tiger," said Ben. "Did you catch any fish yet?"

"Lots of them," said the boy. "We caught a baby shark."

"No way."

"Yeah, way. It was like … this big." The boy stretched his arms to their limit.

As Ben clowned, he weighed any advantage the child's affection for him might have with Elena. No sooner had he earned the imaginary Brownie points, he promptly lost them. Ben's eyes locked onto a stunning girl, who had just entered the cabin. By the time he realized he was ogling, Elena was glaring at him.

"This is Clotilde, from France; Joe's friend." Eric stepped up to make the introductions. "Clotilde, this is our friend, Ben."

They shook hands, Ben greeted her in French and they continued conversing in that language.

"I was just telling Clotilde … I was born in Paris and my mother's French," Ben explained to Elena. As he spoke, he realized how presumptuous it was to assume Elena did not understand French.

"This is Elena, from Boston, she's on vacation," said Ben. "And this is her cousin, Sophia. Sophia is Greek and lives in Argostoli."

He left the women to their introductions and leant against the table. Eric, like some Roman emperor, proclaimed a party underway.

"Everything okay?" Ben asked Elena.

She had disengaged from Sophia and was standing a few feet away.

"Sure," she replied.

Lowering her voice to little more than a whisper, she confessed to a dilemma.

"Sophia wanted to drive back to Argostoli. I had a hard time persuading her to come."

She touched his wrist, holding on to it momentarily, making Ben feel like a co-conspirator.

"There's no way she will stay later than six-thirty," she went on.

That left Ben less than two hours to work on Elena.

"Who's the French girl?" Elena kept her voice to a whisper.

Clotilde had already been introduced to Elena. He interpreted her question as—don't converse in French with her again—or worse, she understood the conversation and was baiting him.

"That's Clotilde, Joe's girlfriend. I've never met her. Eric told me she is a model or actress … aspiring actress."

He kept glancing over at Clotilde despite the risk. She wore a short cotton dress, black, like her hair, which reached down to her lower back. By any standard, this was a woman of outstanding beauty; he could recall seeing no finer. As far as looks were concerned, Elena didn't compare to Clotilde. Shallow though Ben felt, comparing the two, a similar divide existed between his wealth and Joe's. Somehow, this banal thought satisfied him.

Clotilde and Sophia stood by the main cabin door, chatting

away like long-lost friends. Ben thought Sophia looked chic in her black business suit.

"I'll go and bring them over." He adjusted the pneumatic drinks table to a comfortable height. A white leather couch wrapped around, making an intimate space for conversation.

"You two seem to be hitting it off. Come sit with us."

"Sophia was telling me about her grandfather's gallery. I used to work at an art gallery in Paris. We have much in common." Clotilde's English had a heavy French accent. "We both studied art history."

"Why don't we visit the gallery tomorrow in Argostoli," suggested Ben. He hoped to tie Sophia deeper into the plot.

"I'd like that. Is it in the center of town?" asked Clotilde.

"Yes, it's close to the boutiques and restaurants. I can show you the sights if you like," replied Sophia.

Ben decided it was time to isolate Elena from Sophia. He turned to Clotilde. "You must have seen some beautiful sunsets on the trip. Which was your favorite?"

"I think, maybe … Paleokastritsa."

"I was in Paleokastritsa about ten years ago. Were you moored out in the bay?"

"Yes, right out in the channel. It was breathtaking," said Clotilde.

"I bet Sophia knows all the best sunsets in the islands," said Ben. "Have you got any recommendations for Clotilde?"

It was a calculated guess that Sophia would be familiar with Paleokastritsa and probably most of the other Ionian beauty spots. He rose and grabbed Elena's hand. "Let s explore the aft lounge, we've not seen that yet."

Clotilde could keep Sophia occupied for a while; he had to get Elena to himself if he stood any chance of keeping her on the yacht this evening.

She followed Ben down to the stern deck and up a short flight

of steps; he held her hand. The walkway around the boat was narrow with a guardrail about waist high. Eric had called the space
the aft lounge, it sat above the staterooms in front of the main
cabin windshield. A padded, king-size sunbed lay spread out before them.

Ben placed his cocktail in the drinks holders at the head of
the sun lounge.

"That's an unusual T-shirt," said Elena, kneeling. "It was the
first thing I noticed when you walked up to me back there."

The boat was pointing in the direction of their meeting place,
the souvenir shop in plain sight.

He lay to her left.

"I had it specially made to attract gorgeous, intelligent wom-
en."

He turned on his side, leaning on his elbow, propping his head
with his palm.

"Lie down, let's catch some sun," he said.

Elena adopted the same position, their faces less than two
feet apart.

"So what do you think of the yacht?" he asked.

"I'm jealous … tell me more about your friends."

He rushed through a fifteen-second biography on each of
them, making a point to downplay their wealth. This was the
world he inhabited, he had long since stopped concerning himself
whether it impressed.

"By the way, I'm not in the same boat as these guys … no pun
intended. I have a far more modest lifestyle."

"What do you do?" she asked.

"Here goes," he thought, "If she calls me a dilettante it's
over."

"Actually, I don't really do anything. It's a bit embarrassing,
but what can I say? I'm happy…"

"So you're a trust fund brat, then?"

"Something like that, I suppose."

He liked trust fund brat better than dilettante.

"Do you believe that everything happens for a reason?" she asked suddenly.

"Not sure, maybe."

Although his reply was noncommittal, he considered her conjecture meaningless. Such an admission, however, would run counter to his aims.

"I do," she said. "I believe we met for a reason."

"Tell me more."

"You aren't married are you?" asked Elena.

"No."

"We've just met, yet I feel like I've known you forever; like I can just say anything and you'd understand," she paused. "I'm sorry; I bet you think I'm crazy."

"No … I kind of feel the same way."

"I guess what I'm trying to say … I'm at a crossroad; I'm confused by my options."

"What options?"

"To go back to Boston or stay here on the island. It's like I'm resisting going back … back to being an ant in some giant anthill."

Torn between a feeling of genuine empathy and seizing an opportunity, Ben leaned in towards her, putting his arm over her shoulder, holding the back of her neck with his hand. He pulled her head ever so slightly forward, kissing her passionately, but briefly. He sensed her dual emotions: surprise and excitement.

Lust and attraction; he felt both intensely. He broke away from the embrace, not wanting to overplay his hand, keeping his eyes locked on hers. He smiled a cheeky smile.

"What?" he said, as if the kiss had been expected.

She stared at him with an exquisite look, one needing no words; at once demure, yet challenging him—daring him to accept.

Mentally, he put words in her mouth, paraphrasing her expression, "Well hotshot—think you're up to it?"

The mad excitement subsided, like dusk descending.

"Maybe THAT just happened for a reason," said Ben. He was still reverberating from the desire to make love to her, there and then, right on the deck.

She slapped his arm, playfully.

"Stop teasing me. I was serious."

"Sorry, I wasn't teasing. I didn't know what to say," he said. "Where were we? The ant race..."

"I know. I'm being an idiot. Most everybody goes on vacation and thinks about never having to go home."

He felt sure there was a boyfriend lurking somewhere back in Boston. Now was not the right time to ask. He thought it better to wait, let her volunteer the information. Reaching over, he fumbled for one of the mojitos, putting the glass to her lips, tipping it. She giggled as a few drops ran down her chin; he took a sip from the same glass before returning it to the drinks' holder.

"So don't go home then. You'll never know if you don't try," he said.

Ben thought he understood her, "She's in a relationship back home and she's on the fence about it. Now, she's enchanted with new, exotic surroundings and needs to put her relationship, her life, to the test. She thinks I might be part of that test."

It all appeared straightforward, except for the unusual and unexpected depths of his feelings. He steered his thoughts back to the kiss.

"I know we've only just met but I don't want you to go back to Argostoli. Can't you stay for the evening?"

"I can't. Sophia has to work tomorrow. She's has a dinner date with her boyfriend and I'm supposed to go..."

He persisted.

"I have a hotel room with twin beds. You and Sophia can

sleep there. I'm okay on the boat, or I can get another room."

"Ben, I'd love to but…" She hesitated then relented, giving him hope. "I'll talk to her and see."

"We're watching you. Don't get up to anything down there. The Greeks'll put you both in the slammer."

They looked up, startled out of their intimacy. Joe leaned over the flybridge windshield, his arms around the gorgeous Clotilde.

"Take no notice," said Ben to Elena, returning to their conversation. He wondered if Clotilde had seen them kiss earlier.

"Hey, we should exchange numbers in case we get separated later. What's yours?" He yanked the phone from his pocket and repeated each number as she spoke them, punching them into the dial pad, causing her phone to ring.

"There, that's me … wait, let me add a picture," he snapped one quickly. "Assign to contact; done. Look."

Holding up the phone, he looked at the picture. His thoughts sprang back to the girl who once gave him her treasured photo. This one did not kill his passion.

"Let me see that." Elena snatched his phone, as if she'd read his mind. "You idiot!" She laughed, returning the device.

Ben checked the time; it was 5:45. He needed to resolve the issue with Sophia. Now, as Elena laughed, was as good a time as any.

"Let's go and find Sophia. I want to get you booked for tonight. We'll all go out to dinner together. You want to, right?"

Elena's expression clouded over. "Yes, but it's not going to go down well. She won't stay."

"I want you both to stay, but it's you that I'm interested in. If she won't stay, she can drive back on her own," he pressed.

"That wouldn't be fair. It's a long stressful drive … there are no lights, it's all winding bends and cliffs…"

"She'll be fine. She does the drive all the time. It's her job. If you weren't here, she would have driven back on her own anyway."

"I don't know. Where will I sleep? How will I get back to Argostoli? I've no change of clothes."

She struggled, caught between her loyalty to Sophia and a desire to discover what part this man would play in her destiny.

"Let's figure this out. I've got a room, you can sleep there. The yacht's sailing to Argostoli tomorrow; you come with us. Clothes are no problem, borrow something from Clotilde or let's go to a store. I'll buy you some."

"Hmmm. Shopping for lingerie already? I don't think so."

"Tomorrow, all you'll need is a bikini and one of my T-shirts. We'll be diving off the boat at Myrtos Beach."

"I saw Myrtos Beach this morning from the cliff top … it was so pretty."

"There you are then, it's settled."

"Okay, but I'm going to talk to her on my own." Her tone was decisive.

They got up in search of Sophia; she was on the flybridge, still chatting with Clotilde.

"Where've you been?" asked Sophia.

"Sunbathing," replied Elena.

Elena sat next to Sophia and whispered something. Sophia looked surprised. The whispering continued until the two girls excused themselves and left the flybridge.

"What was all that about?" asked Clotilde.

"Elena wants to stay and join us for dinner, but Sophia has to leave," Ben explained. "By the way, what are we doing for dinner?" he said, changing the subject.

15

Elena sat beside Sophia on a slatted wooden bench near the jetty's entrance. They faced the harbor.

"You hardly know these people. Where are you going to sleep? What will Grandmother say if I leave you here?" asked Sophia.

Traditional Greek folk music played over a pair of loudspeakers, mounted on the wall of a nearby restaurant. Elena found herself listening to the song in a bid to escape her cousin's logic.

"I can't stay. I promised Nik I'd meet him for dinner and he's bringing Theo," Sophia persisted.

So Nik's friend's got a name now, thought Elena.

Inventing a minor conspiracy gave her impetus.

"If you're concerned what Aunt Nicia thinks, I'll call her myself."

Three Greek men, in their early twenties, came up to the bench. One of them spoke, his voice coming from out of nowhere, behind Elena.

"Beautiful ladies tonight Club Ecstasy free passes beautiful ladies only for free you come with us."

The girls turned around; Sophia glared at the hawkers. Their leader held a stack of tickets, slapping them on the back of his hand every few seconds.

Sophia launched a tirade, in Greek, and the men beat a rapid retreat. Elena laughed. "What did you say to them?"

"You don't want to know."

The incident broke the tension, lessening Sophia's resolve.

"Okay, call her. I'm having nothing to do with this. I'd better tell Nik that our plans have changed."

They each walked in opposite directions along the esplanade, waiting for their calls to connect. The music grew louder as Elena neared the restaurant.

"Hi, Aunt Nicia, it's Elena."

"Elena, where are you, is everything okay, where's Sophia?"

"Everything's fine. Sophia's fine. She'll be driving back in a few minutes. I just wanted to let you know that I won't be back tonight."

"Oh?"

"Yes, I met some friends, they have a big yacht. Everyone's really nice, Sophia likes them."

"Are they Americans?" asked Nicia.

"Yes, well French and Italian too. They're sailing to Argostoli tomorrow and they invited me," she paused to answer another question. "No, I have a hotel room. I'm having fun, don't worry."

They talked for a few more minutes. Nicia, sweet as always, wished her a pleasant evening before hanging up. Elena suspected Nicia would call Sophia and get a second opinion of her new friends. She returned to the bench where her cousin was waiting.

"She's fine with everything," said Elena. "I feel really bad that you have to drive all the way back on your own."

"Don't worry; I've done it a hundred times. As long as it's still light, there's no problem. Just make sure you bring them to the gallery tomorrow. I need to make some sales." Sophia smiled and checked her watch. "The sun sets around eight; it's already six-fifteen. I'll just say goodbye to Clotilde, then I'm off."

Overcoming an obstacle to be with Ben brought Elena closer to him.

***

Back on the flybridge, Ben stared out over the town, letting the last of the Greek sun weave its lazy spell over late afternoon. The slow transformation to twilight was tangible; he felt it descending as he would a damp mist. Soon night would impose its mystery on the harbor; the first colored lights were already reflecting off the water, the music increasing in intensity; a time for creating memories.

He watched Sophia and Elena walk back along the jetty towards the boat. It was inevitable she would stay with him; the magic of the evening would be sucked away like a vacuum if she left now.

The girls climbed the stairs to the flybridge. Elena emerged first, she glanced at Ben, an almost imperceptible affirmation showed on her face. He could relax now.

Sophia wasted no time announcing her departure. Clotilde hugged her new friend, promising to meet again, tomorrow at the gallery. Joe said goodbye without getting up.

"Take good care of her." Sophia waved her hand towards Ben.

"I won't let her out of my sight." He meant it literally.

Sophia touched Elena's arm on her way to the stairs. "I'll call you later; I'll be checking on you."

Ben had plans for the evening and wasted no time executing them. He addressed anyone in earshot. "I'm going to find Eric and make arrangements for dinner. The restaurant where I met Elena has some great tables by the water. I'll go talk to the owner and reserve something. What time do you think, eight-thirty?"

"Works for me," said Joe.

"Elena, do you need a shower? Let's go and buy whatever you

need."

16

The sun had gone down over the mountains behind the little port of Fiskardo. The night air on the quayside was warm, rich and infused with exotic music.

Joe Marchetti led the party of nine along the promenade for the short walk to Spiro's waterfront taverna. A cloth bag, slung over his right shoulder, rested against his white shirt. On his left arm, the gorgeous Clotilde, in a strapless black dress, attracted the attention of every passerby.

Ben followed, side by side with Elena, a bottle of wine swung like a club in his right hand. He hadn't changed, neither had she; thoughts of the olive colored dress clinging to her freshly showered skin were never far from his mind.

Spiro's taverna was a bustle of activity. Waiters flitted between restaurant and quayside, dodging the crowds of tourists, strolling along the boardwalk. Tonight, empty seats were hard to find. One long table stood out from the others, occupying a prime spot by the water's edge. Two tent-signs bearing the word "RESERVED" rested on its turquoise cloth.

Ben nudged Joe. "That's ours."

An hour earlier, Ben had paid a visit to Spiro, handing him three one-hundred Euro bills as part of an arrangement for the evening.

"Do you want to face the harbor or the promenade?" he asked Elena. "People-watching will be more fun."

"Fine," she replied.

Accommodating nine people required two tables, placed end-to-end. Ben made straight for the rattan loveseat nearest the water, sliding it back, allowing Elena to slide in. Joe and Clotilde sat opposite.

"I'll be back in a minute," said Ben and walked off in search of Spiro.

By the time he returned, his friends were seated. Elena chatted with the couple next to her; the man was Sean, his wife Louise.

"This is Spiro, the owner," announced Ben. "He's promised to look after us tonight."

The guests greeted Spiro. He cleared his throat before delivering his introduction.

"Good evening everybody and bon soir." Spiro smiled at Clotilde. Elena glanced at Ben wondering why he'd staged that for her.

"Thank you for visiting my restaurant. I'm very honored to serve you."

The speech was interrupted by one of the waiters, who arrived carrying a huge bouquet of flowers. He bowed formally and presented them to Elena, surprising both her and the other guests. Diners at the nearby tables paused to stare; a young man applauded.

Ben was still standing next to Spiro; he smiled at Elena over Joe's head. A few seconds later, a second waiter, carrying a glass vase, relieved her of the flowers, placing them in the center of the table. Her eyes narrowed as she shot a glance at Ben. He couldn't tell if she was pleased, angry or surprised.

Spiro let the cheering die down before continuing his welcome.

"Tonight's dinner will be in honor of Elena, who met Ben, my friend, for the first time, here at my restaurant, today."

Applause erupted again. Ben tapped Spiro on the back in a friendly gesture and rejoined Elena.

"I hate you. Everyone's staring at me," she whispered in Ben's ear.

He put his arm around her waist; her head fell gently against his shoulder. The outcome of his conspiracy pleased him. She would never forget this moment.

Spiro passed around menus and started taking the drinks order.

Ben had an announcement of his own. "Tonight, Spiro is going to bring an assortment of his fine creations. They'll keep coming until we tell him to stop. If anyone sees something on the menu that they just have to try, let the waiter know. Bon appétit."

He smiled at Spiro. "I'll have an Alfa beer."

Elena ordered water.

Not to be outdone, Joe took the spotlight. "Put the wine in the middle."

Each of the men had carried a bottle from the yacht; Sean arranged them in the center. Joe stood, put his bag on the table and pulled out three more bottles, lining them up next to the others.

"Six of the best, Sassicaia, the pride of Italy," he said. "None of that Greek piss tonight."

Ben winced, hoping Spiro was out of earshot.

"The Italians copied that wine from the French," said Ben, intending to raise a reaction from Joe.

Joe disliked like anything French. Ben was surprised to learn of a French girlfriend.

"What are you talking about? It's a Super Tuscan," said Joe.

Clotilde sided with Ben. "He's right; Sassicaia is styled after wines from Graves."

"Listen to your better-half, learn something; she's obviously a connoisseur."

"Bullshit, we taught the French how to make wine in the first place, like we taught them cooking and everything else."

With a sweeping motion of his backhand, he flicked the underside of his chin with his fingertips in an exaggerated Italian gesture. He winked at Elena, letting her know he was kidding.

"He's not even Italian," said Ben.

"Be careful or you'll end up drinking the house slop, tonight."

"There are some good Greek wines," Ben protested. "Where'd you get the Sassicaia, anyway?"

"I had it shipped in from Italy, direct to the boat owner's office."

"What's the significance of the wine?" Elena whispered to Ben.

"I don't know. He's always ranting on about it. It is good though, probably three or four-hundred dollars a bottle."

"Ouch," said Elena.

Two waiters arrived, carrying the first round of drinks and baskets of fresh bread. Spiro supervised, taking charge of the wine, uncorking the first Sassicaia with exaggerated ceremony. He poured a tasting sample into Joe's glass. The whole table looked on as Joe pretended to choke on the contents.

"Perhaps, some Greek wine?" suggested Spiro.

"Hey, this guy's funny," said Eric.

Spiro uncorked another bottle, pouring a serving for each guest.

"Enjoy," he said then left.

A young girl in an Athenian goddess costume, carrying a wicker basket of red roses, appeared next to Clotilde. Ben noticed the deep crimson petals against her white dress before he looked up to see the girl's face.

"Joe, wake up. Clotilde needs a rose," he said.

The flower vendor held out an individual rose in a plastic cylinder. Clotilde hesitated, picking two loose ones from the basket.

"Good choice." Ben offered up his water glass as a vase.

"Merci," said Clotilde.

For the last five minutes, Elena had listened to the conversation without speaking. Ben smiled repeatedly at her, keeping her engaged. When she finally spoke, it was to Clotilde.

"Did Sophia tell you about the artists today?"

"Yes, I'm looking forward to seeing their work tomorrow."

"You mentioned working at a gallery in Paris," said Ben.

"Yes, in Le Marais. It was part-time. I wanted a career in modeling but my father is an art dealer; I grew up in that world."

In her preoccupation with Ben, Elena had forgotten to ask Sophia what happened with Pasquali. "I must call Sophia soon," she said to Ben.

Joe handed the flower vendor a pair of twenty-Euro notes. Surprised, she offered one back.

"Keep it," said Joe. "Have a great evening."

The girl, having a seemingly permanent smile, held out roses for Elena. Ben smiled, shaking his head, pointing to the huge bouquet in the center of the table. Elena complimented the girl on her dress and the vendor moved on to the other guests.

"How about you, Ben, are you interested in art?" asked Clotilde.

"Not seriously, I tend to find objects more interesting than paintings. Perhaps some of Modigliani's works … if I had to name a famous painter."

"An Italian of course, what else?" said Joe.

"I think he worked in Paris and was influenced by the French impressionists," said Ben.

"Yeah, well, maybe that's why he painted everyone with ten foot long necks," said Joe.

"I believe his fascination with African art inspired the elongated necks," said Clotilde.

Elena had never heard of Modigliani. In fact, she was unable to remember his name from moments ago.

… it began with the letter M, she thought.

Clotilde was so attractive and sophisticated. It was all she could do not to wilt in her shadow.

It's not her fault; she's not showing off, she thought. I'm the one who mentioned art.

Ben too, was increasingly impressed with the French girl. He reminded himself again to orchestrate the conversation and keep Elena involved. Before he could do that, the first dishes arrived, diverting everyone's attention.

Spiro described each appetizer as though introducing a person.

"This is gemista … tomatoes stuffed and baked; aubergine saganaki, ees delicious; classic Greek salad; dolmades … stuffed vine leaves; tzatziki and kalamarakia … which is pieces of fried squid with lemon juice."

"Outstanding," said Eric.

"Elena, you have to try this," said Ben, lifting the aubergine and stuffed tomatoes plate.

"Thanks, it looks delicious." She scooped up a portion. "This is like eating at my Aunt Nicia's villa. You should see the courtyard where they dine outside; it's magical. I should invite you."

"I think that's all I ever want to do. Spend the whole evening, at the family table, drinking wine, savoring the dishes. How's the Sassicaia, by the way?" he asked, reaching for the bottle.

"Delicious."

Ben poured more wine into Elena's glass then topped up the others, squeezing out the last drops on Joe's pour. "Cheers," he said.

Glasses chinked.

"Time to uncork another," said Joe.

"Hey, Joe, what if we run out of Sassicaia, will you try the Greek wine?" asked Ben.

"Greek wine? Forget about it! Can you imagine … after Sassicaia? I'll just send Alan to the boat for some more."

Elena's phone rang. She excused herself and walked over to the souvenir shop.

"The Greek salad is excellent," said Clotilde. "Back in the States, if I ask for a Greek salad, they'll put lettuce in it."

Ben didn't answer; he sat, transfixed by the vision of Elena, standing exactly where he'd first seen her seven hours earlier. In the muted street light, the olive dress had taken on a different hue; it still clung to her figure, the wellspring of his fantasies.

"Hey Ben, wake up, Clotilde's talking to you," said Joe.

"I asked what Elena does?" repeated Clotilde.

Ben flat out hadn't heard her the first time. "I haven't asked." He wanted to continue his Elena daydream. "And I don't really care. She's from Boston, her parents are Greek; she's staying with family in Argostoli." He kept gazing at Elena. "I think I'm falling in love…"

Clotilde gasped; Joe's jaw dropped.

"Ben!" said Clotilde.

"What the hell," said Joe.

"Well, not yet, but … no seriously; don't tell her for chrissake. I think it's something to do with the atmosphere … you know, here on the island."

"You're a jerk," said Joe.

Clotilde whacked his arm. "Ben's being romantic, Joe. Why can't you?"

"If only he were a true Italian," said Ben.

"No more Sassicaia for you, pal," replied Joe. "Just wait 'til your girlfriend gets back."

"Ben brings up a fascinating subject," said Clotilde. "Studies have shown correlations between falling in love and a sudden change in one's environment."

"I knew it." Ben slapped the table.

"You'd be interested in Why We Love by Dr. Helen Fisher," said Clotilde. "She investigates the brain chemistry behind love. I can lend you a copy. It's interesting stuff."

"I think I read about her research in Scientific American," said Ben.

"Was that the same article with the great English lovers?" Joe waved his hand, dismissing the topic.

"Here's a question for you," Clotilde continued. "What's the name of the hormone associated with love?"

"Serotonin?" suggested Ben.

"That plays a part but it's not the one I'm thinking of," said Clotilde.

"I dunno," said Joe. "How come you know all this stuff?"

"I'll bet Eric knows," said Ben. "He's a biologist."

Clotilde called across the table. "Eric, what's the hormone associated with love?" She glanced over her shoulder at Elena and said in a hushed voice. "Ben's thinks he's been struck by Cupid's arrow."

"Whoa, not so fast," said Ben. "She's kidding, Eric."

"Eh?" Eric looked bemused, trying to follow their gist. "I'm a molecular biologist not a neuroscientist but I think you mean oxytocin."

"That's the one," said Clotilde.

"Women release it in huge quantities during childbirth and breastfeeding," said Eric. "And when you stroke a dog, both human and dog produce it. It's like a bonding thing."

"Where's the goddamn service around here?" said Joe, trying to squeeze another drop out of the Sassicaia.

"Better change the subject before Elena gets back," said Ben. "Besides, there's not much I can do about it now. Aphrodite has spoken."

The waiter arrived, pushing a food cart, just in time to prevent Joe from going into Sassicaia withdrawal. The man studied the empty bottles and looked at Joe, who nodded in the direction of the remaining stash.

Spiro followed, accompanied by a woman. He whispered instructions to the waiter, who began transferring the hot dishes to the table.

"This is my wife, Irilena," said Spiro.

Come Irilena, come see the silly rich Americans, thought Ben.

The silly, rich, and friendly Americans greeted Irilena with applause.

"I have made one dish specially for you," said the wife. She could only speak English slowly and with a heavy Greek accent. "Ees lamb kleftiko, please enjoy."

After the cheering stopped, Spiro announced the rest of the dishes.

Ben's eyes never left Elena, who was still in front of the souvenir shop.

"You asked them to cook a special dish?" asked Clotilde. "I'm impressed."

"Well, sort of," said Ben. "I'm not sure it's so special or they would serve it all the time, right? I appreciate the effort though. Lamb kleftiko's a stew, so she must have started preparing it after I made the arrangements with Spiro. It was nice of her to come out and introduce it."

"Here she is," said Ben, as Elena came back to the table. "How's Sophia?"

"Fine, she got back, no problem. She's having dinner with her boyfriend."

Ben repeated Spiro's description of the entrees. "So, here's kreatopita, a Kefalonia pie; this one's moussaka; shrimp saganaki … I had that already today; sea bass; and this is lamb kleftiko …

you just missed Spiro's wife who told us she'd made it specially for you."

"Liar."

The conversation ebbed as the diners helped themselves to portions of the colorful dishes.

"I want some tuna," said Joe.

"It's not on the menu," Ben replied.

"Is this one of those save the endangered tuna restaurants?" asked Joe.

"I doubt it." Ben readied himself for the imminent banter.

"Quite a few places no longer serve blue fin tuna," said Clotilde.

"I've stopped eating it." Elena sided with the French girl.

"Another save the planet eco-maniac. What's the world coming to?" said Joe.

Clotilde objected.

"Oh no, he's off." Ben knew Joe was teasing Elena, but it wasn't easy to detect.

"No, but I don't think we should exploit species to extinction," Elena replied.

"Take no notice, he's kidding," said Ben.

"Don't let him get started on climate change," said Sean, who had been listening in on the conversation.

"Joe doesn't believe humans can affect the climate," explained Ben.

"That's right," said Joe. "It's a big scam."

Clotilde excused herself and left for the restroom.

Ben poured more wine, topping up each glass to one-quarter full.

The other half of the table became involved in the discussion. Eric shouted over, "Everyone in Joe's family owns a Hummer. His wife, his kids; they all have one. When they go out to dinner or to the movies, they take separate trucks."

Paul Dillon

"They don't want to have to listen to Joe," said Sean.

"It's good for the economy," Joe quipped.

"They're talking about his ex-wife," whispered Ben to Elena.

"Joe doesn't care about the environment or species preservation. He had the designer of his new house cover the walls of his entertainment room in giraffe skin," said Ben.

"How horrible." Elena winced.

"It's true, the designer tried to convince him to use fake giraffe skin … but not Joe," Ben tried mimicking a New Jersey accent, "I can afford the real thing."

"You're kidding me," said Joe. "Have you seen the size of those things? One giraffe covered the whole room; just its neck, alone, was enough for one wall."

"Are we back to Modigliani?" asked Clotilde catching the tail end of the conversation.

They all laughed.

"Joe's unstoppable," said Ben. "No matter what you throw at him, he's got an answer."

"I hope he's behaving himself," said Clotilde.

***

Appetites faded as sauce dried on china. Ben took a long gulp of water and looked at Elena for inspiration. He hoped the waiter would come soon. The evening couldn't have gone better, she had not disappointed, not done anything to switch on his love-safety-valve.

Maybe it's too late now. Even if she starts embellishing her conversation with finger-quotation-marks, I'll no longer care.

He laid his hand over hers, which rested on her leg; the tips of his fingers brushed lightly on her thigh. "You enjoying yourself?"

"Yes," she replied. "But I feel a little drowsy from the wine."

"Drink plenty of water. We'll order coffee, you'll be fine."

Ben withdrew his hand with a gentle squeeze and pondered the evening ahead. Going back to the yacht had no appeal. He was tiring of his friends now; five hours was a marathon for him. After coffee and desserts, he planned to leave for the hotel with Elena.

Spiro returned with a stack of dessert menus. His voice rose just above the music, tempting his tired customers with sweet treats. Waiters cleared the table with effortless efficiency.

Elena agreed to share a zuccotto with Ben who was having difficulty paying attention to the conversation. Joe overheard Ben ordering and seized another opportunity to extol the superiority of all things Italian.

"Zuccotto, eh? Good choice. Couldn't stomach the baklava?"

"I hope Joe's not offending your Greekness," Ben said to Elena.

"No arguments about Italian desserts. I don't like baklava either," she replied.

Ben ordered espresso and a glass of ouzo.

He turned to Elena. "I'm tired, it's been a long day and I'm still getting over yesterday's traveling."

"Me too. Today feels like it's lasted forever ... I mean that in a good way."

"I'm kind of yachted-out," said Ben. "I'm not sure if I want to go back there again tonight."

"I'm okay with that," she said.

"Let's just say goodnight at the jetty then go back to the hotel."

"Okay." Elena pulled a slightly comical face, making him want to kiss her. He did not understand her meaning. The two remained in deep conversation, oblivious of the others.

A hand invaded their world, sliding a dessert plate in front of them. Two spoons lay either side of an upside-down cake, coated with chocolate and sprinkled with white powder. Ben fed Elena zuccotto with his spoon. Only the two of them existed.

Suddenly, the music stopped, breaking their drowsy chocolate spell. Ben looked up. The abrupt silence recalled a teenage memory. A dance hall; the music stops, the lights turn on; a fight is broken up.

Meaningless conversations floated from the other tables, across the sultry air. Joe and Clotilde were silent, watching him. Ben wanted to leave.

"They're in love already," said Joe.

Elena looked puzzled; Ben ignored the remark.

The music started up again, more exotic than before. Sweet chocolate and hazelnut delighted their tongues. Ben soaked up the sensuality of the night; the red billowing ceiling of the tent, the striped walls woven with Arabic window designs. He lounged on the cushioned floor; she danced before him, tempting, promising. However long before she gave herself to him would not matter; let the music play. A tingle ran down his spine.

Spiro set a demitasse in front of Ben; the dark muddy brown of the espresso lay hidden under an orange-yellow froth.

"Ouzo," said Spiro, serving a small glass of clear liquid.

Ben thanked his host and sipped the strong bitter coffee, jolting his senses. The bill would come soon, ending this scene; beginning another.

"If the government gets any bigger, we'll end up socialists, like the Europeans," said Joe.

Sean and Eric were engaged in a political debate with Joe. Ben knew how it would play out; Joe would argue for more free market capitalism, the others making the case for some necessary government regulation.

"It's not such a free market, when big business can lobby congress to further its own agenda," said Sean.

Ben looked up at Clotilde who appeared disinterested. Perhaps he could get a three-way conversation going with Elena and Clotilde, wasting the minutes until they could leave.

Clotilde beat him to the punch. "You're quiet Ben. What side of the debate are you on?"

Ben wasn't going to let her pigeonhole him. He wasn't interested in politics and never joined in discussions unless forced to do so. He struggled to dodge the question yet not reveal his apathy in front of Elena.

"What is Joe debating? Free market capitalism versus socialism?" he said, buying a little time. He'd started, so must continue with an answer; any answer. Spiro was taking forever.

"People will always have opinions. The competing dogmas just change from generation to generation," he said.

"How do you mean?" asked Elena.

Ben wanted to avoid a political debate with Elena. "Well ... consider the future. You could speculate that, in one-hundred years' time, the argument will not be free market capitalism versus socialism."

"What will it be?" asked Clotilde.

"We don't know, but society will advance. Maybe they will look back on the issues of our time as ridiculous; like children arguing over who gets the green M&Ms."

"I don't get it," said Clotilde.

"Take the last century, free market capitalism versus communism or whatever. People were ready to launch nuclear war over the ideology. A few years later, we have forgotten what communism is."

"That's true," said Elena.

"Right. Children born this millennium will have to be taught about communism in history class. Today it's free market capitalism versus socialism; yesterday, free market capitalism versus communism. The further you go back, the more ridiculous it gets; Yankees versus Confederates, Royalist versus Parliamentarians, Catholics versus Protestants, and so on."

"Amen to that," said Elena, excusing herself. "I need the restroom"

The strong coffee had conspired with the pointless conversation to stall Ben's progress with Elena. He got up and followed her into the taverna, looking for Spiro.

***

By the time he returned, Ben's head had cleared.

A street vendor showed his tray of novelty gadgets at Eric's table. Attracting little interest, the man left without making a sale.

Ben walked back to his seat, picked up the ouzo and knocked it back. He remained standing, looking out over the bay, where the lights from the tavernas splashed yellow, red, and orange patterns over the water.

Elena and Spiro came out of the restaurant together, chatting on the way to the table. Ben stared at the harbor unaware of their approach until she put her arms around his neck. He felt her breasts pressing into his back and sensed the texture of dress clinging to curves. She nuzzled her face into his neck.

"Everything okay?" she asked.

"It's a beautiful night, so peaceful."

He wanted to turn around and hold her but now wasn't the time. He thought of the check to keep from becoming aroused.

"It's been a perfect evening," she said.

Ben had to agree; being with Elena was natural, second nature. There was no surprise when she hugged him from behind; it was as though she had known him forever.

He turned; Elena let her arms fall to her side. "I'd better see to the check," he said.

A huge wad of Euro notes lay piled on a silver plate next to the bill.

"How much do I owe?" asked Ben to no one in particular.

"We took care of it already," said Eric.

Ben protested.

"Hey man, you went to a lot of trouble to arrange dinner. Don't worry; we took very good care of Spiro."

The remark was final, further argument was futile. Eric went over to Spiro, shook hands and thanked him for his service. No doubt this would be one of Spiro's more profitable tables this season.

"My compliments to Irilena, please thank her for taking the trouble to make the lamb kleftiko; it was delicious," said Ben.

Elena stood by his side, the others waited in front of the souvenir shop until Ben was finished. They walked away.

"My flowers!" said Elena.

"Better leave them," said Ben. "There's nowhere to put them."

"No way," said Elena.

She returned to the table, lifting the flowers from the vase. Drops of water ran off the stems, wetting her legs.

17

Ioannis Katros led his family along the marble floor of the Church of Saint Gerasimos. Elena stood by her mother's side, surprised by the spectacle's opulence. Incense filled the air, lingering; fueling the solemn chants with an alien potency. For the first time, Elena understood how ritual exploited the senses to strike awe in the beholder.

She whispered to her mother. "The children won't be able to see anything; someone will have to take them outside."

There was no reply.

Elena's mother was second generation American, born of Italian parents. Although not a devout Catholic, Veronica Katros' influence on her daughter favored the Roman over the Greek Orthodox Church. Apart from marriages, christenings, or deaths, on her father's side, the family never attended service.

As Elena waited in line, she struggled to recall the layout of a traditional Greek church. She crossed an antechamber, entering the main space.

Narthex, and nave, she thought.

At the far end, a large screen, the templon, separated the nave from the sanctuary beyond.

This was a church unlike any in Elena's recollection. Standing in the middle of nowhere, its magnificent interior was reminiscent of the Vatican or ancient Constantinople. Every available surface bore icons or frescoes painted in the Byzantine style. Vaulted ceilings, covered with intricate works of art, depicted saints or biblical stories. Each higher ceiling led the eyes upwards to the massive dome, soaring above the nave to gaze upon the image of Christ.

The church benches, removed to accommodate a larger congregation, left an open space of black-and-white, checkered marble. Elena ran her hand along a velvet rope. It hung from an ornate gilded post, defining the aisle. Worshippers, pressing forward, pushed her from behind as she shuffled into position midway in the nave.

There was so much to marvel at, Elena didn't know where to start. From any angle, the templon, intricately carved from white marble, and inset with icons was the focal point. It towered upwards, passing the visual baton to the painted ceilings. Elena looked up; the detailed artwork mesmerized. Only when her neck tired, did the paintings lose their grip, bowing to the elaborate chandeliers. One in particular held her attention. Hanging from the central dome, covered in candles, it had a name she knew; horos. Like a silver ring of Saturn, its icon-encrusted band circled a colossal inner orb. Staggeringly baroque, the inner orb alone was grander than the finest chandelier she had ever seen. A monk standing near the altar pushed the horos with a rod, making it turn back and forth in hypnotic fashion.

This was the awe in which the Patron Saint of Kefalonia was held. With new appreciation, Elena began to consider her father's personal quest with deeper awareness. A monk chanted, another echoed his song. Elena looked across at her father and saw a man electrified in the presence of his saint. She tried to fill her mind with his thoughts, but could not. To her, the terrible truth of his childhood trauma had always been out of reach; a mountain peak obscured by clouds.

From her earliest years, Elena's father had told stories about Saint Gerasimos. She remembered how the saint's body had not decomposed after burial; that it lay in its original robes in a silver and glass sarcophagus. Yesterday, faithful servants had carried his casket from the old monastery, out of the cave where he'd spent his life, laying it to rest at a marble shrine in the church. There it now sat, awaiting its annual journey.

Although absorbed in the ritual, Elena retained the presence of mind to check on the two young boys. Strangely, they showed no sign of restlessness.

Hemmed in by the congregation, she could not see the saint. The activity of the monks, by the templon, suggested his casket lay over to her left. More than once, Elena caught a glimpse of silver over the heads of the worshippers. Soon they would take the sarcophagus and carry it, upright, to the ancient tree planted by the saint in his lifetime.

An elbow nudged Elena's arm, her mother nodded in the direction of her father. The congregation had begun to line up at the front of the church. Ioannis, Nicia and Andreas joined the queue.

"Is this the Communion?" whispered Elena.

"Yes," replied her mother.

Out of the sanctuary, a priest emerged, carrying a silver chalice and a ritual spoon; chanting filled the air.

A young girl bowed her head, awaiting the priest. Elena imagined her chosen for the honor, like some festival princess. The child's mother held a red cloth napkin under her daughter's chin, now raised to receive the blessing. Dipping the spoon into the chalice, the priest administered the communion wine and the young girl passed the cloth to the next in line.

With communicants moving in and out of the aisle, the area

in front of Elena became less crowded. Her pulse quickened as she caught a glimpse of the saint. A woman, returning from the sacrament, shuffled back to her place, once more blocking Elena's view.

Now her father prepared to receive the communion wine. Kneeling before the priest, he turned to the left, fixing his eyes on the saint. The priest held the spoon, just above the chalice, waiting for what seemed an eternity until her father turned his head back to receive the blessing. Ioannis passed the red cloth over to his sister and returned down the aisle.

As he rejoined Elena, she smiled. He did not respond, causing her concern. She tapped his arm and he faced her momentarily. His unfamiliar expression showed a hint of fear. She tried to put her apprehension aside.

A little trepidation was to be expected.

How quickly time passes, the service was almost over.

What message had she missed during the sermon?

Elena regretted her poor understanding of the language. She resolved to ask Nicia, later.

Robed figures gathered around the body of Gerasimos, conjuring suspense like an electric charge. The burnished dome rose into the air, a woman cried out. The scene was far more intense than Elena expected. The casket moved forward, people shouted out, some became hysterical.

Held aloft in his silver and glass tomb, Saint Gerasimos was coming back to his beloved land.

18

Walking back to the yacht took longer than expected. The young boy, Alan, stopped to play with a kitten he'd spotted under a bench near the harbor wall. Elena sat on the armrest, watching the boy coax the tawny cat into the light. Ben and Eric passed time discovering mosquito bites on their legs.

"I need to get something from the boat," said Ben. "Be back in a minute."

No sooner had the kitten emerged than Elena's phone rang, frightening the creature, sending it back under the bench. She pulled the handset from her bag, checking the caller ID: Greg Buchanan. She let it go unanswered. Time had flown; she had forgotten her promise to call.

It's still only mid-afternoon in Boston; he's sure to ring again.

Until now, Elena hadn't considered the night ahead. Rather than making conscious decisions, events seemed to have unfolded around her.

Kismet, she mused.

Tonight was part of a process, a process that could define her future. Now, a choice was imminent, forget Greg's message or respond. Ignoring it would create more tension, weighing on her mind, holding her down. Her thoughts had to be free from conflict, allowing destiny to run its course. The phone, still in her hand, vibrated with a new voicemail. She acted without hesitation, hitting the retrieve option, anxious for a conclusion.

Alan, seemingly bored with the cat, stood up just as Ben returned. "Bye Kitty, bye Ben," said the boy and followed his father to the yacht.

Elena saw Ben approaching; she stepped over to the boardwalk, straining to hear Greg's message above the music and clatter of the tourists.

"Listen, I'm sorry about earlier, I got stressed out," there was a pause. "Forget what I said about deadlines. I mean, I still want you to come back soon, but ... well, just come back when you're ready. Hey, it's late over there; you're probably beat. No need to call me back tonight. Let's speak tomorrow. I love you."

She turned back towards the bench. The cat was out again, nestling against Ben's foot. He stroked its back without looking up.

"Oh, you got the cat to come out. It likes you." She sat next to Ben, patting the kitten's head. "Here, fluffy baby."

"Shall we?" Ben nodded towards the promenade.

Elena picked up her bouquet; a faint whiff of fragrance followed the movement. Her thoughts remained with Greg as they made their way to the plaza. It was sweet of him, conceding to her wishes; she felt relief from the earlier tension.

"Did you get tomorrow's schedule from Eric?" she asked.

"Yes, we need to be back at the boat by one."

"Did you say you had two rooms at the hotel?" She deliberately intended to confuse him.

"Err ... no, one room with two beds. I think I said we can get another room, if there are any available, or one of us can stay on the yacht."

"Let's figure that out when we get there."

Greg's message lingered in her head. His voice had a weak feel to it, she preferred the insistent Greg, the Greg who demanded her. She decided against calling him tonight; a text would suffice. Greg had no way of knowing where she was. He didn't have Aunt Nicia's number and wouldn't call if he did. That would be spying.

"Something wrong?" asked Ben.

"No, I just got a text from Sophia. I need to let her know I won't be back until late tomorrow."

She sat on one of the benches in the main plaza, opposite the cafe with the rude waitress. Her fingers tapped out a reply.

"Hi got your message sorry I didn't get back to you busy with Sophia poor phone service out here going to turn in now call you tomorrow."

There was no need to append with 'love you'; it was only a text message.

***

Ben had the distinct impression that Sophia was not the caller. Something had distracted Elena. A sense of deflation threatened to wipe out the euphoria, the mysterious spell that had bound them together at the restaurant. His objective was clear; the excitement must reappear.

She rose, beaming him a smile. The gesture was like throwing a switch, bringing back the magic. He put his arm around her waist, pulling her into him. Her arm rested on his, the contact tingling.

This was their street. From noon 'til night, for eight hours, the music, people, buildings, the lights, heat and aromas had become their world.

Ben stopped in front of a pink building, which housed a general store. He pointed at two swollen bites on his leg.

"Look at these."

"I haven't been bitten yet." Elena spoke as though boasting

of an achievement.

"That's because you're Greek. I'm going to buy some citronella candles, keep the damn mozzies away tonight. Do you need anything?"

"Should we get something to drink?"

"The hotel bar will be open for another hour; we'll have a nightcap there. Watch these while I go inside." He handed her a green paper shopping bag. "You left this on the boat." The bag contained overnight necessities and a bikini they'd bought earlier.

To idle away the time until his return, Elena took pictures of the harbor. An old lady, standing alone, stared out over the bay. She turned around in surprise as the camera flashed, snapping her profile

Elena was still preoccupied when Ben returned from the store.

"I'll carry the bags, you look after the flowers," he said. "It's not far."

A cooling breeze drifted along the narrow side street leading away from the promenade. Storekeepers stood in doorways, looking bored, hoping to make a last sale.

"The cafes look so lonely at this time of night," said Elena.

They strolled, with linked arms, up the slight incline, stopping once to browse the goods outside a leather store. Barely three hundred yards long, the narrow street ended at a T-junction where a wider road ran parallel with the harbor. They turned left, hugging a stone wall. The dimly lit lane had no sidewalk and the land beyond rose steeply. Here, only the sound of crickets stirred above the distant drone from the quayside.

Presently, they rounded a curve where the ground on the right leveled out.

"We're here," said Ben.

Tall, dark trees hid the building from view until they passed the opening to a parking lot. Fifty yards further, a gravel path led to the hotel, its walls bathed in orange light.

Crossing the black and white checkerboard foyer, they entered the bar. Before Ben had taken in the surroundings, a deep voice called out.

"Good evening."

Surprised, Ben felt as though he'd trespassed into someone's home.

"Hey, good evening," he replied, still unsure who'd addressed him.

"Beautiful flowers for a beautiful lady," said the man behind the bar. "I put them in water for you."

"Thanks," said Ben.

The counter ran along the right hand side of the room, one-third its length. A man and woman, in their fifties, occupied two stools at the far end. The bartender, also in his fifties, went back to his conversation with the couple. No other guests were in the room.

Dropping his bags on a circular table, Ben pulled back an armchair. Elena moved to sit but stopped as laughter erupted at the bar.

"That guy sounds fun. Shall we sit at the bar?" he suggested.

Elena nodded, following him.

The bartender leaned against the counter, chatting to the middle-aged couple. "You liked that … no cheating, eh?"

He stood up as Ben approached.

"I'm still not sure how you did that," said the woman.

From her accent, Ben gathered she was English, from the West Country.

"Watch him, he's full of tricks," she said to Ben.

"What did he do?" Ben moved closer to her.

The woman talked, excitedly; the bartender asked Ben for his order. Politeness required Ben to juggle the two conversations.

"Balanced a fork on a toothpick?" Ben exaggerated his curiosity. He had no idea what she was talking about. "Elena, what would you like?"

"Strawberry daiquiri."

Ben repeated Elena's order to the barman, who appeared not to have understood.

The woman kept up a steady stream of words. "...cork in a wine bottle; amazing how he..."

"I need to see that," said Ben, on autopilot.

"We don't have this," said the bartender. His face seemed fixed in a permanent grin.

He must be referring to the strawberry daiquiri, thought Ben.

He turned back to Elena, "Fancy a mojito then?"

She nodded.

"Mojito?" asked Ben.

The barman, still grinning, shook his head.

"You're out of luck, old chap," said the man at the end of the bar.

"How about any cocktail that contains rum?" Ben continued.

"I make you something, no problem. You like ... lady friend like; special recipe." The man's thick Greek accent added more humor to the already farcical conversation.

Ben's "Okay" was a trifle hesitant.

"Don't worry, the man's a magician, an absolute magician," said the woman.

Anticipating some diabolical concoction, Ben looked at Elena.

"This should be interesting," she said, rolling her eyes.

Ben turned to the couple, his hand rested on Elena's arm.

"Hi, I'm Ben, this is Elena. What were those tricks again?"

He swiveled a bar stool, motioning for Elena to sit next to the couple. She adjusted her skirt, which rode up as she sat. Ben leaned in; his legs touched hers as he rotated her seat to face the bar.

"Tom and Betty Henderson, from Bristol, England," said the man.

"The barman's name is Spiro," whispered Betty.

"Popular name," said Elena.

"Rum cocktail; specialty of the house," said Spiro.

He placed two Collins glasses on the bar.

"Thank you, Spiro," said Ben. He sipped the drink. "Not bad, not bad at all."

"Where you two from?" asked Tom.

"Boston," replied Elena. "My father is Greek-American"

Spiro said something in Greek, Elena attempted a response.

"I didn't realize you spoke Greek," said Ben.

"I don't. Well, I know a few words but the Greeks speak so fast, I can't tell what they're saying. So I always answer with, 'I'm sorry, I don't understand Greek'. That's what I said just now."

"I live in Los Angeles," Ben chimed in with a delayed reply.

"But you're not American," said Betty.

His reply was interrupted as Spiro reappeared, holding a champagne bucket containing Elena's flowers. He held them in front of his face, peeking through the petals like a madman.

"The man's crazy," whispered Ben.

"Spiro, show them the tricks," demanded Betty.

"Man, that cocktail's good," said Ben. "What the hell's in it?"

Spiro wagged his finger and shook his head. Elena let out a laugh, sparking off a domino effect with Tom and Betty, who were quite drunk.

"An empty wine bottle," said Spiro.

He held a cork in one hand, the bottle in the other and set them down on the bar. Chuckling to himself, he stood back to admire his handiwork.

Ben wondered whether he was supposed to inspect them.

"What now?" he asked.

Spiro folded his arms into his white shirt. Satisfied with his dramatic introduction, he picked up the cork, squeezing it into the wine bottle.

"You're going to love this," cried Betty.

Taking the end of a wooden spoon, Spiro forced the cork into the neck until it dropped to the bottom of the bottle. Then, he rattled it around.

"Cool," said Elena.

Betty slapped Elena on the forearm. "That's not it."

All eyes fixed on Spiro. Ben stared at the man's grey beard, waiting for him to speak.

A show of empty hands, followed by a pirouette, produced a white cloth napkin, which Spiro spread neatly on the bar. Placing the wine bottle on the napkin, he flicked the toothpick holder, deftly catching one between finger and thumb. Next, he balanced the toothpick on top of the bottle.

"The trick is to get the cork out. You can only use your hands and any object that is touching the bottle," explained Tom.

Ben had seen a girl perform this trick before, in a San Diego bar. The addition of a toothpick confused him slightly. He decided to play dumb.

"Got you stumped eh?" the woman teased.

"Free cocktails if you can do it," said Spiro.

"I give up," said Ben.

Elena picked up the toothpick and grabbed the bottle, tipping it upside down. She tried to stab the toothpick into the cork. Ben could see this was impossible; the toothpick barely reached it. Even if the toothpick could be jabbed into the cork, there wouldn't be enough traction to pull it through the neck.

Tom ordered single a malt scotch and a gin and tonic. "Another round, old chap?" he asked Ben.

"Not so fast, Tom, Elena's going to win free drinks." Ben could handle one more cocktail but he didn't want Elena getting too drunk.

"Any object that is touching the bottle." Unable to resist, Betty offered Elena a clue.

Ben knew it was nigh on impossible to solve the puzzle, more so with the red herring of the toothpick. He pondered another round. He felt fine, the drink wasn't too strong; one more might work to his advantage later. He glanced at Elena's glass; it was almost empty.

"I give up," she said, putting the bottle back on the napkin.

"Show them … show them how it's done," shrieked Betty, beside herself with glee.

Spiro looked at Ben, who shrugged by way of resignation.

"Watch this," howled Betty.

"Steady on, old girl," said Tom. Even in his semi-drunken state, he was aware that his wife was making a complete fool of herself.

Stepping forward, Spiro began the show.

"Anything touching the bottle," he reminded them.

Shooting a conspiratorial grin towards the hysterical Betty, he moved the bottle to one side and held the white napkin by its corners, letting it drape down like a flag.

"What's next, a rabbit?" whispered Ben.

He glanced back and forth between Elena and Betty. Elena was transfixed, Betty stared maniacally, as if attending a public execution; her mouth wide open, awaiting Spiro to deliver the coup de grace.

Slowly, the dramatic Spiro twisted one corner of the napkin and fed it into the bottle until it looked like, a Molotov cocktail. Ben downed the last of his drink.

Betty will start baying soon, if he doesn't hurry up, he thought.

With a deft movement, Spiro flipped the bottle upside down and juggled the cork into place, allowing it to become snagged in the napkin. Pausing for effect, he pulled on the cloth, trapping the cork in the neck. Seconds later, with a sharp tug, the cork popped out to rapturous applause from the Hendersons.

Elena appeared to be enjoying herself. Ben was undecided

whether to leave now or risk one more drink. He put his hand on Betty's shoulder, "You were right, that was cool."

"You haven't seen anything yet," said Betty. "Spiro, show them the one with the spoon."

"We should be going, it's getting late," said Ben to Elena.

She drank the rest of her cocktail without a reply.

"Another?" asked Spiro, nodding at her empty glass.

She raised her eyebrows at Ben, as if to say, "I will if you will."

"Sure you'll be okay?" he asked.

"I'm fine. I really haven't drunk that much."

"Two more special rum cocktails and whatever Tom and Betty are having," ordered Ben. "Let's take the drinks up to the room," he whispered to Elena.

"Good idea."

Mercifully, Betty stopped talking about bar tricks while she watched Spiro prepare her drink. Her silence pleased Ben; it would be easier to make his excuses and leave.

"Twenty-five Euros," Spiro placed the last of the drinks on the bar.

"Cheers," said Ben.

They chinked glasses. Ben reached into his wallet, putting thirty Euros on the counter.

"We're going to turn in," he said. "We have an early start in the morning. Betty, Tom, it was a pleasure meeting you."

Betty pleaded with them to stay.

Ben got up, offering his hand to Elena.

"Thanks Spiro, you'll have to let me have that recipe," he said, pointing at his drink.

Going over to the circular table, Ben retrieved their bags. Elena picked up the champagne bucket. She struggled to carry it, and her drink, at the same time.

"Spiro, is it okay?" she nodded at the bucket. "I'll bring it back in the morning."

He held up a thumb.

"Efharisto," she smiled.

"Here, give me those," said Ben. "Put the bucket under my arm."

"Okay, I'll take the bag."

They made their way out of the bar, across the foyer, and up the travertine staircase.

"Sorry, there's no elevator," said Ben.

"How early do we have to leave tomorrow?"

"Noonish."

The hotel was silent; there wasn't a soul on the stairs or in the corridor. Ben put the flower bucket on the tiled floor outside his room and rummaged for the key. The huge thing had snagged in his pocket, frustrating him. Finally, the lock clicked and the door sprang open. Light from the corridor flooded into the room. Without turning on the room-lights, he entered, leaving the door ajar. Elena followed him inside.

"I'll put these here." He set the flower bucket on the mirrored table. "Make yourself at home."

The maid had tidied well, the freshly made bed left a good impression. She'd also closed the veranda doors and drawn the curtains. The room was hot and stifling.

"I forgot to pick up the remote control for the air conditioning," he said, drawing the drapes. "It's not like back home, these small hotels charge for the AC."

Opening the veranda doors brought little relief. He stepped outside into the warm dense night. The patio was dark, lit only by refraction from the garden. Elena stayed by the bed, taking in the room.

From the veranda, Ben stared, drawn to her figure, made silhouette by light from the hallway. It was time.

"Close the door and come outside, it's a little cooler. I can go down and see if I can get the remote, if you're too hot."

She placed the carrier bag on the bed and closed the door.

"It's fine. I don't mind the heat," she said and stepped outside. "Besides, there was no one at reception, it's late."

"Cheers," said Ben.

Their glasses touched.

"I'd better light those candles. I don't want to be an entrée for some mosquito tonight."

He slipped back into the room and fumbled around in the carrier bag until he found a disposable gas lighter and the two wide yellow candles.

"Here." He lit the wick of the first one, placing it on the balcony wall. "And here…" The lighter flame flickered over the second candle on the veranda table.

He leaned against the balcony wall, overlooking the amorphous garden. Lanterns, under the dwarf pines, cast shadows across the lawn, reflecting faint beams of light off the low stone walls. A primeval harmony drifted up from the darkness on its way to a sky, clear and scattered with stars. The garden, the crickets were goading him, abetting his desires; he knew she'd respond.

"I've fallen in love with this place," he said. "I call it the Cypress Garden. You can just make out the trees in the darkness."

Elena moved over to him, leaning her back against the balcony, her legs brushed against his.

"Mmmm, I love the smell, the sounds of summer nights," she said.

"It's got a different quality now. This morning, the crows and cicadas were running the show; tonight, the crickets have taken over. I can't decide which I like best."

"The crickets sound just fine."

Ben turned towards her, tugging her arm; the momentum pulled her closer. She didn't withdraw. In a continuation of the movement, he put his left arm around her, drawing her closer still. His right hand felt the curve of her hip. In the instant before their lips met, his eyes searched her face for an expression, for consent to his desire. Their kiss lasted only moments; he sensed her passion match his. Slowly he withdrew, excited, aroused. Inches apart, their faces smiled knowingly. Tonight, he could do whatever he wanted.

Sharing a strange familiarity, they both took a drink. Each believing their intentions understood.

"Something really wild is happening," he said.

"What do you mean?"

"That kiss … it reminded me of something," he hesitated, "… so familiar." He sought to expand but fell silent.

Everything happens for a reason, she said to herself. Wasn't it fate, hadn't Greg himself delivered her into Ben's arms from halfway across the world.

They kissed again … longer this time.

"Let's go inside." He led her by the hand into the middle of the room and kissed her again. The candle lights flickered, like spirits, dancing to the rhythm of the crickets. Her breasts pushed into his chest arousing him further. Ben broke the kiss, eager to feast his eyes on her.

She stood there, her head tilted up, looking into his eyes.

He unzipped the olive dress and pulled it down over her shoulders, revealing her ample cleavage, which spilled over the black lace of her bra. She did not move; he stared, entranced. Time had ceased to register for him. He unhooked her bra, lifting it away, exposing the luscious curves beneath. Hypnotized, like a cobra; he felt their softness, drank in their shape in the yellow candle light until they burned into his memory—a process he was conscious of, could feel happening.

He tried to speak, to express what she was doing to him, but words would not come. Her arms encircled his waist. He touched her breasts, caressing them. They kissed again; he pressed his hands on her shoulders, easing her down until she sat on the bed.

With her thighs stretched out before him, he knelt on the floor, her knees against his chest. He longed to see more of her. With a mind of their own, his hands moved along her thighs, pulling the short skirt up to her hips.

Elena just looked at him, letting him do as he pleased.

Later, Ben would not be able to recall exactly what happened that night. Yes, they made love but it was like trying to remember an elusive dream, only fractions remained.

19

By early evening on the day after the tree house quake, Argostoli had regained its dignity. Talk in the cafes around the main square returned to the humdrum of everyday life. The capital had been fortunate; the epicenter of Sunday's tremor was out at sea. Damage to the town was light.

Come the morning of Tuesday, August 11, the city's mood grew somber once more. At 5:32am, a 6.8 magnitude earthquake struck with an epicenter off the northwest coast of the neighboring island of Zante.

Conversations started and ended with speculation about the days ahead. Some predicted catastrophe, others gave thanks for their safety. Everywhere, neighbor asked neighbor the same questions; whether houses were damaged, if families were safe.

Fortune had not been kind to the Katros house. The early morning tremor was more than just a minor incident; the ceiling in the boy's bedroom had partially collapsed. The boys were unharmed but the outer wall suffered structural damage causing two ceiling joists to shear. Repairs threatened to stretch finances to breaking point. Ioannis's father had assessed the costs and would have to call upon past favors to lessen the burden. It would take several days just to gather supplies. In the meantime, the family decided to move the boys to their grandmother's cottage.

As if Vasilis Katros didn't have enough problems, the very day he planned to begin repairs on the stone barn, more work had piled up at home. He resolved to stick with today's plan and fix the barn. Stamos would help his father; Ioannis would stay at home with his mother.

Mid-morning came and Mrs. Katros announced a visit to the town's open-air market. Ioannis enjoyed shopping trips, if his mother bought wisely or found a bargain, there was usually a little money left over for sweets or ice cream.

Life was tough for Ioannis's mother. Every minute of every day was spoken for; feeding the family, mending and washing clothes, working in the Matsakis' store. If she wasn't doing chores, she made lace with Nessa. Like other mothers in the poor neighborhoods of Argostoli, Mrs. Katros found it hard to escape the drudgery of life and enjoy her children's precious years. All too soon, they would become adults. The recent tremors reminded her to appreciate what little time remained of their fleeting childhood.

Ioannis and Nicia waited on the sidewalk, watching their mother close the front door of the house.

"Yanni, don't let the dog follow us," said his mother.

An old black Labrador, belonging to a neighboring family, sauntered up to Ioannis, rubbing its snout against his leg. Nicia stroked the friendly pet, secretly hoping it would follow them.

"But it wants to come with us," said Ioannis.

Not wishing to scold the children, his mother, shrugged. The old dog would turn back at the end of the street, anyway.

August was no time to be hurrying through the hot, dusty streets, even in the morning. The wise old Labrador turned back, right on cue; a single lazy bark marking its goodbye.

Presently, they turned right, onto a wider avenue; the market was uphill from here.

"Cross over into the shade," said Ioannis's mother.

As Mrs. Katros trudged up the hill, her thoughts returned to self-reflection. She was fortunate, many of the neighborhood children quarreled constantly, adding to their mothers' burden. At least she didn't have those worries. Ioannis and Nicia had run on ahead and waited beside an ice cream sign. She resolved to buy them a treat on the journey home.

The open-air market played a key role in the town's social life. Occupying an acre of flat ground, merchants shouted out their bargains from wooden stalls laid out in a grid pattern. Outside the main entrance, handcarts sold prasopita, kritsinia, and souvlaki snacks.

Of all the goods for sale, Ioannis loved the spices best. Whenever his mother became distracted, haggling with a merchant or talking with a friend, he would grab Nicia's hand, pulling her along the narrow lanes to the spice vendors in the central square. Even if he were blind, Ioannis could find his way there, following the aromas. Sumac, cinnamon, cumin, ginger, cloves, zatar; he liked to read their names aloud from the chalk signs in front of the spice sacks.

Despite the morning earthquake, the market bustled with activity. Ioannis's mother reminded the children to stay close; she knew they would not. Today would end up like all other shopping days, Mrs. Katros would spend minutes looking up and down between the stalls, heavy bags in hand, searching and calling out their names.

While their mother haggled over the price of onions, the children sneaked underneath the merchant's stand.

***

Ioannis and Nicia were playing with a black cat when the aftershock hit. Women screamed, dropping their bags, struggling to stay on their feet. Mrs. Katros gripped a stanchion at the corner of the shaking stall. All around her, boxes fell from shelves, scattering fruit and vegetables over the floor.

Under the onion vendor's stand, Ioannis clung to a post like a drowning rat. Horrified and unable to move, he heard his mother calling but was too shocked to reply. He wanted to reach out for Nicia; she knelt on the floor, crying, in front of the cat.

Everything happened in a flash. The cat, as if possessed by a demon, hissed loudly, arching its back in terror. Ioannis watched, strangely fascinated, as Nicia reached out to the frightened animal, causing it to strike at her hand. The blow drew blood. The cat struck one more time then bolted.

The world under the stall confused and frightened Ioannis. Violent shaking, screams, rolling onions, a demonic cat then brief silence, with only creaking timber, gently swaying above. He let go of the post, crawled over to his sister and put his arm around her. Shocked by the attack, Nicia had stopped crying.

"Yanni, the cat scratched me, I just wanted to help it," she said.

The sense of injustice in her voice caused Ioannis to relive the incident all over again. As with several other moments from that fateful week, he would remember Nicia's simple words for the rest of his life.

"Yanni, Nicia!" His mother shouted.

She called again, this time he responded. Releasing Nicia, he crawled out from beneath the vegetable stall, concerned for his mother's safety.

"There you are. Thank goodness." She scooped Ioannis into her arms, hugging him tight.

Over her shoulder, he saw a chaotic scene. A woman lay on the ground, barely ten feet away; Ioannis recognized one of the market vendors, an old man, knelt beside her. The man rolled up his jacket, creating a pillow for her head. Onlookers gathered round. Everywhere, vegetables, fruits and wooden crates lay scattered on the floor.

"Where's Nicia?" asked his mother. Her lips brushed against his ear.

"A cat scratched her," he said.

"Yanni, listen to me. Where is Nicia?"

"She's there, under there." Ioannis pointed at the stall.

Mrs. Katros bent down, releasing Ioannis. He darted back underneath the instant his feet hit the ground.

Somewhere nearby, a dog barked incessantly.

"It's safe now, you can come out," said Mrs. Katros.

She reached out closing her hand around Nicia's, pulling her into the sunlight. Ioannis held his sister's other arm, the injured hand hung from her limp wrist. Drops of blood rolled down her finger, falling to the floor.

"Are you hurt?" asked Mrs. Katros.

She rubbed her daughter's arms and legs, checking for breaks or bruises. Finding nothing, she hugged the young girl, looking to the sky in relief.

"She's bleeding, Mom," said Ioannis, pointing at the back of Nicia's hand.

"It's just a scratch," said his mother.

She pulled a handkerchief from her dress pocket, moistening a corner with saliva. Nicia winced as her mother wiped the blood from the back of her hand.

"What about Stamos?" asked Ioannis.

The young boy's concern for his brother outweighed his fears for Nessa, even his father.

His mother worried too, about her husband and son working on the old stone barn. It could have collapsed; they might be inside. The woman weighed up the situation, quickly reaching a decision. She must go home, Nessa was in the house alone.

"Yanni, go to the farm and check on your brother. Look

out for them on the road; they're probably on their way back. If they're not at the barn, come straight back home—and stay away from damaged buildings."

Mrs. Katros thought again whether she'd made the right decision sending the young child through the streets alone, so soon after an earthquake.

"If they're hurt, get help, right away." She kissed the top of his head.

"Come on Nicia, we must hurry," Mrs. Katros set off at a swift pace, almost dragging her daughter along. She turned back one time to see Ioannis running helter-skelter up the hill. As he ran, the boy imagined life without his brother and wept. Over and over, he repeated a prayer to Saint Gerasimos.

20

Ben stretched, savoring the freshness of the early morning heat. During the night, he'd woken often. Each time, he'd reached out for Elena making sure she wasn't a dream. Now the bed was empty.

On the mirrored dresser, a bucket of flowers provided concrete evidence of the night before. He turned his head toward the veranda, light streamed in from the half-opened doors. From his vantage point, he could see the stub of a citronella candle, burned down and extinguished on the round white table.

A chair leg screeched along the patio floor, a foot appeared, resting on the table's edge. She was outside.

Rolling to the side of the bed, he let his feet dangle to the ground and sat there, motionless. Relieved that Elena hadn't got up early and vanished, he nonetheless winced at his overreaction. After all, foregoing a cruise for the one-hour taxi ride home seemed unlikely.

Without making a sound, he walked over to the veranda, popping his head around the door then stepped outside. Bare feet on warm tiles always gave him a childish delight and he couldn't help but smile when he saw her.

"Hey, gorgeous."

Elena looked up, cheerful and relaxed.

"Hi."

The black bikini he'd bought yesterday showed off her cleavage, rekindling memories of the night before. He wanted her again.

"You're up early," he said.

"Hmm, I showered already. For the past week, I've been getting up at dawn and reading on my balcony, like a regular trust fund brat. It's becoming a habit."

Her chair rocked back at an angle. She placed the book on her thigh, covering part of her bikini bottom. Her legs were crossed and resting on the table. Dark glasses covered her eyes.

The ever-noisy crows called from the trees.

"I know what you mean about the sounds," said Elena. "They've been at it all morning."

"The birds are excited to see you. I hope they aren't bothering you."

"Why? Are you going to tell them off? No, it's okay; I like them."

The sun's rays washed over Ben's bare shoulders as he looked over the balcony. His garden stretched out before him, clean and fresh; yes, that's how it felt.

"Did you go down there yet?" he asked.

Elena drank from a plastic water bottle then picked up her book.

"No, it looks nice though. Let's go after breakfast—if we have time."

"We don't have to be at the yacht until one."

As he looked over the garden, Ben could think of only one thing, making love to her again. Turning around, he leaned against the balcony rail, his eyes ran the length of her legs right up to the scooped front of her bikini bottom. He lusted after her. Drumming his fingers on the wall, he thought up ploys to get her back into the room.

From where he stood, the position of her arms hid her cleavage. He became fidgety and moved to a better vantage point, over by the door, where she couldn't catch him staring.

"I put some T-shirts on the spare bed; pick anyone you want—they're all extra-large and should fit like a cotton dress."

"Okay."

She answered without looking up.

I hope the damn chapter's not a long one, he thought.

Resigned to wait, he went back in the room, lay on top of the blankets, and closed his eyes. All thoughts centered on how to act when she came back inside. He fantasized about the different ways he would make love to her. Finally, he could stand it no more and headed for the shower.

***

Elena snapped the book shut, laying it on her lap. A blue and white Greek flag peaked out from the pages, printed on her leather bookmark. She flipped it back and forth and wondered what it would be like to stay on the island; to become Greek and never go home. Reading had made her hungry.

***

With ardor temporarily dulled by the shower, Ben looked into the mirror atop the vanity table. A silver champagne bucket covered the top of his white shorts; flowers carpeted his bare chest.

"Ready for breakfast?" asked Elena, as she stepped in from the veranda.

"Sure, I'm starved."

She bent over the spare bed, examining the T-shirts. Ben grabbed her hand, pulling it upwards, and wrapped his arms around her; he was already aroused. A waft of perfume brought back memories of the night before. They kissed. He knew she felt his excitement pressing against her side. Ben untied the bikini straps behind her neck, wondering how such thin strings could support her breasts. He moved to lift the garment away but she stopped him, clutching the straps in her fingers.

"Elena," he whispered, putting his hands on her covered breasts.

Their eyes locked. There was something disconcerting in the way her look articulated his desperation.

"Ben, let's not do it right now, we went a long way yesterday. I need to think about this. We should be careful."

"Elena, I want to be honest with you, so I'm going to say exactly what I feel. I don't want to be crude but I'm almost bursting, I can hardly stand it."

They kissed again, passionately; he tried once again to lift her top away, she resisted. Ben was confused; she wore the same expression as the night before, giving him the green light to do as he pleased. He hugged her, kissed her neck then let her go.

"I'm sorry, you probably think I'm a sex maniac or something," he said.

"Don't be silly. I like knowing how much you want me. I think I told you, I'm a bit confused about the direction of my life right now."

"It's okay. I understand ... Breakfast?"

They laughed, breaking the tension; she bent down again and picked up a white T-shirt.

"This one will do. I'm ready."

Ben chose a black one from the remaining pile, slipping it over his head.

"What do you think?" She modeled the T-shirt-dress for him; a black and white print covered the front, the back was plain.

He sighed, longingly, "Aye, Aye, Aye."

"Who's the woman on the shirt?" she asked.

"Hedy Lamarr—a forties movie star."

"You have some, err, interesting T-shirts."

"Let's go, I think they stop serving at ten," he said.

She grabbed her book on the way out.

Breakfast was self-service. A waitress, in a formal black uniform, had already begun dismantling the buffet as they reached the dining room. Ben suggested an outside table and they carried their trays to the vine-covered pergola adjacent the cypress garden. A whisper of breeze tempered the heat.

As they ate, Ben explained Eric's plan for the day. The yacht would leave Fiskardo sometime after one, sailing first to the ruined castle at Assos then to nearby Myrtos Beach. They'd anchor at Myrtos until late afternoon before leaving for Argostoli. Myrtos to Argostoli was a two-hour voyage; they expected to dock around 7:00pm.

Ben didn't broach plans for the evening. He would need to get a room or stay on the yacht; it would depend on Elena. He suspected she'd go straight to her aunt's villa.

"Can I get you another coffee?" he asked. "I'm having one."

"Please."

He returned with the drinks and they chatted a while longer. The patio had cleared of guests.

"Let me show you the garden," he suggested.

"I can't wait."

The waitress hovered over them, brusquely removing their empty dishes. Taking the hint, they got out of her way and left the table.

"I'll give you the tour." Ben spoke in the manner he might use to a guest in his own house.

She followed him, walking between the stone walls towards the sundial. A crow squawked, hopping around in the branches of a dwarf pine. The bird was close enough for Ben to hear the air rushing over its rapidly beating wings.

"Hey, Elena, want to try something?"

"What?"

"Sit down on the grass."

She hesitated. "Okay…"

He sat first, held her hand, tugging on it until she followed.

"Now lie back." He kept hold of her hand and they stretched out together. "Close your eyes and listen…"

Ben looked up at the cloudless sky, soaking up the garden's voice; the sounds grew richer with the closing of his eyes. Free from visual stimulation, his mind concentrated on her touch and the intense, hypnotic cadence of the cicadas. He remained silent, waiting for her to speak and break the spell. Birds flapped and called, punctuating the rhythm.

"I feel like we're the two people on that T-shirt you wore yesterday," she said. "Is that what they were doing, listening to the forest sounds?"

He liked her idea, "I never thought of that."

He rose, pulling her up with him.

"It's as though I'm part of this place, part of everything that lives here," he said.

"It's like meditating."

They walked on, past the sundial, to the folly at the end of the garden. Ben pointed out the way the architect had built the make-believe structure—a mysterious iron door leading nowhere, overgrown with vines.

Elena touched the rusted ironwork, running her fingers over its decay. A dried leaf, shrunk and twisted, hung from a strand of spider silk, spinning backwards and forwards, holding her attention.

"This bench has some shade," said Ben. "Let's read here."

They sat under the mass of red and purple flowers that covered the tree and its symbiotic vines.

"You know what? I forgot my book," he said. "It doesn't matter, I couldn't concentrate yesterday anyway. I came here an hour before I met you."

"Maybe it was a premonition."

Two crows swooped down from the cypresses, their voices harsh and loud. They landed on the grass by the bench, startling Elena. One of the birds walked up close as if inspecting them; the other kept its distance.

"Aren't they funny," she said.

"See how shiny their feathers are. There's a blue tinge to them in strong sunlight. Did you know they're highly intelligent?"

"Not really."

"Yeah, they use tools and can solve quite complex problems. You know, like placing a square or round shaped peg in the correct hole to get a reward. I even saw a video of a captive bird bending a piece of wire into the shape of a hook to snag pieces of food the researchers had put out of reach."

"Fascinating."

"…And apparently, they can recognize individual people. Like, if someone has been cruel to them, they'll remember." He elaborated, "Some students on campus had to net a bunch of crows as part of a study. After their release, the birds hassled those who'd netted them—even when the students came back to the university years later. Isn't that amazing?"

"How come you know all this stuff?"

"Trust fund brat, plenty of time on his hands—hey, I read a lot."

"You said you weren't married?"

"That's right, I'm not."

The second crow took off, landing on the sundial. The brave one stayed by the bench; they cawed to each other repeatedly.

"Have you ever been married?" she pressed.

"No. I was engaged once. That's the closest I've been."

"What happened?"

"She died in a car accident."

"I'm sorry."

"She was twenty one," A twinge of sorrow crossed Ben's face, an echo of yesterday in the garden. Elena noticed.

"It must have been painful"

"Yeah, it was tough. You know, it's strange but I often think that sadness and happiness are almost the same."

Ben's words reminded Elena of her father, a few days earlier at the Festival of Saint Gerasimos.

"How's that?" she asked.

"It's hard to explain. Let's say you're at the theater, watching a movie, a sad movie. You're a girl, right—you cry at sad movies," he paused, as though awaiting affirmation. "So I look at you as the movie finishes, there are tears in your eyes—you look at me and smile, or laugh. At the same time, you're still crying. It's as though feeling sad is somehow enjoyable. Being sad at the end of movie isn't so bad; some people like it."

Unsure if his meaning was clear, he sought clarification in her expression. The crow nearest the bench cawed several times in quick succession.

"It's almost as though the bird's embellishing your idea," she said.

Ben smiled, "Good, I need some help. Don't mind him; he's the Greek God of Sadness in disguise."

"But you're feeling empathy for the characters in the movie; it's different when it's your own life."

"True; what I'm trying to say," he paused. "Perhaps the more intense the sadness, the more you have to rise above it, eventually turning the sadness into something … something almost exhilarating, epic…"

Ben didn't want to further elaborate and changed the subject, "enough of that; what are you reading, anyway?"

The God of Sadness took off, gliding across the lawn to join its companion. Elena handed Ben her book.

"The Ten Thousand Things—unusual book, do you like it?"

Elena was taken aback. "You've read it?"

"Yeah, but it was years ago."

"I'm not sure what to make of it," she said.

"I remember the garden, the inner bay. The author paints a vivid picture."

"And the curiosity cabinet full of shells."

"Wouldn't it be cool, if I could watch the pictures your mind creates, like I was watching a movie—and you could watch mine," he said.

"You have too much time on your hands. Do you ever think of getting a job, doing something with your life?"

"Well, I'm doing something now. I'm enjoying life," he said. "I'm enjoying the act of existing."

"How Zen-like."

"Maybe."

"Actually, that's why I bought this book. Isn't the Ten Thousand Things a Zen or Tao expression for the way everything in the universe is interconnected?"

"Something like that; is that what interests you?" he asked.

"You could say that. I'm kind of in my Zen-karma phase. I get the impression you think the same way."

Reluctant to continue the topic, Ben didn't answer.

"I'm interested in what you think. I want to be able to," she paused, "just enjoy existing too."

He searched for a hint of mockery in her remark but detected none.

"I don't know much about Zen or karma, so it's hard to say. From what I've read, Zen is, like, gaining knowledge or coming to some realization from within—maybe without a doctrine—I'm okay with that. Karma … well, I flat out don't get karma so can't help on that one."

"So what do you believe in, then?"

"Zen can't be taught, my child," he teased.

"No seriously, I believe we met for a reason; I think you've been put here to help me."

"Well, I'm enjoying the task." He smiled. "But there is no one-minute explanation. Even if I talked for an hour, I doubt I could answer your question."

"I have vays of making you tock."

"You certainly do."

The conversation faded; Elena went back to her book.

While she read, Ben walked around the garden. He paused in front of the sundial, examining its design. A rough-hewn stone, three feet square formed its base. On top of the base, sat another slab; rose-hued, cracked, and etched with markings. A bronze triangle, fashioned into an indicator, cast its shadow on the weathered marble below.

In the corner of his eye, he caught Elena waving her hand in the air, chasing off a troublesome insect.

As he walked back to the bench, he thought it time to find out more about her, about her plans.

"How long are you going to stay on the island?" he asked.

She stopped reading and looked up. "I'm not sure."

"Don't you have to get back to Boston?"

"I suppose so."

"I guess I need to make decisions too. After today, the yacht moves on to Zante," he paused. "What if I wanted to keep seeing you?"

She let the book rest on her thigh.

"And how long might that be for?"

"I can stay as long as I like, I don't work, remember?"

"What about your friends? I don't want to get in the way."

"I'm more interested in you. Will you stay with me again tonight? I'll get a room in Argostoli."

"I can't. I don't want to have to explain to Sophia or Aunt

Nicia why I'm not going to sleep at the house."

Her words disappointed him even though he'd expected such.

"Well, we could have dinner at my aunt's villa. I'd like you to meet her. How about tonight?"

If he accepted her invitation, he wouldn't be able to spend the evening with his friends, which would be awkward. A dreadful thought crossed his mind; now might be his last chance to make love to her. He would have to try again, later in the room.

"Yeah, I'd like to have dinner at your Aunt's. I remember you told me about the courtyard. Will it be okay, do they speak English?"

"Yes, they all do. Aunt Nicia spent ten years in the States. She's such a sweet lady; she's part of the reason I'm still here. I'll call and let them know. I'm so excited."

She reached into her bag, pulled out the phone and walked over by the pines.

Deciding not wait, Ben started back to the hotel.

"I'll see you in the room," he said.

Elena raised her hand then nodded.

***

Being alone gave Elena the chance to leave a message for Greg; there might not be another opportunity later. She didn't want to talk, just keep her promise to call. Greg usually turned his mobile off at night; it wasn't yet dawn in Boston. She dialed the number, hoping not to hear his voice. The phone rang, for what seemed like an age, until a recording finally answered.

"Hi Greg, sorry it's so early but I promised to get back to you. I'm going out for the day with Sophia. I don't think I'll get chance to ring again so voicemail's all you get. I'll try you again tomorrow."

Next, she dialed Sophia's number, her cousin answered immediately.

"Hi Sophia, are you at work?"

Suddenly Elena shrieked.

A huge black flying insect landed on her shoulder. She panicked, flicking it off. The insect pressed its attack, dive-bombing her head; she flailed her arms frantically in a desperate bid to keep it at bay. In the commotion, her phone fell to the grass.

Overcoming the creature left her flustered and she stood, watching its retreat, until it disappeared into the cypresses. In the midst of her fright, she was surprised to have imagined Ben, amusing himself at her antics from the room.

Recovering her poise, she bent down and picked up the phone, plucking a tiny buttercup in the same movement.

"Sorry—no, no, I'm okay. I just got attacked by a giant black bee or something."

She looked up to the balcony, Ben was nowhere in sight.

***

Ben lay on the bed. Memories from the night before filled his mind. He closed his eyes, bringing back a vision of Elena, semi-naked in the candlelight. Surprised by the power of his lust, he prayed she wouldn't be long.

Lust; wasn't it the first stage of love? Love; wasn't that a mystery well on its way to being solved? thought Ben.

His musings led him to recall Clotilde's conversation over dinner at Spiro's and he searched for oxytocin on his phone. It didn't take him long to skim through the first few articles and there it all was; the three stages of love.

Lust, he read. Testosterone and estrogen…

Then an attraction phase with adrenaline, dopamine and serotonin. Finally, attachment and oxytocin. Eric was right, mothers produce the hormone in childbirth and so do both sexes during orgasm.

Whatever the names of the chemicals, he'd once produced them by the bucket load for Maria, and that concerned him. Like an addict daring to test his resilience, he would experiment and felt powerless to do otherwise.

***

Elena had no key; she would have to knock. It was hard keeping his mind off her. For the umpteenth time, he calculated the minutes before they must leave. Eric had told him to be at the boat before one; they had over an hour. Now would be a good time to freshen up, the knock would come at any moment.

He emerged from the bathroom, anxious, impatient, even reckless, and gulped down a glass of water.

This isn't like dating, he reasoned. Today might be the last time I see her. Even if I don't go to Zante, surely I'll have only one or two days more.

Walking out on to the balcony, he checked the garden. She was not there. The reading chair stood back from the table, bringing back the memory of her legs.

The knock finally came, ending his frustration. He opened the door, letting her walk into his arms.

"I missed you, already," he said.

She snuggled up to him, raising his hopes.

"Everything's set. Dinner's at ten; Sophia will bring her boyfriend. Aunt Nicia will cook for us. It'll be such fun."

She broke away, his hand held her arm, only letting go when it reached full stretch. She stood between the two beds.

"I have nothing to pack. When are we leaving?" she asked.

"We have plenty of time."

She pointed at a carrier bag by the veranda door.

"I'll put my laundry in there."

Her olive dress lay stretched out on the spare bed. She lifted it up, exposing the black lingerie underneath.

"I'll get it." Ben picked up the bag, holding its string handles as she dropped the clothes inside; the lacey underwear landed on top.

Elena moved to brush past; Ben reached across, dropping the

carrier on the bed, forcing her to walk into his arms. He put his hands on her hips. "I might not see you again, after today," he said, feigning a childish tone.

"Ah, poor Ben," she sighed.

She looked up at him; her head tilted back, wearing the look from the night before. Their eyes remained locked together as Ben lifted the hem of her T-shirt above her waist. She raised her arms over her head and in a flowing movement, the white shirt lay strewn across the duvet. He undid the straps of her bikini; this time she didn't resist. He pushed her gently down on to the bed.

Ben caught a glance from the eyes of Hedy Lamarr, watching him through ruffles of white cotton as he followed Elena down.

21

Ben and Elena lay entangled together, drenched with sweat. The room was hot. He didn't move; maybe he would never move again and lie there, forever, wrapped around her wet body.

He wasn't sure how long they'd been making love. In the depths of his passion, time ceased to flow; making love to Elena became his only reason to exist.

"That was incredible," he said.

"I know. I love doing it like that," she whispered.

His phone beeped with a message, Elena wriggled free.

"I'll have to take another shower," she said. "You've made me all sweaty, you hog."

"Actually, it was the other way round."

She whacked him on the arm, gathered up her bikini and slunk off to the bathroom.

The text was from Eric. "Don't forget we leave at one."

"Hey Elena, we're running late," he shouted.

"That's your fault."

Ben typed a reply.

'I thought you said one thirty be there soon.'

A tangle of thoughts circled his head as he threw clothes into the suitcase. Plenty had happened in the last twenty-four hours, yet it seemed only moments since he'd opened his eyes and stared at the bands of sunlight through the veranda doors. He dropped the lid down, checking it would close, and stepped out to the balcony for one last look at his garden.

Elena came out of the shower clad in her bikini. He caught a glimpse of her in the corner of his eye and went back inside the room.

"Don't you dare touch me, you're still sweaty," she said, pre-empting any attempt to grab her.

He made his hands like claws and chased her, screaming, back into the bathroom. She stood against the sink, arms outstretched. "Get away!"

His frivolity jostled with a desire to have her again as she cowered in front of him. He got in the shower, letting her escape.

By the time he stepped out of the bathroom, Elena was dressed and reading on the patio.

"I'm clean now, can I grab you?"

"That's way enough grabbing for one day."

"Have you got everything? I think we're ready." He threw his toiletry bag in the suitcase and zipped the lid shut.

Only the green carrier remained; Elena plucked it off the bed and followed Ben as he wheeled his case towards the door.

"It's a pity to leave the flowers. Spiro will have to come and reclaim his champagne bucket," she said.

"The maid can have them." Ben took a twenty-euro bill from his wallet. "Here, slide that under the bucket."

After one last sweep of the room, they left.

Ben's dash along the corridor left Elena struggling to keep up. He arrived at reception before she'd descended the stairs.

Two small boys played chase around a set of matching blue suitcases in front of the registration counter. The children grew increasingly noisy as they waited for their father to check in.

"Carlo. Pazientare!" The mother grabbed the older child by the arm, lifting him off the ground.

Ben reached for his phone, checking the time. He would not make it to the boat by one-thirty.

Elena sensed his impatience. "Hey, it's Greece; fifteen minutes late, an hour, no worries."

"No kidding. What's mañana in Greek."

Carlo's little brother tripped and crashed into Ben's legs. Carlo stood still, feigning innocence, hoping to avoid another tongue-lashing. The father took no notice, leaving the mother to pick up the fallen boy and drag him across the floor next to her husband. She turned to Ben.

"I apologize. The boys are tired."

The woman's English was impeccable though Ben detected no sincerity in her voice.

"No problem," said Ben. He touched Elena's arm. "Hey, there's a diving board at the back of the yacht. I'm looking forward to the beach; it should be fun." He spoke to keep his mind off the delay rather than to initiate conversation.

After what seemed an eternity, the receptionist handed over a room key. Ben wheeled his small case past the pile of blue luggage as the girl behind the counter wished the Italians a pleasant stay.

Ben had prepaid his room. There were no additional charges. Two minutes later, he and Elena traded the cool of the lobby for the stifling August heat and started back to the boat.

"Is it far? I can't remember how we got here last night." Elena flipped on her sunglasses.

"It's a three-minute walk."

Once out of the hotel, Ben relaxed, slowing his pace to match hers. They soon entered the narrow side street with the leather goods store.

"You don't even remember looking at the handbags over

there; were you drunk?" he asked.

"I'm just messing with you," she replied.

A minute later, they emerged from the alley onto the harbor front. The sight of sparkling blue water reinvigorated Ben.

Eric and Sean stood on the jetty, by the boat. The engines hummed gently as they stepped aboard.

"Hey, sorry we're late," said Ben. "We were reading in the hotel garden—lost track of time."

"Sure you were," said Eric. "Sean, do you want to get the line and we can cast off?"

Sean untied the rope then jumped on board; Eric started the winch motor, hauling up the gangplank.

"Give me your bags, I'll stow them," said Eric. He reappeared a minute later. Ben and Elena followed him up to the flybridge cockpit as Sean went aft, looking out over the guardrail from where he signaled the all clear.

The Lamia IV eased into the harbor, gradually picking up speed as it found open water. Soon they reached the middle of the bay. Turning starboard, Eric opened up the throttle and the powerful craft surged forward with a judder.

"We'll have to go back there one day," said Ben. He held Elena's arm and pointed to Spiro's taverna.

The pastel colored buildings receded as the yacht headed southwest out of the harbor and into the channel separating Kefalonia from Ithaca. Elena looked to the hills in the west, searching for Dimi's villa. She imagined him, at the cliff edge, smoking a cigarette and leaning on the balcony, thinking about her, wondering if she'd ever return. So much had changed since arriving in Kefalonia anything seemed possible. As the boat rounded the headland and turned north, the velvet couch flashed into her thoughts.

"What are those?" asked Ben.

"Lighthouses," replied Eric. "Closest to shore is the old lighthouse. According to the guidebook, the Venetians built it."

Now little more than a ruin, Ben thought the circular beacon looked sad without its cupola. Further up the hill, a much taller, square tower stood about fifty feet high.

"The other one is nineteenth century," Eric continued.

Above the rocky shore, small pines stunted by sea winds surrounded the towers.

Some twenty minutes later, the yacht reached the tip of the peninsula at the most northerly point of the island and steered a course south along the wild and rugged western coast.

Ben turned to his friend. "What's the top speed?"

"Twenty-five knots."

"Where are we going, again?" asked Elena.

"Assos," replied Eric. "It's a small village in a sheltered bay about five nautical miles from here. We'll anchor there and have lunch; maybe take a dip."

"Assos is where the Venetian castle is, right?" asked Ben.

"Yeah, but it's quite a hike, especially in this heat."

At a half mile out to sea, the air became cool and pleasant. Ben rested his hand on Elena's; they fell silent, awed by the majesty of the mountainous coastline. She looked up at the cliffs, soaring hundreds of feet above and thought about yesterday's drive with Sophia, the hairpin bends, the precipice below. How strange that she should return to Argostoli on the same turquoise water she had admired from on high.

Down on the aft deck, the two wives basked in their swimsuits on the sun-lounge. Elena looked around for Clotilde, wondering what costume the model would wear today.

Attracted by a deserted cove, Eric steered the boat towards the shore and slowed to a crawl.

"The coastline is certainly spectacular," said Ben.

"You got that right," said Eric. "I'm always on the lookout for the perfect hidden beach. Did I tell you about the one in Corfu?"

"I'm jealous already," said Elena.

"We found this really small bay, too shallow for the boat. The entrance was so narrow it almost formed a lagoon. We anchored close and swam to the shore. The water was only waist deep, with a temperature like a warm bath. We hung out there for hours, didn't want to leave. It was one of those magical, unexpected places you always hope to find on an island cruise."

"Sorry I missed out," said Ben.

"Yeah, you'd have loved it. The cove was sheltered with pines; it was like our own private beach. Oh, and then Alan found this taverna along a dirt path through the trees. There was like nothing for miles around, no tourists, just a taverna. I had the most amazing shrimp dish, just plain, freshly caught shrimp cooked in olive oil, garlic, lemon…"

"Knock it off, you're making me hungry. I want that exact same shrimp dish, right now," said Elena.

"Make that two," Ben chipped in.

Eric continued, "I sat there drinking a couple of cold ones, watching the owner catching these tiny birds."

"Tiny birds?" asked Ben.

"Yeah, little song birds, I forgot what he said they were called. He caught two while I was there."

"Who'd be a titan of the Biotech industry when you could own that taverna," said Ben.

"Yeah, tell me about it."

Talk of the magical cove and the legendary shrimp dish made Eric eager for new discoveries. "This place isn't very interesting." He engaged the throttle and the yacht slid away.

A few minutes out from Assos, Joe climbed up to the flybridge, followed by Clotilde.

"That kid of yours fleeced us," said Joe.

"You been teaching him poker?" asked Eric.

"Don't listen to him," said Clotilde. "We were playing crazy eights, ask Sean."

Clotilde's lime green bikini competed for attention with Joe's Hawaiian shirt.

"Check out the castle." Eric pointed ahead.

Ben looked up at the sun-bleached outcrop. Olive trees surrounded the red-brown walls of the square, roofless fort.

The yacht slowed, gliding into the bay. A thin strip of land connected the promontory to the mainland, forming a sheltered cove with a narrow northerly entrance. The water was shallow, the bottom easily visible. Eric stopped the motor a hundred yards from the beach.

"You gotta be kidding," said Joe.

"Nice," said Clotilde.

Brightly colored houses lined the shore, from the harbor mouth to the castle rock. Several smaller craft lay anchored in the bay.

Before leaving to drop anchor, Eric handed out cold beers from the built-in icebox near the cockpit.

With the village as a backdrop, Ben photographed Elena. Clotilde stood watching them.

"Lean against the guardrail," said Ben. "Now turn you head to the right."

Elena's profile was beguiling. A satisfying sensation, perhaps pride, swept over him. It had been a long time since Ben had wanted to belong to someone.

"I like the T-shirt," said Clotilde.

Ben focused on the monochrome print in the viewfinder. A young, dark-haired woman; her hands raised, touching her forehead, pushing back her hair. A large bracelet dangled from her left arm.

"Hedy Lamarr isn't it?" He heard Clotilde say.

"Yeah, it's one of Ben's," replied Elena.

"If he had any class," said Joe. "He'd have given you the Sophia Loren one."

"Did you know Hedy Lamarr was an inventor?" asked Clotilde.

"Inventor and movie star. Hedy, you under-achiever you," said Elena.

"Yes, she invented some kind of radio technology. Spread spectrum, I think," said Clotilde.

Ben took his eyes away from the viewfinder and rejoined the physical world.

Yet again the stylish Clotilde scored high in his estimation; devastatingly beautiful, art and wine connoisseur, Miss General Knowledge. Once more, he found himself comparing the French girl to Elena. He knew most men would pick Clotilde. Two days ago, he would have done so without thinking. Clotilde was flawless, a classical beauty; Elena wasn't. She had a larger nose, typical of Mediterranean and Middle Eastern people. Now, that feature held more allure than the unblemished Clotilde and he began to feel an elitist pride in its imperfection.

In any case, thought Ben. After you get used to someone, you cease to notice their features.

Clotilde was too perfect; every man could see that. She could never be special to him and him alone.

Ben tapped Elena's arm. "I'm going for a dip, you coming?"

"Sure. Is there a snorkel, the water looks so clear?"

"I'll ask Eric."

***

Down on the stern deck, Ben laid his hands on Elena's shoulders, gently massaging her neck muscles. They watched Sean start the winch and guide the dinghy into the water.

"Sean and Sandra have volunteered to pop over to the village and bring back lunch," said Eric, stepping out of the main cabin. He checked the reception on his phone. "Hey, Sean, call me when you get to a menu."

"Okay." Sean laughed and started the motor. His wife stepped into the craft, steadying herself on her husband's arm.

"Hey, Alan," said Ben. "Get the snorkels and show me how to set up the diving board."

The young boy disappeared into the cabin below, returning moments later with two masks. Passing them to Ben, he rigged up the diving board in less than a minute, looking pleased to demonstrate his seamanship.

"You'll be captain one day," said Ben.

"I already know how to pilot the boat. I skippered it from Paxi to Lefkada."

"No way. What about charts and maps?"

"My dad showed me how to navigate."

"What are you, like ten or something?" teased Ben.

The boy jumped onto the diving board. "Race you to shore," he shouted and plunged into the water.

All alone on the stern deck, Ben grabbed the hem of Elena's T-shirt, pulling it up. She slapped his arm, removing the garment herself.

Sheltered by the rocky promontory, the air in the cove was motionless and blazing hot under the afternoon sun. Ben whipped off his shirt and passed a snorkel to Elena, beckoning towards the step with his palm. "Ladies first."

She leaned over the side, dipping the mask into the water. With the visor full, she flung the water at Ben, drenching his chest before jumping into the sea. He bounded onto the board, diving in after her.

***

Ben was following a shoal of orange fish when he heard Eric shouting.

"What do you guys want to order?"

He flipped over on to his back, sliding the snorkel over his head.

"Do they have the shrimp, in the olive oil and garlic?"

"No, I checked already," said Eric, with a smile.

"How about souvlaki?"

"Souvlaki," he said into the handset.

"Yeah, lamb souvlaki," he relayed.

"That'll do for me," said Ben.

"What does Elena want?"

She was several hundred yards away, over by the outcrop.

"Dunno, a salad … any salad," said Ben.

***

Elena swam for another half hour later before returning to the boat. Ben was hanging off the guardrail, ready to climb out of the water when she slithered up behind, wrapping her arms around his waist. Her breasts pressed into his back as she squeezed him. He flipped around, facing her, relishing the sensation of her slippery body. His mind scrambled, searching for a plan, anticipating any opportunity that might arise where he could make love to her before Argostoli. He kissed her neck as she wriggled free and climbed on deck. Ben swam off to cool his desire.

It was mid-afternoon when the dinghy returned. Ben heard Eric shouting his name and headed back to the boat, cutting through the water with a powerful stroke. He imagined Elena watching him.

As he scrambled back on board, Eric's wife called from the galley. "Ben, do me a favor, take these plates upstairs."

He obliged, making a couple of trips for napkins, utensils, chilled white wine and beers.

Soon everyone was on the flybridge enjoying lunch. Young Alan sat at the cockpit playing a handheld video game, somehow managing to munch a burger at the same time.

"How's the salad?" Ben asked Elena.

"Delicious."

"Joe, you been swimming yet?" Sean wound strands of linguine around his fork, sucking up a loose strand as he popped it into his mouth.

"He doesn't want Clotilde seeing his man boobs," said Eric.

"I might get the scuba gear out later," replied Joe.

"Joe's been working out; he's in good shape," said Clotilde.

She put an arm around his neck and kissed his cheek. "How about you, Ben, do you work out?"

Ben's T-shirt was still on the stern deck. He wondered if Clotilde had noticed the small fold of fat peeking over the top of his shorts; he leaned back, tightening his stomach.

"Usually, but I've been traveling for a month. I try and do some pushups when I'm on the road."

"How many pushups, five?" asked Joe.

"A hundred or so," said Ben, ignoring the sarcasm.

"A hundred at once?" Elena felt one of his biceps, mocking him.

"No, four sets of twenty-five," said Ben.

"More like a hundred sets of one," said Joe.

Alan shouted; everyone looked up.

"He's probably just beaten his record score," said his mother.

The boy came over to his father, in search of praise. Eric high-fived him, letting him squeeze into the circle of adults.

"What did you order, Joe?" asked Ben.

"Moussaka."

"How is it?"

"So-so. You know the Greeks copied Moussaka from the Italians," said Joe.

"Oh, really, I suppose you guys taught both the Greeks and the French to cook," said Elena.

Surprised by her remark, Ben looked up from his lunch and waited for Joe's reaction.

"Yeah but we did a better job with the Greeks," replied Joe. He appeared to have accepted Elena as one of the group. This pleased Ben.

"Joe isn't a big fan of French cuisine," said Clotilde.

"That's right. We taught them to cook then they go and start adding cream and butter and heaven knows what else. The next thing you know, the food's ruined. Italian food is simple with fresh ingredients; tomatoes, a little garlic, olive oil."

"Do you ever cook French food?" Elena asked Clotilde.

"Sometimes, but only when I'm mad at him," she paused. "I don't mind Joe mocking the French, I'm part Italian anyway."

Ben put his fork on his plate. "That explains a lot."

"Yes, my father's Italian."

"Clotilde comes from a distinguished Italian family," Joe said. His face lit up with pride.

"Tell us more," said Elena.

"My ancestor was Josephina Grassini, an opera singer who was quite a star in the late eighteenth, early nineteenth centuries—you've probably never heard of her."

Ben hadn't, but that didn't slow Clotilde's mystique from its meteoric rise.

"You peasants wouldn't know it, but Grassini was a big deal back then," said Joe. "She was the lover of both Napoleon and the Duke of Wellington."

"There's no need to lie," said Ben.

"It's true," said Clotilde. Ben's deadpan humor was lost on the French woman.

"So, not-tonight-Josephine was your ancestor?" asked Elena.

"That was a different Josephine," said Clotilde.

"I don't know what she saw in that pansy, Napoleon," said Joe.

"Joe doesn't have any respect for our great Emperor," said Clotilde.

"Emperor of France? He was Italian! His real name was Buonaparte, not Bonaparte. What a nation, your greatest leader wasn't even French," said Joe.

Ben wondered how much Clotilde might resemble the illustrious Josephina Grassini. Did the two military goliaths go into battle at Waterloo fighting for their countries or was their contest more personal?

"There are some desserts here," Sandra produced a plastic bag from under her seat. "They're all the same, chocolate gateau."

"Thanks, they look delicious but I'll pass," said Elena. "I'll tidy up. What happens to the trash?"

Plates and food containers lay strewn around the bridge, as though the Battle of Waterloo had taken place on board.

"How come you didn't hire a maid?" Ben asked Eric.

"We invited you instead," said Joe.

"There's a dishwasher and garbage disposal in the galley," said Eric.

Ben got up, making room for Elena to slide out from the bench-style seats.

"So get busy then," he said, pulling her to her feet.

His leg darted back to avoid a kick.

"I'll give you a hand." He smiled.

Several trips back and forth cleared the mess on the flybridge. Elena stacked dishes in the washer while Ben flung food cartons in the disposal.

"You must have been a great waitress."

"The best," she replied.

"Hey, thanks for offering to help. That was a nice gesture."

"No problem, it's the least I could do. I feel guilty, not paying for anything."

"Your money's no good here." He wrapped his arms around her waist, squeezing her from behind. "I wish we were alone on the yacht, right now."

He fantasized. She turned around, still in his embrace. Her eyes betrayed indecision, spurring him on. Privacy was just a few feet away, below deck. He held her wrist, stepping back, pulling her towards the stairs.

She resisted. "It's too risky."

Frustrated, he relived the moments from their steamy encounter at the Hotel Dionysus.

A motor sounded from the stern; Eric and Sean winched the dinghy into its cradle.

"Eric must be getting ready to leave. We'll soon be at your fancy shmancy beach."

Minutes later the main engines started; the yacht plowed forward.

22

Nicia lay on the bed, doodling on the bandage that wrapped around her hand. Visions of the hissing cat provided inspiration for her scribbles. Yesterday, after returning from the market, her mother had cleaned the wound with iodine and hot water; it stung. "We have to kill the germs," her mother kept saying.

After applying the final stroke of color to the sketch, she dropped her brush into the water jar and snapped the paint set closed. She was restless. School had closed for the summer. Ioannis and Stamos were at Grandmother's cottage; Mother was next door in the store and Father at the farm. Only Nessa was in the house and Nessa wasn't much fun. This morning, at the breakfast table, her elder sister hadn't so much as said a word; Nicia ate her tiropita and marmalade toast in silence.

By late morning, Nicia had begun to wonder why Larissa Matsakis hadn't come around from next door. Because Nicia was older than Larissa, she felt the girl should come to her; there was something slightly demeaning in having to search Larissa out. In a few minutes, Nicia would go and find her friend. Perhaps they'd go to Grandmother's and visit the boys. She picked up a book from the bedside table.

Although poor, the family managed to borrow, swap or buy second hand books for Nicia. Tutankhamen's Treasures was the latest. The Egyptian pharaoh and his treasure-filled tomb fascinated Nicia. She loved the book's black and white lithographs; the gilded wooden Canopic Shrine, the Lion Bed, the Statue of Anubis. If only the pictures were in color.

"Are you up there," Larissa called from downstairs. The Matsakis' children often came into the house unannounced and vice versa.

"In the bedroom," shouted Nicia.

She tracked the sound of Larissa's shoes tapping on the bare wooden stairs then the landing; in a few seconds, the loose floorboard outside her door would squeak. Larissa came in, without knocking, and sat on the narrow bed.

"Let's go and play in our garden," said Larissa.

Nicia considered the suggestion, picturing her neighbor's yard. A simple rope swing with a red seat hung from a branch in the Matsakis' apple tree; she could play there until lunch.

"I want to go and see Ioannis this afternoon," said Nicia.

"Can I come too?" asked Larissa.

Nicia wasn't sure. "I'll have to ask."

The two girls left the Katros' house; Nicia noted the time on the hall clock. Not long until lunch.

The Matsakis' store, not much larger than Nicia's house, had one sash window with shutters of a faded and delicate blue. Bottles of olive oil, jars and jugs, even boxes of fruit sat in the open window or outside the door partially blocking the entrance. Years later, Nicia would try to remember the display that day but could not. Clear in her mind though, she remembered carrying Tutankhamen's Treasures and that Larissa walked in front wearing a lilac dress.

The shop had a peculiar, unique aroma. Neither pleasant nor

unpleasant, the smell was a strange combination of spice, fruit, paraffin and shoe polish. The two girls walked behind the counter towards the rear. Nicia said "Hello" to her mother who smiled and ruffled her daughter's hair.

A bead curtain hung at the entrance to a small storeroom. Nicia parted the strands of beads with her hands, gliding through as though doing the breaststroke. Larissa shouted something and ran off through the open door at the back of the building, disappearing into the bright sunshine.

A voice called from the gloom. "Nicia, come and look."

She recognized the voice instantly; it belonged to Andreas, Larissa's thirteen-year-old brother. Nicia stopped just short of the door and turned.

"What is it?"

Andreas was holding something in his outstretched hands. Nicia could only make out a head, the head of something alive.

"I found it near the harbor."

Nicia moved closer and realized Andreas held a bird, a seagull.

"It can't fly," said Andreas.

She stroked the gull, her fingertips gliding down its soft neck and back.

"I don't know what to do with it."

"Let's take it to the doctor," Nicia suggested.

"Doctors only treat people."

"Can I hold it?"

Nicia put Tutankhamen's Treasures on top of a wooden crate and held out her hands. Noticing the colorful bandage, Andreas asked if the scratch hurt. He'd heard about yesterday's incident with the cat.

"It doesn't hurt."

Outside in the garden, the bough of the apple tree creaked with the rhythm of a pendulum; Larissa's ankles and black shoes swung in and out of sight from the side of the door jamb.

Stretching out his arms, Andreas offered Nicia the seagull.

She expected the bird to struggle or peck at her, it did not. The injured creature just sat there, motionless. She cradled the gull gently, holding it up to her nose, sniffing its scent.

Curious about the book, Andreas reached down to the wooden crate and examined the cover. Nicia continued to stroke the bird's feathers.

"What shall we call it?" she asked.

"Tutankhamen," said Andreas. "Let's call it Tutankhamen."

Nicia didn't hear the second iteration of the word Tutankhamen. At the moment Andreas spoke, a wall of noise—the same roar that deafened Ioannis a half mile away, reached Nicia with a mind-numbing crash. The ground rushed up, smacking her hard, sending the newly christened bird into the air. For what seemed an eternity, Nicia bounced around on the floor, banging her head several times; she never lost consciousness. When the shaking finally stopped, day had become night. She wondered if blindness had struck, her eyes were open but there was no light.

Andreas's voice came out of the darkness. "Nicia … Nicia…"

"I've lost the seagull," was all she could say.

Her eyes and lungs hurt; she coughed violently.

"Are you okay?" asked Andreas.

"I think so, but I can't see."

"Don't move." Miraculously, Andreas too had escaped injury.

Mature for his years, he had the presence of mind to grasp their plight.

"It's dust from the earthquake. Hold on, I'll try and find you."

Above their heads, a ray of light, thin and diffuse stirred hope.

"Nicia, look up, can you see any light?"

"Yes, I see it."

Disorientated, Andreas tried standing only to bang his head on something hard; he got back down on the floor.

"Don't try to stand; I think the ceiling has collapsed."

Crawling in the direction of Nicia's voice, Andreas inched his way over the masonry.

"Say something," he said.

Out of the darkness, came a reply, "Tutankhamen."

Despite their predicament, Andreas wanted to chuckle; Nicia was somewhere nearby.

With each passing minute, the dust cloud floated slowly to the ground. Sunlight shone down like a torch beam into the center of the room. In the distance, a siren pierced the silence. The shrill sound seemed to trigger a chorus of shouts. Nicia couldn't tell if the cries came from inside or outside the building.

Nicia screamed; something touched her.

"It's only me," said Andreas.

He felt her shape in the gloom, first her leg then her head; he put his arm around her shoulders.

Nicia's fears subsided as Andreas held her. Up above, the ray of sunlight penetrated enough to cast the first shadows over their new world. Nicia's mother called, her voice muffled and distant. Somewhere close by, Larissa cried.

"We're inside the storeroom. I think we're trapped," Andreas shouted.

Timber groaned then snapped, more light streamed in, illuminating their prison. Nicia could see their dilemma clearly now. Behind her, the store entrance appeared impassible, choked with fallen masonry. In front, the rear wall had collapsed to a pile of rubble a few feet high. The ceiling angled down sharply propped up on the debris. She looked at Andreas; his face comforted her.

Nicia's mother called out again. "Nicia, your father will be here soon. Stay where you are, we'll get you out."

Still crouching, Andreas lifted his hand and touched the roof beams. The two children were lucky; the floor above had provided protection from the falling stonework. Someone from the outside would be able to remove enough floorboards to affect a rescue.

"We'll be okay. Your dad will come soon," said Andreas.

His words evoked memories of his own father, killed by an incendiary bomb dropped by a German plane in the Second World War.

Unwilling to wait, Andreas resolved to break his way through and escape their dark cell. He told Nicia his plan. A new voice called from outside.

The boy moved quickly. Standing on a crate, he reached up to an area of floor, already damaged and open to the sky. He thought about his sick mother; she'd been sleeping in the room above.

Without tools, breaking through the boards proved an impossible task. Andreas used a chunk of stone as a hammer and beat the underside of the floorboards but with little success. The work was hot and sweaty. Clear air and sunlight spurred the boy on. He shouted to his sister; Larissa was unhurt and still in the garden. Hearing Andreas's voice, she scrambled over the rubble, climbing the incline, and thrust an arm through a hole in the boards. Andreas held her hand tight like a lifeline thrown to a drowning man.

Down below, something brushed against Nicia's leg. Her heart leapt into her mouth; she screamed. Andreas let go his sister's fingers and jumped off the crate, reaching Nicia in a single bound.

"Tutankhamen," Nicia clutched the injured bird to her chest; tears dripped down her cheek.

In spite of his predicament, Andreas was happy. He kissed the head of Nicia, his Egyptian princess.

23

Eric steered the Lamia IV out of the cove at Assos, round the castle rock then headed south for five nautical miles. The yacht cruised into a small bay formed by two spurs that curved out from the land. Eric anchored a few hundred yards from the glistening white shore of Myrtos.

"I expected there'd be other boats here," he said.

At first glance, Ben thought the beach only accessible by sea; it sat at the foot of steep limestone cliffs rising hundreds of feet into the air. As he studied the vista, he noticed a narrow precipitous road, winding its way down to a dirt parking lot overflowing with cars. A solitary wooden hut blended into the landscape without spoiling the natural beauty.

Colorful parasols stained the pristine white shoreline, each providing shade to a pair of sun loungers.

"Myrtos is one of the most photographed beaches in Europe," said Eric, muddling fresh mint into a glass of lime juice.

Elena pulled the camera from her bag and cycled through the photographs. She stopped at the picture of herself and Sophia, sitting atop the wall overlooking the bay.

"This is the view from up there." She passed the device to Ben.

"Who's the girl in the olive dress?"

"You're supposed to be looking at the scenery."

Eric handed Ben a mojito. "Let's go up top."

Out on the stern deck, the water created ripples of light that danced up the stark white stairwell. Sean had the dinghy ready for launch; Joe prepared diving equipment.

"We have more scuba gear if you want to explore the deep," said Eric.

"I'm not wearing the mouthpiece after he's used it," said Joe.

Ben ignored Joe's remark and turned to Clotilde, "Have you been here before?"

"Many years ago," she replied. "It's a trendy spot, popular with the Italians."

"So Joe, why don't you swim over to the beach and parlez vous Italiano with your paesanos," said Ben.

"Paesani." said Joe.

A shadow passed overhead, everyone looked up. Like a giant gaudy eagle, a hang-glider soared above the yacht. Ben's eyes followed the craft as it banked sharply, swooping back towards the cliff.

Elena gripped Ben's arm. "I think he's in trouble."

With surprising speed the pilot reached the precipice but he was clearly too low. The purple and yellow glider appeared on course to smash into the rock face.

"What's he doing?" said Eric.

Nausea swelled in Ben's stomach at the prospect of witnessing an accident. He cringed as the craft swerved viciously at the last moment then soared back out to sea.

A faint commotion drifted across the water from the shore. People stood, with hands shielding the sun, focusing their attention on the flying daredevil. The kite repeated the maneuver again, hurtling bullet-like towards the cliff, turning seconds before impact.

"Show off," said Joe.

Each brush with death happened at a lower altitude. Finally, the pilot reached treetop height then attempted the spectacular. Like a bird snatching its prey, his feet brushed loose pebbles from the escarpment. Onlookers strained their necks as he bounced off the shale, skimming over parasols to perform a perfect landing on the beach.

"Now that is how to make an entrance," said Eric.

In a slick, practiced motion, the bronze-tanned pilot tethered his craft and ran to the water's edge, plunging into the sea with a powerful dive.

"Well," said Clotilde.

"Couldn't he just drive here, like everybody else," said Joe.

"Watch out Joe," said Ben. "The daring bronze man is swimming towards the yacht. He might be planning to steal Clotilde."

"The daring bronze man will get a harpoon up his ass," replied Joe. "We're off diving, to hell with him."

He led Clotilde down the steps, as though shielding her from imaginary bronze suitors.

"I'm going for a dip, you coming?" asked Elena.

"I think I'll hang out with Eric for a while," said Ben.

"Okay, see you later."

***

Ben realized he'd been in Elena's company for most of the last twenty-four hours. It would be good to take a break, besides he needed to talk to Eric about tomorrow's arrangements.

"I'll fix more drinks," said Ben.

On his way back from the galley, he scanned the water for Elena. She was in the dinghy with the others, heading towards the beach.

"There you go." Ben handed Eric a cocktail.

"Cheers. So how's it going with Elena? It's the first time I've seen you guys apart."

"Hmmm, I was going to talk to you about that."

"She lives in Argostoli, doesn't she? Is she staying with us for Zante?"

"I haven't asked. I don't think so."

"But you're coming?"

"To be honest, I'm not sure."

"That's a helluva strong mojito you just made," said Eric.

Ben lowered his voice even though Elena was nowhere to be seen, "What do you think of her?"

"She seems nice enough. You must be keen to ask that kind of question. Do I detect something more than a casual attraction?"

Ben felt busted.

"Well, now you mention it," he said. "Here's the problem, you're flying back to LA in two days. I want to go to Zante but I doubt she'll come along. I know it sounds nuts, but if she says no, I'll end up staying here."

"When's she going back to the States?"

"She hasn't decided—at least that's what she told me. She might leave tomorrow for all I know."

"Is there a boyfriend?"

"I didn't ask but I get the feeling there is."

"What about tonight?"

"She invited me over to her family's villa for dinner. I already accepted."

Eric sipped his drink. "That doesn't suggest there's someone else."

"But he'll be back in the States. Her aunt's family might not even know him."

In detail, Ben told Eric the events surrounding his meeting with Elena.

"I swear, nothing like that's happened before … at least not in a long, long time. I don't know what's got into me. I've been trying to put things in perspective—it's because I'm on vacation, or on a Greek Island, the heat, even crazy things like cicadas or the color of her dress."

"It's well known that a change in environment can affect your state of mind," said Eric. "And we all respond to visual stimuli even if subconsciously. Maybe you got struck by Cupid's arrow," he laughed, "or the thunderbolt, like that scene in the Godfather."

"Visual stimuli? You promised not to wear your biologist's hat on vacation."

"But think about it. I saw the same girl in the same dress, so did Sean, and Joe, and a bunch of other guys. We didn't go bananas over her. I mean, don't get me wrong, she's an attractive girl—it's as the saying goes; beauty is in the eye of the beholder."

"You don't think she's so hot then?" asked Ben.

"No, I didn't say that, but there are plenty of examples in nature of the power of visual attraction; flowers mimicking female wasps in look and smell, birds of paradise with bizarre plumage and dance rituals."

"I'm not a wasp, though."

"Obviously humans are more complicated." Eric paused to think. "Some guys can get excited looking at a porno mag. It's only ink on paper, not a living thing or even three-dimensional. In biology, the visual experience sparks off the chemistry."

"Spoken like a true scientist," said Ben.

"Was I getting carried away?"

"No I'm fascinated. The problem is, I think I'm falling in love with her—maybe it's obsession."

Eric smiled. "Have you had sex yet?"

"Well … yeah and now I can't stop thinking about it—all the damn time."

"I'd say you should be careful," said Eric.

"I have to keep seeing her."

"One or two days shouldn't be long enough to get hooked."

"Something like this happened a few years back. Remember Nicole? I once brought her to one of your parties. Her father owned a bunch of buildings downtown."

"Vaguely," replied Eric.

"I only saw her four or five times but I could feel myself falling in love. She ended up not returning my calls. It was one of those deals where every time the phone rings you hope it's her."

"We've all been there."

"Although you're disappointed, it's not quite painful enough to hurt."

"You need to find out more about Elena," said Eric.

A combination of hot sun and cool sea breeze had left Ben sublimely relaxed. The two cocktails kept the conversation flowing.

"Isn't there a love-antidote on the market yet?" Ben was only half-joking.

"That's funny," said Eric. "Before I sold Genecular Labs, we looked into that."

"What, developing a love-antidote?"

"Yeah, it was during one of our company-wide brainstorming sessions. We canvassed all our business and marketing people to suggest areas for off-the-wall research. So this one woman, a real smart girl, had charted the success of erectile dysfunction drugs and wrote a proposal for a love-antidote. I mean, they were only two-pagers, not full blown analyses."

"What happened?"

"We canned the bitch, right away."

"What?"

"Just kidding, no, she submitted three ideas—one made it to the research stage. Unfortunately for you, it wasn't the love-antidote."

Ben grinned. "Maybe I can buy some of the ingredients off-the-shelf."

"I doubt we'll ever see such a product," continued Eric. "There'd be issues with the size of the market, whether insurance would cover the treatment, not to mention the negative publicity—think of the headlines—GENECULAR LABS DESIGNS MOLECULE KILLS LOVE!"

"You're a letdown," said Ben.

"I still have the woman's email address. You can start your own company."

"Funny."

Ben stood up, looking over the water, searching for Elena. He didn't want her sneaking up and hearing their conversation. The dinghy was over by the southern end of the beach.

"We're only beginning to scratch the surface of neuroscience," said Eric. "No scientist is even close to a love-antidote—or a love potion for that matter."

Ben checked the icebox for beers. He flipped open a couple of cans, handing one to Eric.

"Did you ever work with oxytocin?" asked Ben.

"We didn't, but I'm familiar with the research. For example, if you inject it into young female rats they start behaving like mothers, fussing over baby rats, even young females that have never mated," said Eric. "Actually, Miss Smartypants suggested a different hormone for her love potion."

"Oh?" said Ben.

"Vasopressin, an almost identical molecule," said Eric. "Researchers experimented with a species of rodent, one that forms stable mating partnerships. They blocked the vasopressin transmitter with an inhibitor, causing the animals to lose interest in their lifelong partners."

"I might need some of that."

They laughed.

The two men fell silent, gazing out over the flat sea. Ben reflected on the complexity of the brain's chemistry, his desire for Elena; of poems and love songs.

Love has to be the ultimate existential experience, he thought.

"You going to mention this to Elena?" asked Eric.

"Hell no. Imagine how that would go down."

"Right," said Eric. "Honey, I love you

—No you don't, it's just the chemicals in your head."

"Honest, Elena, it's still love," said Ben

"Yeah, we're still drunk, even though we know the rum caused it."

Both men chuckled.

The afternoon sun had lost its ferocity, sinking low over the water. Ben became tired. Thinking back, weeks seemed to have passed since he met Elena. He got up and headed for the stairs. "See you later. I'm going to take a nap."

The strong cocktail and the two beers had taken their toll. He lay on the padded cushions of the aft deck lounge, gazing up at the heavens. The sun smoldered, over to the west. High above, a white jet-trail spread wide across the sky, its creator long since gone. He fell into a deep sleep.

24

Ben looked down at an intensely blue scene. Fluted pillars of white marble rose above a roman mosaic floor flooded with crystal water. Streaming from behind, the most intense sunlight he'd ever known illuminated a girl, swimming between the stanchions. Her motion rippled the pool's surface creating reflections that danced up the cerulean walls.

From the shore, a car horn blared, drifting across the gentle swell, entering Ben's dream. Voices floated above him. Familiar though the voices were, they made him uncomfortable lest attaching a meaning to their words rob him of his exquisite illusion.

He sensed, rather than saw, Elena lying next to him. Slowly, he opened his eyes. Sleep had left him deeply relaxed.

Elena was indeed by his side, asleep. Seeing her brought back the delicious memory of his dream. He snuggled closer, hoping to catch a whiff of perfume and, with it, the scent of last night's passion. She bore only the faint tang of the sea.

While he slept, the air had cooled, though it remained comfortably warm. He lifted his head, checking the sun against the horizon; an effort that banished the last remnants of his dream.

His conversation with Eric was still bouncing around in his mind. It was good to get a friend's opinion and he valued Eric's judgment. Mulling over his words, Ben tried to draw conclusions, make decisions. He couldn't go to Zante without Elena—that much was now clear. How hollow would he feel on the yacht without her? At the next opportunity, he must question her. Eric was right. A two or three day romance couldn't hurt but a few days had a habit of turning into weeks. Before the night was over, he must know how long she intended to remain in Kefalonia.

An electric motor whirred, gears ground—the sound of the winch. Someone was hauling the dinghy out of the water.

Resigned to sleep alone tonight, Ben let the disappointment sink in. After dinner at the aunt's house, he would visit the hotel bar, deadening his senses. Tonight, even the Hendersons would provide a welcome distraction.

The main motor fired up, stirring movement in Elena; he put his arm around her, hoping she'd wake. Her bikini had dried in the late afternoon sun.

It's not simply lust, he thought. I really like her.

She opened her eyes, smiled at him, and he kissed her.

"Hey sleepyhead," he said.

"How long was I out?"

"Princess slept for one hundred years."

The boat shuddered slightly as it started to move.

Elena sat up. "I wish we could stay here for the sunset. Can you imagine how beautiful it'll be?"

"You don't say. I already asked Eric—the sun sets around eight and we're a long way from Argostoli. He doesn't want to navigate in the dark for two hours. Besides we'd be late for your dinner party."

"I almost forgot about tonight," she said. "I can't wait to tell Sophia I've been to Myrtos Beach—that's why I went in the dinghy, so I can say I was actually on the beach."

"I thought you'd gone looking for the hang-gliding hunk."

"You don't miss a thing, do you?"

The moment's humor provided Ben an opportunity to address his pressing problem.

"They're sailing to Zante tomorrow. I have to decide whether to go with them—you're welcome to come too."

"I can't."

"So if I stay, will I be able to see you?"

"Yes, we can see each other for as long as I'm here."

"But you don't know how long that will be?"

"I haven't made up my mind yet."

He wanted to ask about a boyfriend but decided to postpone that question. He'd already overplayed his hand by tacitly agreeing to abandon his friends on the vague promise that she'd continue seeing him for who knows how long. For now, he wanted to leave it at that.

"Okay, no worries, they're flying back to LA in a couple of days, anyway. I'm not even done with Kefalonia yet."

Out in open water, the boat was now quarter of the way across the five mile straight separating the mainland from the Pali Peninsula. Argostoli lay to the south. Although only eleven nautical miles, as the crow flies, the journey by sea involved circumnavigating the Pali peninsula, tripling the distance.

A breeze picked up as they approached the tip of Pali; Ben felt a slight chill.

"I think I'll go to the cabin. Are you coming?"

Elena shivered too. "Yes, it's getting cold."

Joe was stowing scuba gear in a hold below the stern as Ben stepped down from the mid-deck. Clotilde, wearing a man's red baggy sweater, sat watching him.

"Mr. and Mrs. Jacques Cousteau," said Ben.

"Who're you calling French?" growled Joe.

"How was the dive?" Elena asked Clotilde.

"Terrific, we didn't go too far, there are some tricky currents here."

"Do you dive often?" asked Ben.

Clotilde stretched the sweater over her knees. "When I get the chance."

There's no end to the woman's talents, thought Ben and walked past her into the main cabin. Eric was at the cockpit; his son sat next to him, a captain in the making.

"Hey Ben, we're going to play Blackjack—if Joe ever finishes stowing the scuba gear. Are you two in?" asked Sean.

Ben looked at Elena; she nodded.

"Sure," said Ben.

Blackjack wiled away the time … the Lamia IV made her way south, hugging the western edge of the Pali Peninsula, a mile off-shore. To the starboard side, nothing but open sea stretched for two hundred miles to the southeast coast of Italy.

At the southern end of the peninsula, the boat steered a southeasterly course, past the small island of Nisida Vardiani, then turned north into the bay of Argostoli.

"I'm out," declared Ben.

Down some five hundred Euros, he'd lost seven hands in a row. Clotilde had scooped up most of his crisp Euro notes; Elena was breaking even.

"I'm going on deck to watch the sunset," said Ben.

Stretching his arms in the air, he slid back in his seat and looked at Elena. "Are you coming?"

"Okay," she replied. "I haven't won anything, so I don't feel guilty calling it quits."

They sat behind the windshield on the deserted flybridge.

"You didn't do too well down there," said Elena. "Clotilde skinned you big time."

"Right, I'll have to find an ATM."

Argostoli lay out of sight, to the east, on the other side of the narrow Fanari Peninsula.

"How does it feel; sailing into your ancestral home at sunset?" he asked.

"It's," she paused, "well, comforting. The longer I stay here the more Greek I feel. I'm going to try using the language more."

They leaned against the windshield; he put his arms around her.

"Are you warm enough in that T-shirt?"

"Yeah. By the way," said Elena. "I have to remind Clotilde about Sophia's Gallery tomorrow. Do you think she'll come?"

"I expect so. I think the plan is to spend most of the day in Argostoli. Zante is only about twenty miles south of here—not far with this boat. They'll not be in any hurry to leave."

The Lamia IV continued north, shadowing the eastern coast of the two-mile wide channel.

"It's an unusual topography, sailing between two peninsulas," said Ben. "We're too early for the sunset, besides, it'll go down behind those mountains."

"I often watch the sun set over Lixouri from Aunt Nicia's orchard." Elena pointed east, to the nearby shore. "Her villa is somewhere over … there it is."

"She must have a wonderful view. I mean, you must have a wonderful view."

The yacht turned east at the tip of the Fanari Peninsula; the bay stretched on for another six miles to the north.

"That's Fanari Lighthouse," said Elena. "It's a great place to watch the sun go down. Let's go there tomorrow."

If Ben couldn't get her to his hotel tonight, he'd make sure it happened the next night.

"I'd like that. So, it's the art gallery in the afternoon, sunset at the lighthouse … and dinner after?" he asked.

"Okay, dinner after."

Not for the first time, Ben thought he recognized the expression on her face, the one he'd seen in the candlelight the night before. In his mind, he saw a green light to continue their passion.

Content, he checked the signal on his phone; it was strong.

"I need to book a hotel."

He found a listing of local hotels on the web and dialed a number. While he spoke to the receptionist, Clotilde appeared, still wearing the baggy sweater. She sat next to Elena.

"...06 2014," said Ben. "Great, so that's two nights. Oh, and I'll need a rental car for this evening. Can you arrange that by eight or eight-thirty?" He paused to hear the reply." I don't know ... a Jeep, yeah, get me a Jeep. Thanks, I appreciate all your help. I'll see you later."

"Elena tells me you're not coming with us to Zante," said Clotilde.

"No, I'm staying here with her."

"That's so romantic," said Clotilde.

"Well, I can't leave her alone with sex-crazed Greeks everywhere."

The girls laughed; Ben did not. With a twinge of jealousy, he entertained the idea of Elena looking for a Greek man. That would make sense—bring her closer to her roots.

Enough daylight remained for the craft to steer without lights. Close to land, the temperature rose once more. Clotilde removed her sweater; Ben tried not to ogle her stunning figure.

"Are you still coming to the gallery tomorrow?" he asked.

"It's all settled," said Elena. "We arranged everything when you were on the phone."

***

The boat slowed to a crawl. Elena looked out across the water. A mile ahead, the old stone Drapano Bridge crossed the lagoon, linking Argostoli to the mainland. Elena was getting used to seeing the landmark bridge, first from the cemetery, then on the drive to Fiskardo. She thought back to that morning, only yesterday.

Before Dimi, before Ben—and what to do about Greg? Very soon, decisions have to be made.

***

Just north of the commercial port, on the outskirts of town, Eric steered into the marina, maneuvering the boat with skill, bumping it gently against the moorings.

"I'll find a taxi, can you get the bags?" asked Ben.

He was in a hurry, there might yet be a chance of persuading Elena to join him for a cocktail at the hotel. Dinner with her aunt was at 10:00pm, as long as he got her back to the house by 8:30pm, she would have time to shower and get ready.

Hailing a cab proved difficult, the yacht had docked on the edge of town and traffic was light. He decided to walk in the direction of the port, hoping to find a taxi stand. Frustrated and hot, he hiked a half-mile before finding a hotel. He went inside and asked reception to call a cab.

Twenty-five minutes had passed since he left the others. Ben gave the driver instructions, first to the jetty then to the Royal Ionian Hotel. He was in no mood to chat.

The car pulled into the parking lot and stopped.

Ben pointed to the yacht. "Please go a bit further."

The driver reluctantly moved.

"Just here. Thanks. Wait a moment, I'll be right back."

He rushed across the tarmac and bounded up the gangplank, landing on the deck with a thud. Elena was still chatting with Clotilde in the main cabin; no one else was around.

"Whatever happened to you?" she asked.

Ben described his difficulty finding a taxi. "Where is everyone?"

"Joe's taking a nap; the others went for a look around. Clotilde didn't want to leave me on my own."

"We'd better go, the car's waiting."

Elena had their bags ready; Ben grabbed them and left.

"See you tomorrow," Clotilde called from the stern deck.

Ben opened the taxi door, letting Elena slide in to the back-seat; she clutched a green carrier bag. The driver packed Ben's case in the trunk. "Royal Ionian?" he asked.

"Please." Ben got into the back seat next to Elena. Tired, hot, and sweaty from his exertion, he finally had a minute to relax. The sedan sped along the port road, passing the Lixouri-Argostoli ferryboat; his hotel was only a few blocks away.

"How are you for time?" he asked.

"I'm shattered," she replied. "I just want to get home, take a nap, and get ready for dinner."

Suddenly, Ben remembered the rental car; he hadn't factored in the additional time. There would be paperwork to sign, payments to make; the hire company might even collect him and drive to their location. The taxi pulled up outside the hotel. Ben and Elena had hardly spoken on the short journey. He too felt exhausted and decided not to ask her to join him, there was a risk of spoiling what had been a perfect day.

"What's your aunt's address?"

"I'm not sure—I know how to get there but not the address. I'll text you when I get home. The concierge will give you directions."

For a moment, Ben entertained the sickening possibility that she wouldn't text him, that he'd never see her again. His panic subsided; her number was stored on his phone.

The driver got out, popped open the trunk and carried Ben's case to the curb. Reaching into his wallet, Ben pulled out his last hundred Euro note.

"Here, take this to cover the cab." He passed the money to Elena.

"No, that's way too much," she protested.

"It's okay, give me the change later."

He kissed her and opened the door. Elena said something to

the driver, in Greek. Ben waved her goodbye from the roadside.

25

Clouds of dust from falling rocks and shattered houses darkened the sky. Vasilis Katros ran towards Argostoli knowing in his heart that devastation waited.

***

Luck—he would detest that word after today—was on his side for the moment. He'd been alone, working in the fields, when the earthquake struck. No warning prepared him for the elemental force, the earsplitting crescendo that heralded the cataclysmic event. Shockwaves, brutal and unearthly, threw him to the floor, bouncing him across the ground. Memories flashed through his mind, a day from his youth, a storm at sea, the fear of drowning. Movement was futile; never had Vasilis experienced tremors of such savagery and duration. When the shaking finally stopped, he got to his knees and stared at the crumpled heap that was once his barn. Luck, was not being inside.

***

Running on adrenalin, he reached the outskirts of town in minutes only to have his worst fears confirmed. He flew, like a man possessed, leaping and stumbling over the piles of debris that littered the pavements. Everywhere, panic and terror held sway.

Vasilis had visions of his house, a smoldering ruin. Deep in his heart, the certainty of personal tragedy had taken root. He couldn't imagine otherwise.

Every building he passed had been destroyed. Each time Vasilis turned a corner, a new pile of debris sparked the memory of a person he'd known, a friend perhaps lost. Out on the streets, people were dazed, angry, crying or just plain scared. More than once, he saw men digging franticly in mounds of rubble, hoping for a miracle, that a loved one might have survived.

A hysterical woman called out to him, begging for aid. Vasilis pressed on, unable even to shout an apology. He wanted to help, now wasn't the time.

Another cry, desperate, someone he knew. Vasilis slowed only enough to yell out a reply. "My family," was all he could say. Somehow, speaking for the first time brought home the full extent of the devastation. His town had been destroyed, utterly, every last building.

Closing in on his neighborhood, a terrible dilemma became manifest.

Go home first or get the boys?

His house was closest but Stamos and Ioannis had only their grandmother for protection.

Panic mounted as he turned the corner—what used to be the corner—of his street. No matter how many times he deliberated, Vasilis always reached the same conclusion; his world, his family, revolved around his home, he had to go there first.

His terrace was no different from any other he'd passed on the frantic dash through town. Some houses had walls, some lay in a heap; none were habitable. Outside his door, Vasilis bent over double, exhausted. His chest hurt, breathing was painful. Preparing himself for the worst, he took stock of the damage.

His property had fared better than most. The ground floor, at least, was recognizable. Wooden shutters, ripped from their latch-es, hung erratically around the windows. Dark green and freshly painted, they made an odd contrast to the missing or shattered panes of glass. The upper-storey facade had disappeared entirely, exposing ceilings and interior walls to public view. Vasilis thought it strange to see his bedroom from the street. Two framed wed-ding photographs were gone, only their hooks remained. His bed-room door, hanging ajar, now led nowhere.

The pavement was surprisingly clear of debris; the masonry from the first floor had fallen inside. Vasilis shouted the names of his daughters, Nessa and Nicia; he called for his wife. Some inner demon tortured him with the horrible question:

Which one do you most want to survive?

He resisted the demon's nagging and pushed against the front door; it wouldn't budge. He tried again, this time throwing all his weight into the effort. The entrance was blocked; the bottom of the door smashed by the debris piled up behind.

"Dad."

He gave up his efforts just as Nessa shouted him. She was standing outside the ruins of the Matsakis' store. They rushed towards each other; she threw her arms around his neck.

"Thank heavens you're safe. Where's your mother? Where's Nicia?"

He thought to ask Nessa where she'd been when the house collapsed but there just wasn't time.

"Mom's in the garden next door," Nessa paused. "Dad … Nicia is trapped…"

"Trapped, where?"

The word 'trapped' sickened him, invoking visions of Nicia crushed and dying in the rubble.

"In the storeroom at the back of the shop. She's trapped un-der the floor with Andreas." Nessa's breathing came in gasps as she spoke.

"Show me. Is she hurt?"

"No, I think she's okay. Mr. Tsakampikas is helping free her."

The teenager led the way through the ruined store; its collapse seemed imminent. The roof perched precariously on what remained of the side and internal walls. Vasilis followed his daughter over the mound of rubble that, earlier in the day, had displayed produce from his farm. Anxious voices shouted somewhere in the ruins.

Dumbstruck by the absolute devastation of his neighbor's business, Vasilis struggled to make sense of it all. He could not imagine how the building had collapsed in such an odd fashion. On the side abutting his house, everything had caved in; it was possible to scramble over the debris and go through to the garden beyond.

The rear facade, like the front, had disintegrated and now lay on the ground. The partition between the shop and storeroom remained standing for most of the building's length, except where he and Nessa now scrambled. A load-bearing wall, it continued upwards to the first floor, supporting the roof. As he climbed over the fallen section of masonry, he caught his first glimpse of the garden beyond.

His wife sat on the ground, obviously hurt. She watched Mr. Tsakampikas lever up a piece of flooring. The nails shrieked against the wood as he pried the board loose.

A body lay next to his wife; Larissa Matsakis buried her head in the chest of the motionless form.

Vasilis rushed over. His wife's face, black with dust, seemed to belong to a stranger. Tears and sweat ran down her cheeks, joining like tributaries of some great river. He knelt beside her, reaching for her hand. An ugly red welt, seeping with blood, stretched along her leg, from knee to shin.

"You're hurt." Vasilis stared, aghast.

"Don't worry, it's not serious."

"Have you heard from Stamos?"

"No, I tried to go, but I can hardly walk."

He wanted to comfort her, to stay with her. He hoped she'd understand.

"I have to go, I'm sorry."

"No, no, you must."

"I need to see Nicia first."

Vasilis squeezed his wife's hand, kissed her cheek and rose. He felt sorrow for Larissa too. Her eyes never left her mother who lay beside her, barely conscious. Vasilis ruffled the young girl's hair. "Look after her, I'll try to come straight back."

Every passing second became more pressing than the last. Vasilis would have given five years of his life for an extra few minutes to help free Nicia. He ran up the incline of the fallen floor to where Mr. Tsakampikas, hammer in hand, had prized two boards loose.

"Theo, I'll never be able to thank you enough for this." Vasilis laid his hand on his friend's shoulder. "I have to go find the boys."

"Don't worry. I'll have Nicia out soon. My family are out helping others, I'll go back to them after your daughter is safe."

"Let me talk to her." Vasilis assessed the scene.

Without saw or crowbar, the rescue would take thirty or forty minutes. Equipped with only a small hammer, Mr. Tsakampikas struggled to smash the floorboards and dropping heavy masonry was too risky with the children just below.

Vasilis shouted through the hole in the floor. "Nicia, are you hurt?"

"I'm alright, Dad," echoed the reply.

"Mr. Tsakampikas will get you out in no time; I have to go and find the boys. I'll be back soon, I love you."

Vasilis's eyes welled up as he left his family at the Matsakis' ruin. He ran, brushing away tears with his shirtsleeve. The half-mile dash to his mother-in-law's house was going to be the loneliest journey of his life.

He passed families heading out of town to their farms or to the hills. Like a funeral procession, they trudged through the street, mournful, carrying only those possessions needed to survive.

Long before he reached the grandmother's cottage, a somber rationale dawned. Vasilis fought desperately against the tide of logic threatening to crush his spirit. He asked himself again, If both boys were unharmed, wouldn't at least one of them have gone back to their mother's house by now? He knew the answer with a dreadful certainty.

***

People had begun to organize. Those not injured, or caring for the injured, went door-to-door accounting for the occupants.

Neighbors had gathered outside the shell of his mother-in-law's home.

Exhausted and covered in bruises from stumbling through the debris, Vasilis called out as he approached the crowd. He recognized some of their faces, including Mr. Sklavounakis, the owner of the adjacent property. The man moved quickly towards him, his actions confirming Vasilis's worst fears.

Mr. Sklavounakis threw his arms around Vasilis, preventing his passage. Vasilis struggled to break free; a second man joined the fray, forcing him back.

"Let me pass. I have to go inside."

Blind to reason, Vasilis drove forward like a tormented bull; a third man grabbed his arm.

"They're not inside, they're not inside," shouted Mr. Sklavounakis.

"Where the hell are they?" yelled Vasilis.

His strength was waning fast; he no longer made headway. Slowly, Vasilis's struggles diminished, his shouts became sobs.

Mr. Sklavounakis spoke in Vasilis's ear, "I'm sorry." The innocent words came laced with dread.

"What's happened? Dear Lord, what's happened?"

"They're over there," Mr. Sklavounakis's voice was fateful, solemn.

He signaled the other two men to let go. Broken, Vasilis followed them across the street where a patch of bare ground served as a makeshift hospital. A single pear tree grew in the center of the small dusty lot. Volunteers rigged ropes and blankets from the lower branches of the tree, over to a wire fence, sheltering the injured from the blazing sun. Three women tended the wounded in the shade of the improvised tent.

Doors, salvaged from the wreckage, served as stretchers for the injured and the dead. The blood drained from Vasilis's face at the sight of several doors draped over with blankets.

A brown dog pushed its nose under a shroud then ambled away towards the tree.

Mr. Sklavounakis put a hand on Vasilis's shoulder. He pointed to the tent. "Your boy is over there."

Vasilis rushed over. Ioannis lay, uncovered, his eyes wide open, staring at the cotton ceiling.

"Yanni."

He threw himself to the ground, cradling his young son's head. Ioannis didn't move.

"We don't think he's seriously hurt," said Mr. Sklavounakis. "His leg was struck by something—probably a wooden beam. It's badly bruised but not broken. If you can fashion a crutch, you should be able to take him with you."

"Yanni, where's Stamos?"

There was no reply.

"Yanni, where's Stamos?" Vasilis asked again.

Ioannis stared unblinking at the blanket above, oblivious to his father's question.

"He was speaking when we found him," said Mr. Sklavounakis. "He's in a state of shock, there's not much we can do except wait until he snaps out of it."

Vasilis staggered to his feet like a condemned man resigned to his fate. He faced Sklavounakis, burying his face in the man's shoulder and listened to him recount what had happened.

"Your boy was lying on the kitchen floor when we arrived. His grandmother was in the same room. I'm afraid she's dead. We don't know how; there are no visible injuries."

Sklavounakis paused, searching for the words to carry on.

Vasilis lifted his head off Mr. Sklavounakis's shoulder. Like a proud man presenting a stoic face to his executioner, he waited for the guillotine to drop.

"I'm truly sorry…" Sklavounakis could hardly speak. "Your oldest boy was killed … he must have been in the garden at the time; the outbuilding collapsed on top of him."

For a moment, Vasilis was a child again, his careless behavior had caused an accident, injuring his sister; he stood trembling before his father. An immense sadness welled up from his stomach to his throat, rendering him speechless. He tried to utter an apology but could not. A feeble squeak, audible only to himself, was all he could manage.

He followed Sklavounakis towards the shrouded bodies, as though living a nightmare. Still mute, his expression implored the man to point out his son. Sklavounakis lowered his eyes to a body at their feet and gently shook his head.

"It's better that you don't see him," he said.

Vasilis Katros dropped to the dirt floor and lay on his side, his back to the dead boy. Using an arm as a pillow, he stayed on the ground for an eternity, lacking the will to move. Voices existed all around him, legs and feet moved in the periphery of his vision.

A foraging party of ants marched across the dry earth carrying a dead insect, many times larger than themselves. Their efforts meant more than his life; he hoped the ants made it safely home.

26

Freshly showered, Ben left his room and walked through the air-conditioned lobby of the Royal Ionian Hotel into the hot sultry night. The balmy air acted like an elixir, restoring his amorous mood.

A bunch of carnations wrapped in magenta paper nestled in his left hand. In his right, a hand-drawn map sketched the route to the villa. The hotel's parking lot was half a block away; he walked at a snail's pace, determined to reach the car without a single bead of perspiration sticking shirt to skin.

The sight of the red Jeep brought a smile. One hour earlier, the car hire representative had delivered the vehicle, sparking off a moment of amusement.

"On this island," the woman told him. "A Jeep means anything resembling a Jeep."

In this case, his Jeep was a Suzuki. Despite his persistence, no actual Jeeps were available—he really didn't care. Stepping into the open-topped car, he fired up the motor and unfolded the map.

Navigating around the unfamiliar town at night wasn't a concern. He had navigation capability on his phone and he could always call Elena if he got lost. Ben felt confident of arriving in good time.

He studied the directions. Arriving at Argostoli by boat had given him a general idea of the peninsula's topography. Elena had pointed out her aunt's house from the yacht, he knew it was on the western edge of the narrow peninsula; the Royal Ionian lay on the eastern shore.

"Be careful, there are many one-way streets," the hotel concierge had warned.

Mindful of the advice, he turned out of the parking lot into the street, concentrating on the first 'very important' turn.

The route took him past the town's main plaza, its lower side lined with restaurants. Tables filled the sidewalk, extending out over the road and into the square. Classic Mediterranean late-night dining; the scene hummed with activity, whetting his appetite for the evening ahead.

Getting out of Argostoli proved easier than expected. Once he'd located Gerasimou Germeni Street, a straight run uphill took him to the top of town. A couple of twisting bends later he found himself on the lighthouse road. He was almost there.

Elena's message had said 'turn right after you pass the stone house with pine trees in the garden'. Her instructions were precise. Ten minutes after leaving the hotel, Ben turned into the long private drive leading to Aunt Nicia's villa.

He pulled up alongside a Mercedes roadster, switched off the engine and dialed Elena's number. She answered after two rings.

"I'm outside," he said.

She told him to wait.

Ben spent the moments anticipating her outfit—it was too hot for jeans. She'd said, 'come casual, it's a typical Mediterranean al fresco family dinner.' He remained in the car, watching the front of the house.

Lanterns hung from ornate posts, illuminating the driveway

and immaculate grounds. The villa had a classic and timeless charm though its date had to be post-earthquake. In the orange-tinged light, the color of the pale walls was difficult to identify; the window frames were probably bright blue.

The door of the house swung open and Elena appeared. She wore white three-quarter length curve-hugging pants and a sleeveless top; its neck high and scooped. A silver pendant hung from a black chain decorating the plain outfit. Tied-back hair completed her look.

She walked across the drive to the open-top car and leant against the door. "I like the Jeep."

"It's a Suzuki, but…"

Ben got out, holding the carnations.

The gift brought a smile. "Flowers, again; you shouldn't have."

"I didn't. They're for your aunt."

Before they entered the house, she reminded Ben of his role.

"Remember, we've only just met. I'm thanking you for the boat trip."

"Got it."

Once inside, she led him along a wide corridor tiled with brown terracotta squares. They passed a wooden staircase, entering the kitchen through a pair of pine doors. Tempting aromas of garlic, spices, and roasting meats filled the air. Ben hadn't eaten since Assos; he was famished.

Outside, through the open doors, he got his first glimpse of the courtyard. Elena hadn't overstated its charm.

Two women prepared food. A small television tuned to a Greek news channel sat on the counter.

He recognized Sophia immediately, even though she faced the counter. The older lady had to be Aunt Nicia. She wiped her hand on a cloth towel and turned towards him.

"This is Ben," said Elena.

"These are for you." He held out the carnations.

"Oh, how lovely, thank you." Nicia's serene disposition appeared to match Elena's description or perhaps his preconception amplified the impression.

"I have heard so much about you," he continued. "It's nice to finally meet you."

"Now Elena, what have you been telling him?"

"Just that you're the happiest woman on the planet," she replied.

Sophia turned away from her task to shake Ben's hand. As their hands clasped, he wondered how much Elena had told her of the night before.

"Thank you for taking such good care of my cousin," said Sophia. "She told me all about her adventure."

"We had a fun time."

Elena watched her aunt closely, trying to gauge her first impressions of Ben. Already an influential figure in her life, Nicia's disapproval would be a significant setback.

"Why don't you take Ben into the courtyard and introduce him to Andreas," suggested Nicia. "We'll be serving soon."

"Do you need any help?" asked Ben.

"No, No thank you. You go on outside."

Ben followed Elena into the luxuriant night. The whirring of the kitchen fan and the chatter of the television dissolved into slow, melodious piano, perhaps a nocturne, the silence between its notes filled with the natural harmony of night insects. Ben felt he could cut the air with a knife such was its substance.

Elena nudged his arm. "I told you the courtyard was a magical place."

Her statement went unanswered as Ben adjusted to the change in light. Lanterns, hidden in foliage, cast muted colors from the walls.

Two men, one wearing a fedora, sat at an enormous table under a pergola covered in wisteria. Thick fluted candles, flickering in the faint breeze, added warmth to the men's faces.

As Elena's ethereal-white figure approached, the man in the hat rose. Much older than the other, he was over six feet tall and athletically built. She introduced him first.

"This is Andreas, my uncle."

Andreas removed his hat, revealing a head of thick, grey hair.

"Hi, I'm Ben, pleased to meet you."

The man smiled, welcoming Ben to his house. Ben recognized the smile as genuine; he liked Andreas instantly.

The other man, in his early thirties, remained seated until Elena introduced him as Nik, Sophia's boyfriend. His greeting, more reserved, reminded Ben of last night's cancelled dinner arrangement. He hoped there were no ill feelings. Nik sat down before Andreas. Ben looked him over again. His hair, medium length and dark brown, was untidy. A moustache and short beard added to his unkempt look.

***

A dozen people could easily sit at the wooden table; only six places were set. Elena showed Ben to his seat, opposite the men, and went back to help in the kitchen.

Silence followed Elena's departure, Ben searched for a topic of conversation but his mind was blank.

Andreas spoke first.

"What would you like to drink?"

Both men were drinking red wine. The label on the bottle faced away from Ben.

"I'll join you in a glass of wine, if that's okay."

The moments of silence before Andreas spoke were anything but awkward; the tranquility of the courtyard wouldn't allow that. Andreas poured the wine. Ben watched the red liquid tumble into his glass, all the while increasingly attentive of the melody flowing out of speakers hidden in the vines above.

"Chopin?" he asked, with a reasonable degree of certainty; he did know the name of the piece.

"Yes, Moravec. Do you like Chopin?" replied Andreas.

"The music suits your garden," Ben turned towards the kitchen, distracted by women's voices.

Sophia pushed a rustic wooden cart across the terracotta floor, the wheels rattled. Nicia and Elena followed a couple of steps behind. Ben considered helping but, unsure of the protocol, remained seated, sipping wine. The label now faced him, a Côte Rôtie from one of his favorite producers—a good choice, not too expensive. Two more unopened bottles of the same vintage stood to Andreas's right. He complimented the host on his selection.

Before the cart reached the pergola, Elena moved in front, placing trivets on the table. Each of the protective placemats bore painted motifs of common fruits. Ben focused on the one nearest to him; red and green apples on a faux, cracked-plaster background. The women quickly covered the trivets with sizzling iron skillets, his apple motif becoming a dish of baked tomatoes, onion and zucchini, sprinkled with sprigs of rosemary.

Two tiered, the serving cart held hot plates on top, cold below. In no time, the space between the diners teemed with mouthwatering dishes. Two glass bottles of olive oil with cork stoppers followed by three bowls of mixed olives completed the serving.

"The olives are home grown, there's an orchard in the back." Elena pointed in the direction of the rear wall. "I'll show you after we've eaten. The orchard runs all the way down to the sea ... we can see the lights of Lixouri across the bay."

The women took their seats.

"Please, help yourself," said Nicia, signaling the start of dinner.

At some point during the serving, the music changed from piano to flamenco guitar with a female gypsy vocal; Ben couldn't remember exactly when. He looked at Andreas, curious whether he had some remote device, controlling the selection.

The music mystery distracted him; Elena was talking, pointing up at the house.

"That's my bedroom, I've been getting up at first light and reading then I go back to sleep again. It's so beautiful watching the sun come up behind the villa and lighting up the bay."

He turned to look at the balcony outside Elena's room. Uplighters, hidden in the baskets of bougainvillea, illuminated the upper storey. Ben spotted a bird's nest under the eaves, close to her bedroom window.

"Have you seen the swallows?" he asked.

"No. Apparently, I just missed them."

"It's a pity," said Nicia. "Her room's a great place to watch them hunting for insects over the orchard."

Ben found her description evocative. He began telling Nicia about his childhood in the countryside outside of London ... his love of summertime, of swallows nesting in barns, swooping low over the fields of barley. As he spoke, he was that young boy again, transported back to a summer long ago. He stood under a group of sycamores by a rusted iron fence. It overlooked a field, left to pasture, and covered in wildflowers. Twilight made silhouettes of distant trees. Behind the fence, a ditch attracted swarms of midges, irritating him. Somewhere nearby, his parents ate dinner in the garden of a country pub. Over the meadow, swallows swooped and dived in the half-light; tonight their memory created his vision of Nicia's orchard.

With a touch of regret, he shook off the memory. The music, the wine, the courtyard were a heady, intoxicating mixture.

He turned to Andreas. "Elena told me you have a gallery in Argostoli. We are planning a visit tomorrow with some of my friends. Have you had it long?"

"We opened," he paused to calculate, "about six years ago."

At the mention of the gallery, Sophia spoke for the first time. "We got some nice pieces from Dimi yesterday. I have the best ones exhibited already."

"What did you think of Dimi?" Nicia asked Elena. "He's a wonderful artist."

Elena wasn't sure how to respond. Dimi still intrigued her and kept appearing in her thoughts.

"I'm not a good judge of art," she said. "But Dimi and his wife were charming. We had lunch in their garden."

"Is art your main business?" asked Ben.

"It's more of a hobby," replied Andreas.

Ben wondered if Andreas had bought the gallery for Sophia's benefit.

Andreas didn't answer the implied question about his occupation. Ben thought it impolite to press. As though she'd read his mind, Elena supplied the answer.

"Uncle Andreas owns a chain of gas stations, mostly on the mainland."

"It's a very small chain," said Andreas, "We are comfortable, but we are not Onassis."

"Did you know Onassis owned one of the nearby islands?" asked Sophia.

"Really, which one?" Elena twirled wine in her glass.

"Skorpios Island," Sophia continued. "It's near Lefkada, Clotilde probably passed by there the other day. I'll ask her about it tomorrow. Nik's boats take the tourists there…"

Nik had kept a low profile, talking mostly with Sophia. Ben thought it a good opportunity to bring him into the conversation. "You must know quite a bit about the history. I'm interested."

Nik's voice was melodic, somewhat at odds with his designer-ruffled appearance. "Skorpios is a popular destination, although you can't land there. Onassis started that whole own-your-own-island thing back in the sixties. It's where he married Jacqueline Kennedy or Jackie-O as she became known."

"Who owns it now?" asked Ben.

"Onassis's granddaughter, Athina—though she never visits."

"How about that," said Elena. "Having your own island and never visiting."

"There are always rumors that some famous person is going to buy Skorpios. Madonna, Bill Gates… What's for sure, when it's sold, it'll be the most expensive private island in the world."

The conversation centered on Nik for the next few minutes. Ben learned he owned a small car hire business in Argostoli and operated a couple of cruise boats.

Andreas poured the last of the Côte Rôtie, topping up each glass; the iron skillets had long since gone cold. Sophia removed the empty dishes, making space on the table.

"I'll make coffee and bring the desserts." She took the cart back to the kitchen.

"Tell Ben the story of how you came back to Kefalonia," Elena begged Nicia.

"It's getting late, I'm sure he doesn't want to hear about that."

Elena insisted. "I don't care if he doesn't. I want to hear it again."

"Please, I want to hear," said Ben.

"Oh dear, where to start…"

27

It was after midnight by the time Nicia finished her tale. Sophia had brought a second pot of coffee. Three bottles of tentura liqueur sat on the table.

"What do you think; isn't that the best happy-ever-after story?" asked Elena.

"Yes," said Ben. He turned to Nicia, "I've often wondered what it must be like to live through a disaster. Hopefully, I never get to experience one."

The music had stopped, mysteriously, as Nicia began her recital; now, only the crickets broke the silence.

Nik stretched, "I'm tired. I think I'd better be going."

He pushed back his chair, awaiting any objections; Sophia put her hand on his. He rose, saying his goodbyes to Andreas and Nicia in their native tongue.

Only Andreas remained seated. Nik walked around the table to shake Ben's hand.

"It was a pleasure meeting you." Nik's tone was sincere.

"Likewise, I hope we meet again soon," Ben replied.

Sophia followed Nik into the house as Nicia cleared the dishes; Andreas stayed in his chair, sipping tentura.

"I'm going to show Ben the orchard." Elena addressed her uncle.

He nodded.

Ben and Elena set off across the courtyard, pausing to look at the water fountain before disappearing through the gates in the rear boundary wall.

Only a few days into a new quarter, the moon's pale light cast the orchard in shadow. A large table sat underneath a group of pines in front of the olive grove.

Elena leaned back against a wooden chair.

"This is where I have breakfast; there's a nice shade. It gets hot, even in the early morning."

Bright lanterns, placed in the branches, illuminated the first few rows of olive trees. A pale cat looked back from the shadows, its eyes glinting.

Ben peered into the semidarkness.

"How far back does it go?"

"Right down to the sea. It's not far, a couple of hundred yards, maybe. Shall we?"

They entered the ghostly orchard. The cat moved further into the darkness. As Ben moved deeper into the grove, his eyes adjusted to the gloom. Spaced seven or eight yards apart, the olive trees bore a light scent of fruit, sometimes overpowered by whiffs of jasmine, though he saw no plants. The dry, course grass brushed Ben's feet through his sandals. Elena stumbled; he grabbed her hand, keeping hold.

"I should've brought a flashlight," she said.

"What and ruin the mystery tour."

"Glad you're enjoying it but it's almost over," she said. "Here's the bench at the cliff edge."

Ben could barely make out the seat ahead, a black shape against the faint moonlight reflecting off the water.

Resting a hand on the bench, Elena leaned into him. She pointed across the channel, away to the right, where the lights from the town of Lixouri glinted over the bay. They sat in the darkness, a darkness brought to life with the voice of a thousand crickets.

"What did you think of Aunt Nicia's story?" Elena asked him again. "I'll never tire of it."

"You want something like that to happen to you?"

"I don't have a childhood sweetheart, so we can rule out that possibility."

Her answer somehow reassured Ben. "Something's bothering you though."

"Well yeah! This whole place is bothering me."

"How'd you mean?"

"You were there tonight; didn't you feel the magic?"

"Sure, I'm still feeling it. The sea, the crickets, the smell of the night … you. What else is there to live for—oh I forgot the food and wine."

"I'm being serious."

"So was I."

The time for Elena to open up was close; perhaps he'd get to know everything soon.

He made his move. "What about Boston?"

"I'm not sure I want to think about Boston," she hesitated. "It's a reminder that I'll have to leave Kefalonia."

She started to explain her reason for coming to the island.

"It was around the end of the first week that I began to think about not going back home. I thought the whole idea would wear off after a few days but it's taken root," she paused. "And now you've appeared and messed things up even more."

"Why don't you start at the beginning? What do you do in Boston?"

"I work in advertising—mostly writing copy. I'm pushing my

luck taking so much time off." Her voice hinted at some internal conflict. "I'm getting a whole lot of hassle over my extended stay. I've tried working from my bedroom, trying to complete a project, but I can't concentrate... I don't know, it all seems so pointless when you compare Nicia's life, or even Sophia's. I'm so weary of all the corporate bullshit in our world."

Ben stayed silent.

"It's the difference in lifestyle," she continued. "Rushing around everywhere, crazy deadlines, stuck in traffic, no time for lunch, too tired to enjoy dinner, TV advertisements bombarding you twenty-four-seven."

Ben pushed up closer, putting his arm around her.

"Stress is a killer, they say."

Touching her fueled his desire; her soft feel excited him. Now was not the time for lust, he had to get to the bottom of her issues.

"Let's think this through. You're on vacation; the island is charming, you're captivated," he paused. "Okay, that's normal. Everybody, at some time, has taken a holiday and not wanted to return—some actually pull it off. There's nothing wrong with that. Most people just end up going home ... and after they get back into a routine, they forget all about their idyllic island."

"I know what you're saying ... and it's true, but there's more to it than that."

"Like?"

"Like, who's to say I don't belong here. This is my family, my family's roots." She pointed at the house. "Aunt Nicia came back ... look at her; she wouldn't swap her life for anything."

"True."

"And there's Sophia ... she's more Greek than me ... she spent half of her life in the US and prefers it here. I love Sophia as much as anyone that I know in Boston."

"So stay. What's stopping you?" Ben's tone was matter of fact.

Soon he would find out whom else she loved in Boston. He pulled his arm from around her waist, resting it on the back of the bench.

Elena hesitated, "Well ... I don't speak enough Greek for one thing and I'll need to get a job. I don't think there's much work on the island, outside of tourism."

"None of those things are real barriers, if it's what you want."

Elena didn't respond; they sat in silence. Ben was calm, listening to the crickets. He doubted Elena was conscious of them at this moment. She looked lost in her thoughts.

Finally, he asked the question. "Is there somebody special back in Boston?"

She took a few seconds to consider her response. "Somebody, yes ... special, not really."

"Do you want to talk about it?"

"There's isn't much to tell," she replied. "How about you?"

Ben answered emphatically. "Nobody special."

She didn't respond. He let the silence continue, trying to gauge her mood. One more question then he would need to swing her thoughts away from Boston and back to the island.

"How long before you have to go back ... the job I mean?"

"What's today, Saturday? If I go back, it will have to be before the end of next week."

Enough was enough. Ben felt the magic of the evening disappearing, drip by depressing drip. For a moment, he existed on another bench, cold and wet in a dreary industrial part of London. Heavy trucks thundered through the rain-drenched streets, their terse noise, devoid of joy, obliterating the crickets' clement song.

"Well, I'm going to stick around until you make a decision. Who knows, we might both end up staying a while," he said.

She considered his statement. Was he serious? If so, would she want to stay with him? She wasn't sure; really didn't understand him. He was so different from the people she knew. Maybe he'd lived in LA for too long. Whatever the answer, his words comforted her.

"Don't you have to get back to LA?" she asked.

"I don't have to get back anywhere. Let's rent a villa, like your aunt's, and stay 'til the end of summer."

He watched the Boston Elena retreat and waited … waited for the sensuous Elena to reappear.

"Very nice, Mr. Mysterious. Tomorrow, I'm going to have to find out what makes you tick."

"At the moment, you make me tick." His remark implied impermanence; he regretted it immediately.

Hoping she hadn't made the connection, he bent over to kiss her; she responded. The girl from Boston faded away.

Somewhere in the orchard, an owl screeched, breaking the spell of their kiss. Its call, a single note, repeated four or five times in short bursts then stopped. Elena pulled her lips from his.

"We can't, I told you before," she said.

Ben's hand was between her thighs; he didn't remember putting it there.

"They might see us," she said.

His hand nestled further.

"It's too dark to be seen from the house … let's go somewhere out of sight."

"No," Her answer was resolute.

They had agreed to this, Ben had to admit.

"Tomorrow, then, promise me, tomorrow."

"If you're good," she smiled, removing his hand. "Come on, it's late, we should go."

They left the bench and headed back through the orchard. Ben ached with desire.

"It's been a lovely evening," said Elena, offering him encouragement.

His passion both pleased and excited her, but deep inside, a warning sounded.

As they neared the house, the lights hanging in the pines cast olive tree shadows over the ground, laying down an indelible image in Ben's memory. The owl called out again.

"It's somewhere over there," whispered Ben, pointing to their right.

Again, the creature called.

"In one of those two trees."

They crept closer, Ben wondered if the noise of the crickets would disguise their approach.

Elena spotted the owl first.

"It's there, I can see it," she tugged at his arm.

Ben strained his eyes in the shadowy light, following her fingers; he was within five feet of the tree.

"Yeah, I see him," whispered Ben.

The owl was a mere seven inches high. It sat on a branch two yards above their heads.

"Look at its eyes," said Ben.

"It's so beautiful," she whispered.

The bird had a mottled plumage; its paler feathers reflected the light from the lanterns. It sang again, calling four times in quick succession before flying off into a darker part of the orchard.

"We'll have to keep really quiet," said Elena as they sneaked back into the courtyard.

Ben silently thanked the owl for a magical end to their evening.

Under the pergola, the table looked sad and bare. Only the candles remained, extinguished. Ben glanced back one more time before they entered the kitchen; he would always remember Nicia's courtyard.

No one stirred as Elena opened the front door. She followed Ben over to the Jeep; he climbed into the driver's seat.

"I wish I wasn't going back to the hotel alone," Ben complained one more time.

She leaned against his door and kissed his cheek through the open window. Hard metal separated them.

"What time tomorrow?" she asked.

"I'll call you in the morning, maybe at ten or ten-thirty."

"Okay." She turned and walked back to the house.

He gazed longingly as her white figure hurried over the tarmac; every curve committed to memory for recollection on the drive home.

She waved once from the door and went inside.

Ben drove back to Argostoli, concerned about his feelings … his obsession for Elena.

28

The strange mercurial bells reminded Elena of high school and her music teacher, Mrs. Adams, flailing her arms, striking the metal plates of her glockenspiel. Repeating a series of three chimes, in rapid succession, the joyous bells heralded the appearance of Saint Gerasimos to the expectant crowd.

Lowered from its resting place, the silver casket stood upright on the church floor. Four men, in lay clothes, waited to act as bearers. It was time. Bearded monks slid wooden poles, with slow precision, into metal rings on each side of the sarcophagus. Heaving the weight onto their shoulders, the porters raised Gerasimos into the air.

"Let's get in line," Elena nudged her mother's arm.

The men received the order to move and headed to the exit a few yards away. Jostling for position, worshippers poured into the aisle, inching their way behind the saint.

"I wish we were outside," said Elena's mother. "We'd get a much better view. I want to see him looking down at the crowd."

The bearers paused at the threshold, awaiting a signal to proceed; the bells stopped momentarily. Elena stood on tiptoes, straining to see; only a silver dome and cross was visible over the heads of the congregation.

A monk waved a hand, striking up the brass band. The entourage crossed the shaded portico to the church steps. Fifteen seconds elapsed and the bandsmen fell silent again.

Gerasimos appeared to be inspecting the crowd from the top of the steps. Elena gripped her father's arm; his stoic expression remained fast.

The bells resumed their hypnotic tempo. Sunlight showered the silver coffin as the bearers edged forward. The band struck up a march and the procession began. An official photographer, crouching on the steps, snapped shot after shot, backing away like a cur as the saint descended.

Elena crossed the portico and squinted in the sun's glare. She flipped the black hat onto her head, tipping its brim over her eyes and took in the scene. Awash with color, two brass bands led the procession, light blue tunics for the lead, ivory for the vanguard. Banners and standards lined the route, blue and white flags of Greece, yellow of the Orthodox Church. Color and music were one in celebration; the band expressed joy in synchrony with the relentless pealing of bells.

Bearded monks, some in black robes, others white, swung incense burners ahead of the saint. One of the clergymen handed his censer to a young man, picked at random from the crowd. Dressed in jeans and T-shirt, the man held the smoking orb swinging it back and forth, sending wafts of scent floating in the sweltering air.

"I hope Dad's okay," said Elena.

Her mother seemed lost in own thoughts and stared straight ahead without answering.

From her elevated position, Elena looked down at the casket. Solid embossed silver called to mind museums, antiquities, cathedrals... A large cross sat atop a dome which rested on the heavy chunk of a square cornice. As she descended the stairs, the sarcophagus disappeared behind rows of nuns, walking five abreast, in the wake of their saint.

Nicia left her husband's side, dropping back a few paces.

"It's quite an occasion," she said.

"Truly," said Elena. "How far do we walk?"

"Two, maybe three hundred yards," Nicia waved her hand. "Over there, past the bell tower to the big plane tree. Gerasimos spent the last twenty years of his life here." She pointed to the right, over a stonewall. "We call these the threshing fields. This is where he dug the forty wells, raising crops to support the monastery and the poor. This place is sacred to the island."

"How's Dad taking it?" asked Elena, "He looks kind of strange."

"It's hard to imagine what he's going through but it's a necessary process," said Nicia. "I'm sure it will work out fine."

"I hope so, I'm still a little concerned."

"All we can do now is show our love for him." Nicia returned to Andreas.

A military guard in camouflage dress flanked either side of the saint, their polished rifle barrels poked up above the crowd like itinerant railings. Elena singled out one of the soldiers; tall, strong with close cropped hair under a black beret.

Perhaps, she thought. If my father had never left the island, I'd be a Greek woman and might have married such a man.

It wasn't long before the procession reached its destination by the magnificent plane tree. Here, in a quiet courtyard, the majesty of the ancient tree inspired Elena. She looked at the silver coffin then imagined Gerasimos, a living man, digging the ground, planting the young seedling in the earth.

More than four centuries old, she found the timescale difficult to conceive and thought only about the leaves, falling, year after year, over generations of monks, toiling in the fields, eking out an austere life. Although a symbol of longevity, she thought the tree a reminder of the fleeting nature of her father's, and ultimately her own, existence.

A prayer finished, a priest chanted, a monk stepped forward. White bearded, draped in black with flat-topped headdress, two ornate pendants hung from gold chains on his chest.

"Who's that?" asked Elena.

"The Metropolitan, head of the Kefalonian Church," answered Nicia. "He's the equivalent of a bishop."

The crowd hushed as the man prepared to deliver the litany.

Unable to understand, Elena focused on her father. As the Metropolitan reached the highpoint, tears appeared on her father's cheeks. Oblivious to his surroundings, Ioannis Katros stared up at the plane tree, his face elated, yet crying like a little boy. Elena interpreted the expression as a struggle between sadness and joy.

The sermon ended with a tumultuous response from the bell tower; the bearers lifted the saint, turning around to begin their march back. For the first time, Elena got an unobstructed view of the silver casket. Painstakingly intricate, its quality appeared to be the work of the finest artisans. Four sculpted feet supported the base. Inside the sarcophagus, the body of Gerasimos stood upright, visible through arched glass panels. Above his head, a dome and cross rested on a molded cornice.

Mrs. Katros spoke. "It's time to get the boys."

Elena tugged the sleeve of her brother who took the children from their grandfather as part of a prearranged plan.

With tears in his eyes, Ioannis set off after the bearers, quickly overtaking them on their slow trek back to the church. Elena followed. She wanted to be there when he joined the pilgrims, the sick and the suffering, to lie, face-up, in the path of the saint. When she caught up with him, he was already on the ground.

A woman wailed, beseeching Gerasimos for a miracle. Her sorrowful prayers pierced Elena's heart but she kept her eyes locked on her father. Finally, she thought, he looked at peace.

The sarcophagus bore down on Ioannis. A man in a green polo shirt swung incense in its path as the saint passed over a young boy. Moments later, the mournful woman, now singing a hymn, pulled the child into her arms, looking for her miracle. Elena turned her head away, as though from an accident, afraid to witness disappointment on the mother's face.

Incense wafted over her father. The saint was almost within touching distance of Elena; she could see his face clearly. Seconds later, it was all over. Gerasimos granted no extra time, bestowed no visible favor, before moving on to the next pilgrim.

Andreas helped Ioannis to stand. The family gathered round, Nicia touched her brother's shoulder.

"Are you okay?" Elena asked.

Her father nodded but did not speak.

Nicia smiled but the gesture did little to reassure Elena.

"There's still one more ritual," whispered Nicia.

Kissing the feet of the Saint, thought Elena. "Shall we?" she replied.

As they neared the church, people jostled around the steps. Elena looked up as the Metropolitan opened the casket's glass door to the chanting of prayers. She had a clear view of the rite.

Perhaps Gerasimos is looking out over his land, storing up its beauty for another year, she thought. Perhaps he's breathing the air of his beloved fields once more.

The first man in line placed his head inside the sarcophagus and bowed low towards the saint's feet. He moved away, his place taken by his wife; the crowd inched forward, waiting their turn.

With each step higher, the aura emanating from Gerasimos grew stronger, filling Elena's senses. As she watched her father stand before the casket, a strange realization struck; the mummi-fied presence overshadowed the living beings around it.

Ioannis made his bow, taking longer than both Andreas and

Nicia; stealing a few extra seconds for a secret prayer or to utter some long-prepared words. He turned away, leaving Elena face-to-face with the legend that her father had crossed an ocean to see.

Saint Gerasimos's face looked towards the heavens, his mouth slightly open. For a split-second, fear gripped Elena; so intense was the moment. Taking a deep breath calmed her, leaving a tingling sensation all over. She tried to imagine her father's emotions but felt like an intruder interrupting an intimate conversation.

"I'm his daughter." Her words, spoken in Greek, issued almost imperceptibly.

Elena bowed her head before Gerasimos, down past his faded robes, their original patterns still preserved, down past the thick gold chain hanging round his neck with its large ornate cross, down past the smaller cross and the ceremonial belt, down past the mummified hands. Elena bowed, whispering a prayer for Stamos and her father.

29

Elena read the message again.

"Hi hope I didn't wake you let me know if you can talk now and I'll call you love you greg"

Stepping off the veranda into her room, Elena prepared to go down to breakfast. She did a quick calculation of the East Coast time difference; it was 1:00am in Boston. Greg was staying up late, trying to catch her before she set out for the day. He was checking up on her. If she didn't call in the next hour, he'd be asleep.

By the time he wakes up again, I'll be with Ben.

She mapped out the day, deciding when to slot in a call to Greg.

1:00pm the gallery, maybe some shopping after: the lighthouse at sunset, say 6:00-8:00pm: dinner after that and then... What did I promise last night and was Ben serious about renting a villa?

There'd be time to call Greg in the late afternoon or she could do it now. She sat on the bed to clear her mind. Today or tomorrow, she would have to make travel plans or say goodbye to her job and possibly Greg too.

She looked over the spacious, country-style bedroom, comparing it to her own. Last night's clothes lay draped over a stool, adding a touch of chaos to the perfectly manicured room. A brown and beige fern-patterned rug covered the center of the wood-planked floor. Laid at a diagonal to the dark green walls, the carpet formed a diamond shape. The bed, dressing table, and chest of drawers were all hand-painted; pale cream with floral designs. Interesting objects littered the dresser; antique perfume bottles, candlestick holders, silver things with unknown uses, an old pewter...

What was that—an incense burner fashioned into a boy's head?

She got up, tidied her clothes and went out to the balcony, hoping the view would provide inspiration. Her book lay face down on a rustic table. The scene belonged to Ben, not Greg, the courtyard, the pines, the olive orchard, the bench from last night, the bay, Lixouri. Greg would have to wait; she would text him after visiting the gallery.

A knock on the bedroom door reminded her of breakfast; it was probably Sophia.

"Just a minute."

She checked herself in the mirror. Her deep purple, ruched, halter bra-top showed off just enough cleavage; enough to drive Ben crazy.

She opened the door. Sophia entered.

"Morning," said Elena.

"Are you coming down?" asked Sophia.

"Yes, I'm just deciding what to wear with this top."

"White probably."

"I have the pants from last night or a white mini—he's seen the pants already, the mini it is."

"Are you getting serious about him?"

"I'll tell you over breakfast."

Elena finished dressing. They went down to the kitchen where Aunt Nicia busied herself making coffee. Food was laid out, buffet-style, on the counter.

"Help yourself to whatever you want. Take one of those trays and go out by the orchard. I'll bring the coffee to you," said Nicia.

Two minutes later, the girls sat, chatting, under the pines.

"It seems like forever since we last had breakfast here, before our trip to Fiskardo," said Elena. "But it was only the day before yesterday."

She brushed a fly from the edge of her plate.

"I forgot to tell you, I got a message from Dimi," said Sophia. "He was asking about you."

"Oh?"

"He wanted to know how you were, and he asked if you wanted to model for him before you go back to the States."

"Teaser—no he didn't," said Elena.

"No really, listen."

Sophia retrieved the voice message and handed her cousin the phone.

Elena missed the first part, besides it was in Greek. She strained to pick out any familiar words; it was definitely Dimi—his deep voice was unmistakable.

'Elena'—he'd said her name all right, 'ómorfo korítsi'—that meant beautiful girl. She couldn't decipher any more.

"I can't understand what he's saying." She handed the phone back to her cousin.

Sophia listened to the message again, repeating it word for word. "He said, say hello to Elena for me, such a beautiful girl. When is she going back to America? I'd like her to model for me."

"What's the Greek word for model, I want to hear for myself."

"Pozaro."

She listened to the message again. "Is he serious?"

Elena thought of her reflection in the mirror minutes earlier—before she had put on her skirt. She wondered what it would be like posing, half-dressed, in his studio?

"He sounds serious," said Sophia.

"He's crazy, what about his wife?"

"What's she got to do with it?" Sophia appeared confused. "Anyway, didn't she suggest it? He told me she never goes into his studio and he never goes into hers."

"Am I supposed to decide; is he waiting for a reply or something?"

Elena wondered if now was the moment that Sophia would say 'Fooled you!'.

"You don't have to get back to him … not unless you want to."

She wanted to ask Sophia how long the sitting would last but decided against it.

"You were telling me about Ben," said Sophia.

"Oh yes," Elena paused, "I need to talk to you … I really need your advice, I have some decisions to make. How much time do we have before you open the gallery?"

Sophia checked her phone, eager to hear more.

"It's only eight-thirty, we don't open for another two hours; we've plenty of time."

"He's really crazy about me—at least I think so."

"What makes you say that?"

Elena started to say something but checked herself. Sophia was sharp; she needed to be careful.

"Well, I can just tell … and he dropped out of the last leg of the cruise to be with me."

"You didn't sleep with him did you?"

"No, of course not." She thought back to the hotel in Fiskardo. "We stayed in the same room, but there were two beds," she paused, "I mean we kissed a bit, but nothing serious."

"What will Greg think?"

"I'm not going to tell him, so he'll never know," she quickly corrected herself. "There isn't anything to tell him, anyway…"

Elena heard footsteps and looked towards the courtyard. Uncle Andreas approached carrying a tray.

"How are my beautiful girls this morning?"

"Fine." They both spoke at the same time and smiled.

"Coffee is served."

He placed the tray on the table and bowed in the manner of an old-fashioned butler. After making small talk, he headed back to the house. As soon as Andreas was out of earshot, Sophia and Elena continued their conversation.

"I'm going to look up some flight options," said Elena.

"You're going back?"

"I haven't decided yet. If I stay longer than a few more days, I won't have a job to go back to. Plus, Greg will drive me crazy. He left a message this morning to call him right away—there'll probably be another quarrel when we speak. I can't take much more of that."

"I can check the flights before I go to the gallery, but I thought you were thinking of staying. I haven't asked Grandmother, but I'm sure you could stay as long as you want."

"Ben said we could rent a villa."

"Why would he say that if you've only just met? I thought you said nothing happened between you."

"It didn't."

"How can you be sure he's serious, you hardly know him? Even if he does rent a place, he might get bored with you in a few weeks and go back to LA. Who knows what he's got going on there."

Elena sipped the coffee. "You're probably right. It's a bit risky."

"It sounds like you've all but decided to go home then." Sophia didn't attempt to mask her disappointment.

"Almost, I'm going to call Greg this afternoon. I'm actually starting to miss him. It's so funny how you get used to a person. I'm definitely not looking forward to going back to work though, and I'll miss the island so bad. Still, I'll have one more look at Ben then, tomorrow morning, I'll either buy a ticket or…"

She didn't complete the sentence, a few seconds of silence ensued.

"What about love? Don't you love either of them?"

"Well Greg … yes, of course. It's too early to tell about Ben. If I stayed with him, I'm sure I'd fall in love."

A curious expression crossed Sophia's face, as if she thought their idea of love differed.

"Even if he does rent a house, you don't have to move in with him," Sophia continued. "Just stay here with us and see how it goes."

Elena didn't reply.

Ben won't rent a villa unless I agree to move in, she thought, he'll just stay at the hotel, until I give in.

"I thought you loved the lifestyle here," said Sophia. "You said you wanted to try something new."

"How will I know without deciding on Ben? If I stay, he'll stay too and I'd want him to. That means I've rejected Greg."

"If you stay, you're rejecting him anyway; Ben or no Ben."

"Well, Ben's just changed the whole situation—what can I say."

The look of disappointment on Sophia's face prompted a lame response.

"I can come back with Greg—every summer—we'll vacation for a month at a time."

Sophia got up. "I'll get the laptop."

Elena dialed Ben's number. She'd forgotten their arrangements for the day.

As she waited for him to pick up, a snippet of last night's

conversation flashed into her mind.

'At the moment, you do'—that's what he'd said. Sophia was right; he'll stay until he's bored then go back to LA—Sophia's always right.

It was beginning to make sense to Elena. She'd met Ben for a reason and that reason was to confirm Greg as the right choice. It would be a wise decision to pick solid and dependable over massive uncertainty.

Sophia returned with the laptop. Elena got up and walked into the orchard, the phone to her ear.

"Morning, how did you sleep last night?" she asked.

"With difficulty, I was thinking about you," Ben replied.

"Liar."

"I only just got up, what time is it?"

"Nine-ish," she paused. "Hey! Guess where I am?"

"Where?"

"The olive grove—under the tree where we saw the owl."

"I wish we'd taken a photo," said Ben.

"Too late, he's not around." She looked around the orchard. "Just a bunch of crows."

"Well, say 'hi' to them for me."

"I will," she smiled. "Listen, what time are we meeting today?"

"I thought maybe we'd grab some lunch then go over to the gallery. How about I pick you up around noon?"

"Okay, it's a date. I'll see you later—I have to catch Sophia before she leaves. Bye."

She hung up, her mood uplifted. The orchard was taking on the aura of a sacred place; walking amid the shadowy trees at midnight, the little owl. Now, as the morning sun filtered through the branches, it became Ben's champion—a second in his corner.

I still have twenty-four hours to decide, she thought.

"Hey, Elena," Sophia was calling from the breakfast table.

She rejoined her cousin.

"There are available flights. Do you want to book one?"

Elena's stomach tightened. "Which day are you looking at?"

"I checked for Wednesday. If you're going back to work the following week, you'll need some time to recover."

"Can we just reserve it?"

Sophia scrolled down the screen. "Yes, I think so."

"You know what, let's decide later," said Elena. She'd just remembered her existing ticket. "Greg said he'd take care of the flight. I don't want anything to do with it."

"Whatever you say," Sophia closed the laptop cover. "You know I don't want you to go."

"I know," Elena put her hand on Sophia's arm. "Hey, Ben's picking me up at noon. We're having lunch then going to the gallery. Do you want to come?"

Sophia pondered the question. "Are the others coming?"

"He didn't say."

"Why don't you see if you can arrange that and I'll join you?" asked Sophia. "I'm hoping to sell plenty of inventory to your rich friends."

"Okay, no problem."

Ben's going to buy me one of Dimi's paintings, thought Elena. He just doesn't know it yet.

30

Andreas Matsakis's gallery stood in the center of Argostoli on a pedestrian-only street, a short walk from Vallianou Square. Sophia led the party out of the cool marble interior of a nearby Italian restaurant into the oppressive midday heat.

"It's not far, just at the end of the block, on the opposite side," she said.

Elena smiled, remembering that her cousin had chosen the lunch venue after hearing about Joe Marchetti and his love of all things Italian.

"He'll be in the right frame of mind to invest in some art— Pasquali, the Italian's, art," she had said.

That was a nice place for Sophia to say goodbye to her new friends, thought Elena. She's become quite close with Clotilde.

On either side of the gallery entrance, bay windows with gold-painted architrave housed minimalist displays. The elaborate molding extended above the bays, forming arches clad with a dark green marble. Carved into the fascia, and picked out in gold leaf, were the words Gallery Vallianou.

"Please come in." Sophia waited outside the door, her palm

outstretched.

The business specialized in ceramics. Long tables and custom stands displayed the larger pieces; glass cabinets lined the walls. At the rear, a small exhibit room housed the works of local painters.

The manager stood near the register, talking to an elderly couple, the only customers. She excused herself upon seeing Sophia. "How was lunch, dear?"

"Delightful." Sophia let her guests file in. "These are the friends I told you about. It's their final day on the island; they're leaving for Zante this evening."

"I bought some Greek pastries earlier," said the manager. "But, of course, you've just eaten."

The party split into two groups; Sophia stayed close to Clotilde, pointing out the period and style of each section.

"Most of our collection consists of handmade, hand-painted replicas of museum pieces, but we have some creative originals based on classic styles."

Clotilde stopped to admire a piece.

"This is exquisite. It's from the Geometric period, isn't it?"

Is any subject beyond her expertise? wondered Ben.

"I'm impressed," said Sophia. "Yes, it's a doll, a child's toy, from about 900 BC."

"I'd like it," said Clotilde. "Can you ship to the States?"

"Of course."

Clotilde picked out several more reproductions from the Minoan and Corinthian periods.

***

Elena was pleased for her cousin. Their trip to Fiskardo had reaped an unexpected dividend.

Bored with the ceramics, Elena meandered to the back of the shop and into the small art exhibit. She recognized Dimi's three paintings immediately. They hung on the wall opposite the door, the white orchid piece in between the other two. She became impatient to tell Ben that she'd met the artist the day before yesterday.

As she waited for the others to reach the annex, Elena wiled away the moments, reliving the morning at Dimi's studio: Mikka, the tabby cat, the red velvet couch with the woolen blanket, Dimi adjusting her pose…

"There you are." Sophia disturbed her daydream.

"These are all Dimi's work." Elena had waited until Clotilde and Ben were in earshot. She spoke the words with confidence.

"Yes." Sophia addressed the others. "Dimi is one of the gallery's favorite artists."

Elena pulled Ben over to the white orchids. "This is where I was … the morning before we met—at this artist's studio."

Sophia and Clotilde moved closer to the picture.

"These are interesting," said the French girl. "There's a bold, yet dreamlike quality to them. Tell me more about the artist."

"He's a local. His work sells well, in the three to five thousand dollar range," said Sophia. "We've probably sold fifteen to twenty pieces in the last two years."

"Do you like these?" Elena grabbed Ben's wrist and pointed to the white orchids. "This one's my favorite."

She listened to his reply with half an ear as Sophia told Clotilde more about Dimi.

"Would you like it?" Ben studied the painting. "It can be a memento of our day in Fiskardo."

Despite thinking the gift too expensive, Elena wanted the picture.

"That's so nice, thank you." She threw her arms around him and kissed his cheek.

"Steady on there, girl. I'll end up buying the whole collection if you keep doing that."

"Sophia, wrap this one up." Elena pointed at the white orchids.

"I was going to take that," said Clotilde.

"We beat you to it," said Ben.

"No seriously," said Clotilde. "This type of work is popular at the moment. I have some contacts in New York that might be interested. Does he have enough material for an exhibition?"

"Of course," said Sophia.

"I'll take the other two." Clotilde pointed at the adjacent paintings.

"Wonderful." Sophia reached in her bag, pulling out her phone. "Why don't I give Dimi a call; he'll be pleased to hear we've sold three of his pieces."

Clotilde's favorable opinion of Dimi's work boosted Elena's self-esteem, as though she'd discovered him herself. She mused about Dimi becoming famous in New York.

"Dimi, hi, it's Sophia. I'm at the gallery."

Speaking in English, for the benefit of her guests, she continued.

"Elena is here with her friends from Los Angeles. They just bought your three pieces." She paused for Dimi's response. "Yes, White Orchids, Spring Tulips, and Under the Cypress Trees."

Elena thought about Dimi's promise to paint the purple doors. Now that would be something I would like to own.

"One of Elena's friends has contacts in New York. There might be some interest in your work." Sophia paused then looked at Elena. "Yes, she's here—hold on."

Elena shook her head but Sophia held the phone at arm's length, her finger over the microphone. "He wants to talk to you."

Reluctantly, Elena accepted the device.

"Hi Dimi." She waited for his voice, he remained silent long enough for her to feel uncomfortable.

Finally, he spoke. "I've been thinking about you since our little talk. I ask myself, is Elena going to stay on our beautiful island or will she go back to America?"

What if he asks about modeling?

"Just a minute…" She covered the microphone and turned to Ben. "The reception's really poor in here; I'm going to step outside."

A puzzled expression crossed Ben's face. Elena left the room

"Sorry, Dimi, where were we?" The heat on the sidewalk made her gasp.

"I didn't realize you were with someone," said Dimi.

"No, it's okay, really."

"Sophia told me all about you going back to Argostoli on the yacht."

"That's right. I waved to you from out in the bay, near the old lighthouse. You didn't wave back."

"After you left, I looked down at Fiskardo from the patio and imagined you strolling along the promenade. I hope you had a pleasant afternoon."

Exactly how much did Sophia tell him? she wondered.

"So, is Elena going back or has she been transformed?"

Dimi's voice calmed and excited her in equal measure.

"I still haven't decided." She answered as though he were a trusted friend and counselor. "But it's looking like I'll go back sometime next week."

"Maybe you need to be persuaded to stay."

"Dimi, I met someone, right after I left you at the villa."

Elena's openness surprised her.

"Tell me about him."

"There's isn't time, maybe later."

"Did Sophia ask you about sitting for your portrait?"

Deep down, she had been waiting for him to ask.

"Ah … yes … but I didn't think she was serious."

"Perfectly serious, I think it might do you good to get away for a few days and stay at the villa."

"I don't think I can get away." She wanted to use Ben as an excuse but decided against it. "I've never done any modeling before, I'm not sure it's for me."

"It's only a portrait," explained Dimi. "You might end up immortal—like Mona Lisa."

She thought of the velvet couch. "How would you paint me?"

"However you want me to see you."

"Dimi, I have to go back to my friends; Sophia has your number, I'll call you."

"Remember a lover is like a painting."

"Bye, Dimi."

A last minute thought flashed into Elena's head.

"Wait, how long will it take … if I say yes."

"A day, maybe two. We do some sketches, take some photographs, then I finish the picture later."

Dimi's tone soothed her. Why shouldn't she model for him? There was nothing in it.

"Will I need to pose…" She hesitated. "Will it be a nude portrait?"

"Not unless you want to. I hardly ever paint nudes, if that's what you mean. Clothes are much more interesting; they tell a story." Dimi's hypnotic voice droned on, "You have to express how you want to be seen in the moment—imagine it's two hundred years in the future and someone is looking at your portrait; how do you want them to see you? How does the island makes you feel? We can work on a pose; you have very beautiful legs, I have some ideas how to show them."

"Dimi, I have to go. I'll let you know if I decide to come back to your studio."

She hung up.

During the call, she had wandered twenty or thirty yards down the street.

Buying time to collect her thoughts, she stared into a shop window. The glass reflected her image with just enough clarity to check her appearance. A manikin, wearing a short black dress, stood on a raised platform a few feet to her right. She moved in front of the figure, using the black dress as a mirror and thought about how she'd pose.

"There you are." Ben startled her. "Whoa, that would look good on you."

He thinks I'm window-shopping, she thought.

"Why don't you go inside and try it on; you can wear it to dinner tonight."

"No thanks."

Dimi's call had affected her; she wanted to get away from Ben, from everybody. The pressure was building; Greg would be waking in Boston right about now.

"I shouldn't have accepted the painting in there. I wasn't thinking—it's too expensive."

"What's wrong, are you okay?" asked Ben.

"I'm fine, but I'd like to go back to the house. Can you drive me back?"

"Well … sure, we should say goodbye first. I think they're about done in there."

They walked back to the gallery. The manager busied herself with the transaction details.

Elena returned Sophia's phone and pulled her to one side.

"I can't accept Dimi's painting," she whispered. "Would you mind taking it back?"

"Why, what's wrong?"

"I wasn't thinking." She looked at Ben over by the door. "If I book a ticket in the morning then I'm not going to see him again—it's just not right to take the gift."

"Okay, no problem, I'll reverse the charge on his card."

"Thanks."

Minutes later, everyone was in the street saying goodbye.

Elena hugged Clotilde. "It was so nice meeting you, thank you for everything. I had such a wonderful time."

She shook Joe's hand.

"I'll get your contact information from Ben; let's keep in touch," said Clotilde.

"Okay, have a safe trip back to the States."

"We're not going back just yet. Joe wants to spend a couple of weeks in Italy—it's only a stone's throw away," said Clotilde.

"You kept that quiet, Joe," said Ben.

"We might hire a boat, sail around the Adriatic.—We'll need a skipper—I'm not driving the damn thing," said Joe.

"He promised me a week in Venice," said Clotilde.

"Don't let him take you scuba diving in the Grand Canal," said Ben, "You don't want to get slapped around the head with one of those Gondola oars."

"We'll keep that in mind," said Clotilde.

"Hey, I'll see you all on the boat later." Ben started to walk away. "I'm going to drive Elena home."

***

Parked at the hotel, the jeep was only a few hundred yards from the gallery. They walked back in silence. The change in Elena's mood confused Ben.

Who is this Dimi? Why does she not want the painting and why does she want to go home so early?

The energy-sapping heat of mid-afternoon dampened his spirits even further as they entered Vallianou Square. Two young men on scooters slowed down to ogle Elena.

"Do you want to get a cold drink?" he asked; cafes lined the eastern end of the plaza.

"No, I'm fine thanks."

His best course of action was to forget the incident with Dimi and concentrate on the evening ahead. The open-top drive back to the house might revive her spirits.

The Royal Ionian was just off the square; they reached it a

couple of minutes later.

"Last chance for a drink—ice-cold, frosted glass." He forced a smile.

Without replying, she pressed on to the Jeep.

As he opened the passenger door, Ben thought about changing his plans and going to Zante.

"Be careful, the seats will be hot," he said.

The parking lot didn't have shade. A bottle of water, left in the drinks holder, promised refreshment. His fingers pressed into the thin plastic but the water was too hot to drink.

As they got underway, he tried to make conversation. "Things went well for Sophia at the gallery."

His remark reminded Elena of the white orchids.

"I'm sorry about the painting, I hope you understand," she said.

"It's okay, don't worry—it's not a big deal. I'll have it, it's a nice picture."

"I had Sophia reverse the charge to your card," said Elena.

"Okay, no worries," he paused. "When we rent the villa, we'll go back and buy it again."

She did not laugh; his words disturbed her.

The Jeep sped up the hill, heading to the edge of town. By now, Ben had become familiar with the route to Nicia's villa.

"Ben, I'm going to go back to Boston. I think you should go with your friends to Zante."

Her admission shocked him even though she had warned him earlier. The reality of driving her home for the last time hit hard.

The Jeep reached the top of the hill, marking the edge of town. He accelerated hard on the open road.

"Don't be mad," she said.

Ben slammed on the brakes and swerved onto a dirt lot. The Jeep skidded to a halt next to an abandoned trailer, showering dust clouds into the air. He turned off the ignition, taking a big deep breath.

"You're not leaving today; you can't have bought a ticket yet."

"No, but when you drop me off, I'm going to make a phone call to Boston," Ben winced as she spoke. "I'll probably agree to go home and I don't want to ruin the rest of your trip."

He replayed the words in his head 'I'll probably agree to go home'.

It had always been a possibility. Faced with that reality, he considered his options.

Elena laid her hand on his arm; Ben still gripped the steering wheel.

The road was deserted except for the occasional passing car. Tall trees bordered the lot, sheltering the Jeep from the merciless sun. The woods were alive with cicadas, their noise so loud as to make conversation difficult.

Had he heard correctly, did she really just tell him she was going home?

A flurry of emotions surfaced as he struggled for a response. His disappointment was hard to conceal—she must have noticed it. The rational Ben argued: two days isn't enough time to become emotionally attached. A twinge of heartache was all he needed to bear. It was a good thing, then, to say goodbye as soon as possible.

When he spoke, the words seemed to come automatically; he didn't consciously make a decision; the outcome was inevitable—he had no say in the matter.

"I don't care about Zante, it's just another island; it can't be any better than this. Those guys are flying out in two days; I'm not missing out on anything. I'd rather spend the time with you."

"I just want to be honest with you," she said.

"Wild horses couldn't drag me away from you," he bent over and kissed her. Moved by his words, she responded.

The screeching insect cacophony melted away as a car horn blared, abrupt and insolent. It blasted again then again, keeping time with shouts and cheers. Ben tore himself from Elena's embrace to watch a blue sedan, packed with teenagers, speeding away. She pulled down her skirt, brushing Ben's hand away, hauling him out of his delirium.

31

Elena sat at a large oak table under the shade of a cluster of pines. She rocked an empty coffee cup back and forth in its saucer and contemplated tomorrow's excursion. Earlier, over breakfast, Sophia had invited her to visit the studios of two artists. Elena looked forward to seeing more of the island. Sophia's description of Fiskardo and the scenic coast road painted a vivid picture.

A pale, scrawny cat stretched out, sunning itself, on the steps by the iron gates at the back of the house. The cat sidled away as Nicia appeared carrying a tray of coffee and pastries.

"Where were we?" asked Nicia as she sat opposite her niece.

"You were trapped under the floor of Uncle Andreas's store and you'd just found the seagull," said Elena.

"Ah, the seagull, I held on to that bird all through the ordeal and wouldn't let go, even after the rescue."

"What happened after they pulled you out?"

"We waited in the garden for my father to return. You can only imagine our shock when he arrived carrying Ioannis but without Stamos. Mother never recovered from losing Stamos; none of us did, especially Ioannis."

"What were my dad and Stamos like as children?"

"Your father idolized Stamos. It was always, Stamos this, Stamos that. And Stamos was very protective of him."

"I've never experienced loss, it's hard for me to imagine." Elena noticed tears forming in her aunt's eyes and changed the subject. "So, if all the buildings were destroyed, where did you stay?"

"I remember the first night like it was only yesterday. We went down to the harbor with everyone else. Fortunately, it was the middle of summer, so sleeping outside was bearable. We had casualties; all our neighbors did. The only option was to wait at the port until help arrived. I didn't sleep that night, the ground wouldn't stop shaking," Nicia sighed. "The first rescue ship arrived early in the morning, just after dawn. I'll never forget it, a British Navy vessel, the HMS Daring. The whole town assembled on the quayside, waiting silently for the crew to come ashore; it was quite surreal. Some of the wealthy families approached the captain first, trying to buy passage off the island. Thankfully, he refused to negotiate; his first priority was helping the injured."

"Did my dad get help there?" Every time Elena thought of her father as a boy, she brought to mind the sole photograph from his days on the island.

"Yes, and your Grandmother too; it was such a terrible time. You have to remember, there wasn't any drinking water. Everywhere you could hear people calling out for water. It was like a vision of hell."

"What about water for the injured? Did they get priority?"

"We bathed their wounds in seawater. I remember your grandfather bringing buckets from the bay to wash mother's leg. Early the next morning, at around eight, more ships arrived from the Israeli Navy. We were fortunate—they were in the area on a training exercise," Nicia paused. "The Israelis started ferrying the injured to Patras, on the mainland. Andreas's mother left on one of those ships. Andreas and Larissa stayed with us. The British gave us food and water—I'll never forget the freshly baked bread they handed out every morning. Anyway, the medics patched up mother's leg and made a crutch for your poor father, he was hobbling around everywhere. After the British and Israeli ships landed, a huge American cruiser arrived. It was too big to dock in the harbor and stayed out in the middle of the bay. All the ships dispensed provisions and the Red Cross dropped supplies from the air."

"And you still had the seagull. What happened to it?"

"I honestly don't know." Nicia poured herself more coffee. "We ended up living on the farm in one of the big black tents handed out by the sailors. I woke up one morning and the seagull was gone. I was heartbroken that it had left me."

Elena tried to picture the young Nicia, searching the fields for the bird.

Nicia continued, "Father told me it got better and flew back to its family. I heard mother talking about it years later, she said the bird had died and father buried it before I found out."

"Do you remember its name?" Andreas leaned against a pine tree.

"Morning," said Elena. She hadn't noticed her uncle arrive.

Andreas sat next to his wife.

"Do I remember its name? Of course," said Nicia.

"No. Does Elena remember? Her father told her the story often enough," said Andreas.

"Tutankhamen," Elena smiled.

"The days following the earthquake were the saddest of my life," said Andreas. "I still remember the beauty of old Argostoli, the majestic bell towers, the elegant mansions with jasmine cascading down from the balconies, its scent filling the air. It hurt so much, seeing our town turned to rubble."

The pale cat slunk back to his sunspot, stretching out his front legs with a yawn.

"Ioannis didn't speak for days, we were worried sick," said Nicia.

"He didn't start talking again until he was able to walk without the crutches," said Andreas. "But he wasn't quite the same boy. I never heard him mention Stamos again. The young Yanni disappeared along with his brother that summer. I think your grandfather hoped I might become a surrogate brother, but then we got separated."

"How did that happen?" Elena asked.

"The economy of the island was ruined," answered Andreas. "There was no work. Eventually, everyone left on the ships bound for the refugee camps in Patras. One hundred thousand out of a total population of one hundred and twenty-five thousand; most ended up in Athens. My mother didn't survive. Larissa and I went to live in Athens with my uncle. We were lucky; things worked out well for us."

Nicia brushed an insect off her husband's shirt and picked up the story. "My father wanted to take Andreas and Larissa to America but getting the paperwork proved impossible. Nobody wanted to take responsibility for tens of thousands of refugees."

"You ended up in Boston because of grandfather's brother, didn't you?" asked Elena.

"That's right," said Nicia. "My father's younger brother—his name was Stamos too—made his way to America after the war. He sponsored us through one of the relief agencies."

"I hardly remember him," said Elena. "He died when I was little."

"Uncle Stamos was a hardworking man; by the time we arrived in the States, he'd built the bakery into a thriving business and was able to offer father work."

Elena rocked backed on her chair and caught sight of the large ferryboat crossing the channel to Lixouri. She imagined the scene in the bay, fifty-six years ago to the day.

"Where was the big American cruiser anchored?" she asked.

Andreas pointed to a spot, over by the lighthouse. "That was the USS Salem, but we didn't leave on that ship."

"We had to wait for the Greek Navy to arrive," said Nicia. "It took them nearly two weeks to get here. Father wouldn't let Andreas and Larissa look for their mother alone, so we all left on a Greek ship bound for Patras. Father planned to return … he didn't know, at the time, that he'd never come back."

"For a while, we lived in a refugee building, a school in Patras. We hated that place; it was hot, crowded, and there was no privacy," said Andreas. "We found Mother at the nearby hospital. She managed to get word to her brother who came to collect us. Mother died a few weeks later."

Elena had no words of consolation to offer. There was so much tragedy. She let the couple continue reminiscing. Each took their turn with a snapshot of memory; this time Nicia. "I wanted to go back to Argostoli, but the authorities wouldn't let the evacuees return. That's when we contacted the relief agencies; they got word to Uncle Stamos in Boston."

"Larissa and I left for Athens two months before Nicia sailed for the States," said Andreas.

"Yes, we traveled from Patras and boarded the big liner at Athens. We had an address for Andreas, so we were able to contact him."

"Larissa and I were there to wave you off to the new world."

The old couple smiled; a lifetime of shared memories brought a tear to Nicia's eye. "For me, it was very sad, I didn't want to go to America, I missed Andreas. At the port terminal, he promised to find his way to America and bring me back home."

"That's just unbelievable," said Elena. "It's the most beautiful thing I can imagine. Hold on, I have to take a picture."

She pulled the camera out of her bag, taking a couple of

snaps of her aunt and uncle.

"Back then things were different, so different than how you grew up in America," said Andreas. "We didn't have arranged marriages or anything like that but our families were close; we just knew."

"I knew," said Nicia. "I knew one day Andreas would come, when the time was right, and he did." She placed her on her husband's arm.

"Nicia had my address in Athens. Once the family got settled in Boston, she wrote and we kept in touch. My uncle's business expanded and I worked my way up. I was fortunate to have the resources to travel to the States a few times and visit Nicia. When she turned twenty-one, I asked her father for her hand and we returned to Athens. Then my Uncle died, I took over the company, ran it from Athens for a couple of years until we moved back to Argostoli."

"We raised our children in this house," Nicia said.

Elena glimpsed life's purpose in the contented faces of her aunt and uncle. She shivered at the beauty of the moment, and yet, a touch of sorrow crossed her heart. Two white butterflies flew out of the orchard, capturing her attention. They disappeared in the pine branches only to reappear, circling the breakfast table above her head. Spiraling around each other, the delicate creatures drifted towards the house, over the flowering vines that blossomed on the courtyard wall, their wings touching, gently kissing in a timeless ritual dance.

32

Ben's Jeep pulled into the driveway outside Nicia's villa. The mid-afternoon sun had dropped behind the house, leaving the forecourt in shade.

"What time should I pick you up?" asked Ben.

"Seven. It's only a few minutes to the lighthouse from here," replied Elena.

"Seven it is."

She opened the door, swinging her legs out of the car. Ben grabbed her hand.

"You won't change your mind when you call Boston?"

"No. Sunset and dinner, come what may."

She kissed his cheek and stepped down, striding towards the house without looking back.

Weary, Elena went directly to her bedroom and opened the veranda doors; sunlight streamed into the room. She read Greg's message one more time before texting a reply.

'Hey sleepy head you must be up by now call me'.

She hit send and closed her eyes.

If he's awake, he'll ring straight back.

The handset rang within a minute.

"That was quick," she answered.

"Yeah, I tried to get hold of you earlier." Greg's tone was friendly, yet insistent.

"Sorry, I couldn't talk this morning; Aunt Nicia had just made breakfast. By the time we'd finished, I figured you'd be asleep. It wasn't urgent was it?"

"Well sort of. It's got to the point where I'm done waiting, so I came to a decision."

"What decision?" Elena looked over the orchard to the bench at the edge of the bay, sparking memories of the night before.

"I'm going to fly out there. We can spend some time together," he continued. "I could use a break."

His determination reassured, yet disturbed her.

"I said I'd let you know in a few days."

"I can't wait any longer—it's killing me. I didn't sleep much last night."

"You're crazy; you can't just come out here. What about your clients?"

"Just watch me. Here's the deal; either you tell me that you met someone else or I book you on the first flight home. If you say there's no one else, then I'm coming out to bring you back." His tone struck a balance between calling-the-shots and concerned lover. "So what's it going to be?"

Elena was impressed; Ben would never say anything like that. She kept silent for as long as comfort allowed, letting him sweat. She pictured him standing in the kitchen of his big house, phone against his ear, dreading to learn of a rival.

"I haven't met anyone. What are you thinking?" Elena spoke with as much indignation as she could muster.

"I'm sorry. I'm not accusing you but..." A moment's silence followed. "Listen, I know this isn't the time or the place, but I think we should get married."

"Are you serious?" Elena didn't doubt that he was.

"Yeah, I mean—you don't have to decide now. I'll ask you formally when you come back, but, hell yeah, I'm serious."

Even though Elena realized how much Greg loved her, she was genuinely surprised. Her first thought was to break the news to Sophia, to Nicia, to anyone who would listen.

"Greg, I don't know what to say … let's talk after I get back. I was about to tell you I'd decided to go back."

"Amen to that … when?"

"Anytime you like, just book the ticket. I'll leave it all up to you."

This was the moment when Elena resigned herself to leave Kefalonia.

"All right, you got it!"

Elena didn't feel elated, only relief in finally reaching a decision.

"Greg, I'm tired, we walked all over town today. I'm going to take a nap. Would you mind?"

"No, you go right ahead. Get some rest, I'll send the flight details later. Bye, I love you."

"I love you, too."

She hung up, not even caring that a return ticket sat on the table beside her.

He can buy another. I don't care anymore. I want this to be over.

Elena lay down on the bed. A slight breeze blew from the bay bringing the scents and sounds of the garden into the room; she fell into a deep therapeutic sleep.

***

Somewhere close by, a phone rang, startling her. Elena desperately wanted the ringing to stop; the shrill, unnatural sound disturbed everything around her. She was with Ben in a meadow; the air teemed with the richness of summer. A line of tall trees bordered the pasture, which stretched into the distance, tapering to a point on the horizon. Ben's hand tugged hers and she crouched beside him in the long grass. Their eyes met, level with the wildflowers, making the meadow appear to stretch on forever.

"If you listen," said Ben. "You can hear the grass ... the flowers growing."

Bees hovered everywhere, attracted by the festival of color. Elena listened until the drone of insects faded into oblivion. Pollen grains, at first unnoticed, danced before her eyes. For an instant, she became one with the life around her, feeling indescribable joy. The phone rang again, making the insects rise in unison, a few inches above the meadow. There they floated, momentarily, only to drift back down. She wanted to keep listening to the flowers but the phone wouldn't stop ringing.

Elena opened her eyes. She longed to return to the meadow and recapture her moment of elation.

Deflated, she picked up the handset. Greg's number topped the recent call list, a message notification flashed. She dialed the service.

"First new message, received at four thirty-five pm on August twenty-second, two thousand and nine, from 617..."

"Get on with it!" she yelled. "Stupid cyber voice."

"Hi, it's all taken care of. You fly out Wednesday via London, to Logan. You get in at 6:50am. I'll pick you up at the airport. Talk to you later. I'll email the tickets."

Dates and times made going home real. Elena chose to remember her dream; reality came with a touch of sadness.

The phone rang again.

"Dammit." She found herself yelling once more.

Sophia's caller ID lit the screen.

"Hi." Elena switched to a friendly voice.

"Where are you?" asked Sophia.

"At home, I fell asleep."

"Sorry, did I wake you?"

"No, I spoke to Greg, it's all settled. He's booked my flight."

"Oh … great," Sophia didn't sound too pleased.

"Listen, I'm still half asleep. I'll tell you about it later. What time will you be back? Ben's picking me up at seven."

"I'll be back by then."

"Okay, see you later, bye."

Elena hung up.

Ben's picking me up at seven. The words echoed inside her head. What am I going to do about Ben?

Still drowsy, she went out to the veranda.

The view over the olive grove will help me think.

Sat at her favorite reading spot, she picked up her book, flipping through the remaining pages.

About a half hour to finish.

The late afternoon sun inched towards the Pali Peninsula as the story drew to its conclusion. Outside, summer sounds cascaded over the rich imagery of the prose; together they formed an indelible impression. One passage evoked her dream and she felt again that fleeting moment of bliss, which had vanished at her touch.

The orchard, the vines in the garden, the insects, Kefalonia; these things were becoming part of her.

She laid the book on her lap and reached for the bottle of water under her chair. Elena took a long drink, reflecting on what she'd just read. She longed to discuss it with someone.

Not Greg, she thought. He would never read such a book. Back in Boston, neither would I.

Tonight, she'd talk with Ben. After all, she thought. We met for a reason…

Sophia's voice drifted up from the courtyard. Elena rose, looked over the balcony, and called down.

Their voices brought Aunt Nicia out from the kitchen. "Come

outside, we're having drinks," she said.

"I'll be right there." Elena grabbed her bag and hurried down to join Nicia and Sophia under the shady pergola. A carafe of chilled white wine sat on a tray.

"Where's Uncle Andreas?" asked Elena.

"In town. He'll be back for dinner," said Nicia. "Will you be joining us?"

"I'd love to but I promised Ben we'd watch the sunset at the lighthouse. We're dining out afterwards."

"Such a nice young man, did he enjoy last night?"

Elena took comfort from Nicia's approval of Ben.

"Yes, he had a great time. He asked me to thank you again."

Nicia smiled and looked at Sophia. "How did it go today?"

"One of the best days we've had in a long time," replied Sophia. She proceeded to tell Nicia about Ben's visit to the gallery. Elena paid no attention and wondered if Sophia had already broken the news about leaving on Wednesday.

Her dream brought Ben back into focus. She looked forward to seeing him, and considered whether something might happen to make her change plans. Now was not the time to tell Sophia of Greg's marriage proposal.

"Ben bought Elena one of Dimi's paintings but she refused it," said Sophia.

"It was so expensive," Elena protested. The wine made her lightheaded. Nicia scooped up the carafe, topping up their glasses.

"Dimi wants to paint Elena's portrait," said Sophia.

"That's nice," said Nicia.

"I don't think I have time," said Elena.

"Why not?" asked Nicia.

Nicia's tacit approval of Dimi's request made Elena consider the logistics of getting to the villa and back before returning to Boston.

"Didn't Sophia tell you? I booked a flight home for Wednesday."

Nicia adjusted her glasses. "You're leaving us so soon? It feels as though you only just got here."

Elena explained the problems with her job, blaming pressure from her boss for the decision.

"Well, we're certainly going to miss you."

"I'll miss you all too. I'm going to come back to Kefalonia every year and visit you."

She imagined staying at the villa, married to Greg, him sharing her bedroom. Greg would like the house but would never see the courtyard, or the orchard, in the same way as Ben.

Her indecision pestered like a nagging itch.

Maybe I'll go to Dimi's for a couple of days to get away.

The prospect of seeing Ben every day until Wednesday stirred up decidedly mixed emotions.

She turned to Sophia. "How would I get there?"

"Where?"

"Dimi's villa."

Sophia hesitated, "You can probably hire a car tomorrow, drive to Fiskardo, and come back on Tuesday."

"I'll think about it later, seems like a lot of hassle." Elena finished the wine and excused herself; Ben was due in one hour.

33

Elena and her two nephews climbed the steps in front of the Church of Saint Gerasimos. The older boy spotted Nicia under the portico and ran on ahead. Relieved to be back in the shade, Elena let go the hand of her youngest nephew and glanced down. Dust stains on her polished shoes added yet another reason to regret taking the two boys to the gypsy bazaar.

"Did you buy anything?" asked Nicia.

"No, there wasn't much to see, they're already packing up," replied Elena.

"They were just selling junk. It was hot and smelly," said the eldest child.

Elena ignored the boy. "Have we decided then?"

Nicia looked pensive. "Your father wants to visit Stamos's grave."

"I think he should."

"Yes. It's long overdue, he said so himself."

"What else did he say?"

"I didn't press him. He'll need some time to collect his thoughts. It must have been quite emotional back there. I'm sure he'll open up when he's ready."

"Where is he now?"

"I left him over by the monastery, talking with one of the monks."

"I'll call him and let him know we're ready to leave."

The younger child pulled Elena's sleeve.

"Won't be long now," she said, ruffling his hair.

Scores of people headed for the parking lot. Cars crawled like a funeral cortege along the boulevard, past the gypsy campsite.

"Hi Dad, where are you? Everyone wants to go." Elena paused to hear his reply. "We're under the portico at the front of the church…"

She hung up, turning to Nicia. "He's on his way."

Old nephew chased young nephew around and around, repeatedly bumping into Elena. The gypsy camp excursion had sapped her energy, and with it, the last remains of interest in the festival. She longed for the air-conditioned cool of the car, to sit and close her eyes—if only for a moment.

Relief, in the form of the boys' parents, took more grueling minutes to arrive.

Free of her young charges, Elena reached for her phone and dialed Sophia's number. Her cousin had just rounded the corner of the building, Elena heard the other girl's phone ring; they looked at each other and laughed. Andreas followed behind.

"Let's go," said Sophia. "I'm starving."

"We're just waiting on Dad," said Elena.

"We saw him on the promenade with your mom," said Sophia.

"Speak of the devil," said Andreas.

Elena waited until her parents were within earshot. "Can we go now, please, I need something to drink."

"And eat," said Sophia.

"What about something from those stalls across the road?"

Elena's mother asked.

"I don't think so," said Elena. "We've already been; it was horrible. Come on let's go."

Confused, Ioannis apologized for spending so much time with the monks.

"I'm sorry, Dad. I didn't mean to complain. I've just got really tired suddenly."

Walking to the parking lot was like trekking across the Sahara for Elena. Her feet hurt; every stride was an effort. She endured her torment in silence, only to be confronted by a car hot enough for baking bread.

"This is hellish," said Sophia.

"I've got the air conditioning on full-blast," said Ioannis. "Leave the windows down for a couple of minutes."

The car pulled out of the lot, turning onto the tree-lined boulevard. People walked in the street, spilling out from the church steps with little regard for traffic.

Ioannis stopped at the curbside. "We have to wait for Andreas; we'll follow him to the cemetery."

An old gypsy woman sat motionless on a large boulder by the side of the road. She stared into the inferno of the stationary vehicle, right at Elena, trapping her. The woman took no notice of a black haired boy, wailing, a few yards to her right. Tears streamed down the child's face, his sobs grating on Elena's nerves. She hoped Andreas would come soon. The people in the car watched the scene with indifference, as though empathy was impossible, burned out of existence in the roasting heat. Nobody spoke.

Distracted by a flash of white, Elena turned away from the two gypsies as Andreas's Mercedes pulled alongside.

"Let's stop for lunch on the way back," she called.

Andreas nodded; speech was too much effort. He rolled up his window and the sedan moved forward, leading the family's own private cortege.

On both sides of the boulevard, men loaded trucks, piling them high with boxes, furniture, bedding, every imaginable thing. The gypsies dismantled their camp with surprising efficiency.

How different the clothes of the gypsy children; reds, oranges, silk sashes, studded belts, gold braid.

Four girls lay on quilts, strewn over their wares, in the back of a wagon.

Such pretty girls, thought Elena.

The youngest pouted, leaning over the side of the truck towards the car. Elena reached for her camera but the moment was lost. Too tired to care, her head lolled back against the seat; she let her eyelids close. It would be so nice to fall asleep.

***

A dull thud, followed by an animal squealing in pain startled Elena, forcing open her eyes. She leaned out of the window. A man, standing in the bed of a high-sided truck, struggled to haul a yellow Labrador onboard. Sophia let out a sigh of revulsion.

"What just happened?" asked Elena.

Sophia pointed at a youth by the roadside. "That kid just tried to throw the dog into the wagon."

Elena realized the dull thud was bone hitting the metal tailgate. She felt sick.

Ioannis rolled up his window. The car crawled behind a procession of others, heading away from the monastery. Elena hoped the pace would pick up soon.

34

The motor churned, sending ripples across the surface of the marina. The ripples turned into a swell as the boat pulled away from its mooring and maneuvered out into the bay. Ben stayed on the quayside until the faces of his friends disappeared around the headland towards the lighthouse.

With over an hour until sunset, he gunned the Jeep into life and sped off down the port road as if to perform the impossible and wave to the boat on the other side of the peninsula.

The afternoon had turned out well. After driving Elena home, there'd been a farewell party onboard the yacht. His friends agreed he should stay behind with Elena; they'd hardly even taunted him.

Away from the main square, the airless side streets remained deserted. Ben followed the now familiar route to Nicia's villa, letting his mind wander back one hour, to the chinking of cocktail glasses and a farewell chat with his best friend. Good old Eric, no matter the problem, he always found a positive perspective. A couple of mojitos and Eric's persuasive rhetoric had banished Ben's sullen mood.

If Elena decides to leave—fine.

He would enjoy her company one more time, perhaps the last. Whatever transpires must be memorable. That was his only criteria.

Ben cruised through the town, resolved to make the most of the evening, his spirits high.

Passing the stone house with the pine trees, he turned into Nicia's drive and called Elena. She appeared a minute later wearing the same clothes as earlier; Ben leaned against the hood, as he'd done at noon.

"Déjà vu," he said, opening the passenger door. "I was hoping you wouldn't change."

"Why?"

"I've been thinking about that outfit all day."

She changed the subject. "What did you do this afternoon?"

He told her about the farewell party, exaggerating how everyone had spoken highly of her. As he slipped the Jeep into gear, a white Mercedes pulled alongside. Andreas rolled down his window. "Will you be joining us for dinner again tonight?"

"I don't think so," said Elena. "We're going to the lighthouse to watch the sunset. I told Aunt Nicia I'd be dining out with Ben. Don't wait up for me."

The two cars pulled away.

"I'll be sorry to leave this place," said Elena.

Ben realized she'd intended to convey her fondness for Andreas and Nicia but inadvertently revealed the outcome of her phone call with Greg. He showed no reaction, if she wanted to discuss her decision that was up to her, he wasn't going to broach it.

A few minutes later, they reached the northwestern tip of the Fanari Peninsula and a sharp bend in the road.

"It's over there." Elena pointed to a white structure a hundred yards from the highway then swung her hand to the right. "You can park here."

She hadn't given much warning. Ben swerved onto a strip of dirt bordered by a thicket of giant reeds. He brought the Jeep to a halt, plunging its nose into the rushes with a satisfying rustle. By the time he got round to the passenger side, Elena was already sliding out of the car. Her short skirt reminded him of their moment of passion, parked up under the trees by the abandoned trailer. He wondered what the evening might bring.

***

Barely twenty-five feet high, and smaller than Ben had imagined, the Agioi Theodoro Lighthouse stood at the end of a promontory, reached by a concrete pathway. More akin to a gazebo or folly, the tower sat inside a circle of Doric columns, half its height.

A stiff breeze whipped up as they made their way along the track. Ben thought it strange, for they'd walked less than a hundred yards. Here, the ground covering of vegetation disappeared, replaced by boulders, starkly contrasted in the fading light.

"This place is sort of wild and craggy but peaceful, all at the same time," said Elena.

They stepped inside the Doric columns, circumnavigating the base of the tower. Ben stopped to look at a plaque, inscribed with Greek lettering—perhaps a list of names. Five rusty screws fastened the tablet to the wall.

"Are you warm enough?" he asked.

The temperature around the lighthouse was much cooler than he'd experienced anywhere else on the island.

"Yes, I'm fine."

"I see what you mean about wild and craggy." Ben peered out over the jagged black rocks on the bay side of the building; they had an almost sinister appearance.

"Uncle Andreas told me the promontory is manmade."

"Well they could've used some smoother stones." Ben waved in the direction of Lixouri across the channel. "The sun will set behind those hills. We won't see much from here."

"Just you wait," she replied.

A tall boy, maybe eighteen, wearing a black Nike T-shirt picked his way over the sharp rocks. A beer bottle hung lazily from his hand.

Elena watched the youth's slow progress. "It looks dangerous out there."

"And irresistible," he said. "I'm going to the water's edge. Coming?"

She shook her head and sat down on the only smooth boulder in sight.

Ben trod carefully over the crags and stared out at the dark water, its surface menacing. To the south, the inlet opened into the Ionian Sea; to the north, it stretched into the distance. Elena was right; a wild spirit inhabited the rocky outcrop, yet it was hard to imagine a more peaceful place.

Nearby, a young girl and a man in his fifties gazed out to sea. Like the teenage boy, they clutched beer bottles. Ben assumed them related.

He made his way back to Elena and sat beside her.

"I wanted to ask you about the book, The Ten Thousand Things," she said. "I finished it this afternoon."

"Do you like it?"

"Well, I didn't understand it. At the end, there were all these dead people—ghosts I suppose, and things like sea shells and somehow everything was connected."

He shrugged. "You didn't get it—that makes two of us."

Shadows swept in like a tide. Across the bay, an orange glow shone above the hills.

"I want to understand what it means—what it feels like to be connected to everything." She felt comfortable confiding in him. "I've been thinking about meditating, maybe taking some classes when I get back home."

"You should." Ben ignored her reference to returning home.

"I have friends that swear by it."

The father of the teenage boy made his way gingerly over the rocks towards his son; the young girl remained motionless, staring out over the waves.

"What about you, have you ever tried meditating?" she asked.

"Not yet, I'm saving the transcendental stuff for a rainy day."

"Be serious, don't you strive for anything?"

"I can pretty much have whatever I want … go where I want."

"Isn't there something you want that you can't buy?"

He touched her arm. "Well, I'm interested in you."

"I can be bought," she joked.

Dusk, wild and beautiful, was full upon them. The lights of Lixouri twinkled across the bay. Above the town, the sun had begun its descent behind the hills, creating a deep red glow. Now the distant peninsula itself was changing, assuming a dark, featureless dimension, flat like a charcoal drawing. Over the water, a purple cloak smothered the sky.

"It's a magical place," said Ben.

"Told you so."

Movement, over by the lighthouse, caught his eye. He looked back, through the white Doric columns, where a bald man embraced a younger woman against the tower. Ben hoped they were in love.

Suddenly, he recalled the afternoon cocktail party. "Funny you should mention wanting something you can't buy. I was chatting with Clotilde on the yacht earlier," he paused. "Guess what she wants most, something not even Joe's money can buy?"

"No idea. What?"

"Our French friend got all emotional; it seems she'd pay any price to hear Josephina Grassini sing. Think about it, there were no recordings back then—all that is left of the woman that captivated both Napoleon and Wellington are words describing her magnificent voice."

"Maybe it's better that way. Clotilde can imagine her ancestor in any way she chooses. I see what she means though; just to hear a few notes, just one time…"

They went silent.

The sky, the water, everything was shrouded in shadowy magenta gloom. Ben photographed the ferryboat with its flickering yellow lights, plowing through the waves, on its crossing from Argostoli to Lixouri.

"I didn't tell you about my dream," said Elena.

The pristine beauty, the desolation, the magnificent sky … urged her to reach out and touch Ben.

He held her hand.

"Dream?"

"Yes, this afternoon. I fell asleep after you dropped me off. I dreamt we were in the middle of a meadow, listening…" She paused. "No—you were teaching me to listen … listen to the grass, the flowers … growing. But insects flitted around everywhere, buzzing, distracting me." She paused, unable to convey the emotion clearly. "Then, as though I'd known forever, I became part of the landscape and it part of me. I have never felt more alive … that was when my phone rang … it was Sophia." Bending the truth caused her to delay. "I wanted so much to climb back into the dream, but the moment was lost."

Her words resonated with him.

"I used to do that—when I was younger, not so much now."

"Listen to things grow?"

"Well not exactly; more like sensing than listening. I grew up in a northern climate, where everything springs up fast in the brief summer. That's when you can lie in the middle of a field and feel everything growing around you." He paused to embrace a childhood memory, and with the recollection, his voice assumed a note of sadness. "I haven't done that in years … maybe I wouldn't be able to feel it anymore."

A camera flashed, attracting their attention. The teenage boy had made his way across the rocks to the edge of the treacherous waves. In the purple darkness, he leaned forwards, stretching out his arms like a soaring bird, holding the pose and reaching to the sky. Time after time, his ghostly silhouette found substance in the flash of his father's camera.

"I'll never forget this sunset," said Elena.

"Me neither. It's nearly dark, and yet, I don't want to leave. You know, this is the type of experience that can lead to falling in love." Ben spoke from the heart, unconcerned how she'd react.

"Is that what you're feeling?" Her intonation conveyed no surprise.

"I think so—well, we only just met but let's say I'm on the edge, overlooking the cliff."

"That's dangerous." Her hand squeezed his arm tenderly, but it held a dagger. "You know I'm going home on Wednesday."

"I guess," Ben's attempt to disguise his disappointment failed, making the reply feeble.

The family moved away from the lighthouse leaving Ben and Elena alone.

"Tonight will be our last," she said.

Ben rose, pulling her up by the hand

"So let's make it a special one." He led her across the boulders, back to the tower. The wind gusted through the white columns, Ben pressed Elena against the wall, she didn't resist. With the rhythm of a beating heart, the light from the cupola bounced off the rocks, illuminating their kisses.

35

After leaving the festival, the entourage had stopped for lunch in the monastery village. The journey back was uneventful; Elena slept most of the way, waking just outside the cemetery gates.

The graveyard at Drapano lay two hundred yards north of the old bridge, across the lagoon from Argostoli. Cypresses formed its border and many fine trees grew in the grounds.

Cemeteries fascinated Elena. For her, intrigue lay hidden in every marker, even the humble. Tombs that had fallen into disrepair held the most attraction. These, more than the grandiose, embodied her concept of death. One memorial, close to the Katros monument, inspired her to reach for her camera. Rusted railings bordered the grave, each topped with a decorative iron pinecone. Neglect had left many of the finials missing with only a rusty dowel to mark their passing. Inside their tarnished confine, red and yellow wildflowers strained their heads above the weeds. Some of the flowers, blown by the breeze, kissed the corroded pinecones unconcerned with their decay.

"It's a pretty place," said Nicia. "I like to come here at least twice each year."

"Who maintains the graves?" asked Elena.

"Andreas takes care of everything. I always bring fresh flowers when I visit." Nicia held two bundles of red roses.

"Dad, aren't the two monuments beautiful?" Elena clutched her father's arm.

He stood next to Andreas, in front of two adjacent plots dedicated to the Katros and Matsakis families. Choked up with emotion, Ioannis could utter little more than a murmur of agreement.

Nicia, aware of her brother's grief, sought a distraction and turned to her husband. "Why don't you explain the history of the monuments?"

Andreas moved forward to speak, his back to the Matsakis mausoleum. For the benefit of the children and their American mother, he explained the Greek custom of disinterring the dead two years after burial. "In Greece, we wash the bones with wine and place them in an ossuary."

"That's creepy," said the oldest boy; his mother shushed him.

"The urns are usually kept in church vaults; we keep ours here," Andreas continued. "I bought these plots the year Nicia and I moved back to the island."

A flowering tree grew behind the Matsakis tomb, its lush foliage and red blossom provided stark contrast against the white mausoleum. The main edifice stood chest-high, two carved wreaths decorated the fascia. From the top slab emerged a life-sized marble figure, a woman, her head bowed and veiled. Flowers lay in the crux of an arm; a hand covered her face under the veil. The statue's robe flowed over the flat surface, disappearing behind.

"We relocated both my parents here." Andreas spoke with no trace of sadness. "Father died in the war, mother was interred in Patras after the earthquake."

Elena attempted to read the lettering carved between the

wreaths. She could make out the Greek names and dates but not the sentence above.

"What does the inscription say?" she asked.

"'The only moments that matter are those we remember,'" said Andreas.

Elena thought the sentiment strange, even unsettling. "Whose quote is that?"

"Andreas's grandmother always used to say that," replied Nicia. She stooped, placing a bouquet of red roses in a glass vase at the foot of the Matsakis shrine.

"It was a terrible mess trying to bury the dead after the earthquake," said Andreas. He moved over by the Katros tomb. "Greek custom calls for the body to be buried within twenty-four hours but it was not possible for Stamos."

For the first time that day, Ioannis spoke without being asked a question.

"We had to wait for the rescue teams to take care of the dead. It was two days after the earthquake before we could bury Stamos and Grandmother."

"We thought you didn't remember," said Nicia.

"But I've always remembered everything."

The green iridescent wings of a dragonfly caught Elena's eye, distracting her just at the moment of her father's admission. The creature hovered over the Katros monument as if revealing a secret.

Kneeling behind his tomb, the white figure of a boy, in a hooded robe, buried his head into folded arms on top of the flat marble shrine.

Just like a schoolboy asleep on his desk, thought Elena.

Nicia placed the remaining bouquet in a receptacle, mid-way in the fascia. The uppermost petals partially covered an epitaph carved into the shrine.

"What does it say?" asked Elena.

Ioannis read the message, his voice strong with a hint of pride. "'For the brother that we had.'"

More than the sermon at the plane tree, more than the saint passing over Ioannis, this was the defining moment for Elena. The moment she witnessed her father, accepting his brother's death and embracing his memory.

She photographed the beautiful tombs, recording every detail, until Nicia tapped her on the shoulder, motioning her to leave. As she walked away, she took one last shot of her father, standing alone by his brother's grave.

The only moments that matter are those we remember. She never knew Stamos, Ioannis held those memories. Someday, she might stand by the Katros mausoleum again, honoring her father, and count the moments that mattered. This day held many, of that she was certain.

36

Ben and Elena left the lighthouse, heading back towards Nicia's villa. Without streetlights, bends seemed to appear out of nowhere on the narrow lane.

"Do you need to change before dinner?" asked Ben.

Elena's hair blew back in the balmy night air. "Not unless you want me to."

He took his eyes off the road, stealing a glance at her. "You look great."

"I freshened up earlier, so let's go; I'm yours for the evening."

"Any restaurant recommendations? Our last night should be somewhere special."

"Our last night is going to be special but I don't want to eat at a fancy place," she replied. "I'd prefer plain and simple. Drive past the house, then turn right at the junction, there are plenty of tavernas. It's outside Argostoli and touristy but…"

"Sounds okay to me."

"Hey, that was Nik's car." Elena leaned over the door and looked back. "He must be on his way to see Sophia."

"Nik was quiet last night, is he always like that?"

"Sophia says he's shy, until you get to know him. She's serious about their relationship."

"Sophia seems to know what she wants."

"She does. I think you just have to make a commitment and stick to it." After a moment of self-reflection, she added. "That's what Sophia keeps saying."

Colorful beach gear hung from racks under the white canopy of a market at the corner of the intersection.

"Left or right?" asked Ben.

"Right; this is Lassi. Drive a little further, there's curbside parking."

Lassi wasn't more than three quarters of a mile long. Restaurants, small hotels and car rental businesses lined its one main street. Ben drove until Elena spotted a row of quaint tavernas; he pulled in to the curb.

"The food will be similar wherever we choose," she said. "Well, apart from that Chinese place."

"Pick any. I don't mind."

"Somewhere up here," she pointed at the hills above the town, "is the cave where Saint Gerasimos lived when he arrived in Kefalonia—he's the patron saint of the island, by the way."

"A taxi driver told me the story of the mummified saint."

"Did I tell you, I'm only here because my dad came to attend the big festival; it's held every August in honor of Saint Gerasimos."

"You mentioned your father, but I don't remember a festival."

Restaurants vied for the steady flow of tourists promenading up and down the sidewalk. Tent boards, chalked-up with specials, stood outside every building. Ben stopped to browse a menu displayed in a glass case. "How about this one?"

"Why not, let's see how nice their patio is."

A middle-aged man greeted them at the top of an elevated entrance. His manner, relaxed and friendly, suggested a family owned restaurant. Ben liked the atmosphere of the place. Romantically lit, and tiled with a lavender hued stone, the outdoor terrace had charm in abundance.

"For two?" The man motioned to a crowded section, overlooking the street.

"How about over there, by the fountain?" Ben pointed in the opposite direction. "It's more secluded."

"Much nicer," said Elena.

"Americans?" asked the owner.

"Yes," said Ben.

They chose a table under a wooden lattice, covered in vines, forming a green roof above their heads.

Elena ordered a piña colada. Ben asked for a mojito—he was out of luck.

"Then just make me a rum cocktail." It was too much to hope for a repeat of Spiro's fine concoction at the Hotel Dionysius.

The man smiled, nodded and left.

Elena smiled too, she was also thinking of Spiro's nameless drink and the night that followed. She looked up at the canopy of leaves, "I'm glad we chose this place, it's nice here."

Dressed in shorts and a short-sleeved shirt, Ben was sublimely relaxed. The night air, dense and warm, seemed to hug his skin, at times making him conscious of its existence.

"You're still a mystery to me," said Elena. "Tonight, I want to learn what makes Ben Anderson tick."

"I hope you won't be disappointed."

"How about you?" she continued. "What do you want to talk about?"

"About you, what makes you tick." He thought his reply a little unimaginative but didn't care, as long as the topic wasn't Boston and her boyfriend. "Oh, your father and the saint ... you were telling me about the saint."

She curled her fingers, looking at her nails, and began the story of the 1953 earthquake…

"But he was just a kid," said Ben. "How come he blames himself?"

"Who knows … he was only nine, paralyzed, in the middle of one of the worst earthquakes ever," she paused. "And Saint Gerasimos is a big deal here, even more so back in the fifties. It's not such a stretch to imagine a child believing his prayers had been answered."

"Yeah, I understand, but why the guilt?"

"I think he believes that if he'd prayed for Stamos then Stamos would have been spared too."

"And that's been eating at him all these years?"

"Yes, I mean, not like driving him crazy or anything—and it was half a century ago, but he wanted to come back and ask the saint for forgiveness. Closure is how we'd think of it today."

"And did he?"

"Yes, he did. He even visited his brother's grave—which was beautiful—both the grave and the visit," she paused. "You've heard about the miracles attributed to the saint?"

"No."

The owner reappeared with a basket of bread. A second, younger man carried a drinks tray. Ben tasted his cocktail.

"Man, that's good … what's with these Greeks and rum cocktails?"

Clearly, the host didn't understand the remark, but he smiled at the obvious compliment and asked for their order. Ben extended his palm towards Elena who shook her head. "Can we have a minute?"

The two men left and Elena picked up the festival story…

"Did you see him?" asked Ben.

"Who, Saint Gerasimos? Sure, they paraded him around in a glass coffin. Then everyone lined up to kiss his feet."

"You're kidding."

"Well not exactly, I sort of leaned inside the casket and bowed … ceremoniously."

The proprietor returned. Ben suggested a few appetizers; Elena nodded.

"Oh and a bottle of…" Ben pointed to the most expensive wine on list, an Agiorgitiko. The owner thanked them and walked away.

"They only serve Greek wines, but they're very inexpensive. I hope it's decent." Ben switched back to the earlier topic. "You didn't tell me what the mummy looked like."

Elena described the surreal, almost chilling, close-up encounter with the four-hundred-year-old saint.

"It was a very emotional experience—heaven knows what my dad felt."

"That's a great story."

"Can you imagine? Saint Gerasimos lived in a cave, right here, in the hills above this restaurant." She looked up at the pergola, as though to see through the vines.

"I guess he enjoyed meditating." He was only half joking.

A young girl in a blue dress jumped off her seat at a nearby table and ran to the fountain. Ben's eyes followed the girl, who scrambled on top of the mosaic-tiled wall and stood, like a princess, surveying her subjects. He lost the thread of Elena's conversation … he heard her repeat the word 'meditation', he caught 'Zen' and 'spirituality', but was further distracted by an old lady, perhaps the young girl's grandmother, chasing the child around the fountain wall, trying to coax her down.

"I'm sorry," said Ben. The drama with the young girl was happening behind Elena.

"You weren't listening, were you?" She slapped the back of his hand.

To avoid being caught out, Ben summarized, merely guessing the context. "We were talking about Gerasimos and meditating …

that led to the subject of your own spirituality and so to Zen—was I right?"

"Well, this whole trip's been quite a revelation for me." She turned around to see what was distracting him. "Come on then, spill the beans." She waited for him to continue—he appeared bemused. "What's with all this Cypress Garden, crows, listening to grass, then?"

"I never mentioned listening to grass—that was in your dream, I believe."

He tipped his glass vertical, draining the last drop of rum cocktail. Pieces of ice shifted, spilling drink down the side of his mouth, wetting his shirt; they both grinned.

"You promised me … in the Cypress Garden," she insisted.

Her words brought the brevity of their relationship into context.

Was it only yesterday, we lay on the grass in the garden of the Hotel Dionysius.

He continued, "I have vays of making you tock; that's what you said."

"See, you remembered."

Tired of chasing the young girl around the fountain, the grandmother went back to her table and enlisted the help of the father who, at the insistence of his wife, got up to retrieve his daughter. Pulling a camera out his pocket, he crouched low, taking a picture of his princess, before whisking her high into the air. The girl giggled, basking in her father's attention.

"What the hell's going on back there?" Elena turned round.

"I'm thinking what vay you have in mind for making me tock," said Ben.

She smiled, smug in the knowledge that she could make him sing like a canary at will. He knew it too.

Engrossed once more in their own world, Ben and Elena chatted, oblivious, as two waiters materialized. One setup a retractable stand, the other lowered his tray on top and arranged dishes on the table. While they served, the owner arrived, carrying a wine bottle in a wicker holder. He presented the label to Ben, who nodded without reading it.

"Have you noticed how good the tomatoes taste?" Ben passed the plate of Greek salad to Elena.

The proprietor poured a tasting of wine into Ben's glass, Elena helped herself to the salad.

"What do you think they sprinkle on the feta cheese?" she asked.

"Fine," said Ben, glancing quickly at the owner. "I think it's oregano—you're the one who's supposed to be Greek."

The host finished the pour, setting the bottle on the table. "Would you like to order entrees?"

"Not yet, we'll order later." Elena stared into Ben's eyes, giving him that look, the look he'd come to associate with pleasure.

Soothing music played in the background, his mystery cocktail was strong. He looked around, committing the scene to memory; the fountain, the vines, the girl with the blue dress, the curiously shaped bottle on his table, holding the flickering candle. Tonight was going to be a night for storing memories.

"Why do you think I know anything about eastern philosophy?" he asked.

Elena didn't answer. Ben wondered how to proceed, wary of treading on her beliefs and spoiling the evening. Her notion that everything happens for a reason held absolutely no meaning for him.

Maybe something I say will make her change her mind about leaving on Wednesday. If so, I've no idea what.

Elena held an unusual attraction for him, strangely sensual, yet familiar like his car or wallet. Each hour he spent with her, the more entangled he became—an addict, powerless to resist. How he was going to miss her! Not for the first time, the word obsession formed uncomfortably in his mind. This was the moment where the neurotic in him began its rhetoric, trying to ruin his last evening.

"How's the wine?" he asked.

"Keep it flowing."

"Are you coming back to the hotel later?"

"It wouldn't be much of a last night if I didn't," she replied. "Where were we, crows and karma wasn't it?"

Ben was already on his second glass of wine. He looked across at the luscious cleavage showing between the purple spandex of her halter-top and prepared to sing for his supper.

"I'm sorry but I just don't get it—karma I mean." He spoke in his most sympathetic manner. "I'm not closed to any particular idea, but you have to make some pretty staggering assumptions."

"Such as?"

"Past lives for one, the existence of a soul ... a soul that is ... conveniently undetectable, those kinds of things."

He waited, nervously, for her reaction, hoping he hadn't gone too far.

"It doesn't have to be past lives, you can apply the principle to your current life too."

"Like reaping what you sow?"

"Exactly."

"Well, as with any supposition that can't be tested, you either believe it or not. Whatever makes you happy, I say."

"Yes, I believe in Karma and, yes, I want it to be true," she paused. "So, if you need evidence, or proof of everything, how do you ever find any meaning in life?"

"Maybe we can find common ground with Zen—isn't that where you reach awareness from within, without rituals and such?"

"And you've done that?"

"To a degree," he said. "I guess you could say that."

"Is it spiritual?"

"In a secular way … there aren't any actual spirits involved."

Ben poured another glass of Agiorgitiko and caught the owner's attention, waving him over. "We'd better order entrees. Are you still hungry?"

"Yes, I know what I want," she replied.

The proprietor took their orders; Ben tilted the wine bottle indicating another. "Oh, and more water please."

"You still haven't explained your interpretation of Zen yet, that's what I wanted to hear," said Elena.

"You can't define Zen; it's self-realization."

"You're cheating," she said. "Stop holding out on me."

"Okay, but after cocktails and a couple of glasses of wine, I'll start rambling," he paused. "How to describe the connectedness, that's what you wanted, right?"

"Right."

"Imagine yourself in a place," he continued. "It could be somewhere familiar, a woodland glade, a trout stream or somewhere magnificent like the Sahara, under a full moon with millions of stars."

"I'll go with the Sahara."

"Good choice." Ben paused, setting down his fork. "The desert reminds me of a passage in a short story. The author describes a man sitting motionless for hours, staring out from a hill over an oasis of palms. 'We'll never understand what he's doing,' the writer says. 'He's not meditating or contemplating philosophy; rather, he is enjoying the act of existing.'"

"And that's why we are all connected?" she asked.

"That's one way of looking at it. Most indigenous cultures believed their land itself to be alive, rather than full of individual living beings. I believe, as a species, we are predisposed to think this way, but in the West, we repress this notion and so a forest has no intrinsic value unless it can be exploited for our own needs. I can't help thinking that the earth itself, if viewed from space, must be considered to be alive."

"So we're all part of one Great Spirit?"

"You could call living organisms the Great Spirit. Life is a never-ending pattern, each being playing its part to make a whole. The owl last night, the olive trees, the grass, a worm, a spider—they're all connected … but together they make, say, an olive orchard; a piece of natural art. When he enjoys the act of existing, perhaps the Bedouin sees his landscape as an art form."

The entrees arrived causing Ben's focus to drift back down to the table. In vino veritas. He realized he'd been babbling on without regard for Elena. The waiter opened the second bottle, pouring more of the red liquid into his glass.

"So, as I was saying, you can sit in a meadow or a forest or wherever and feel everything growing … existing around you. It's not that different from meditating," said Ben.

"Not everyone is tuned in to that."

"Tuning in is a good analogy. We've got careers, credit card payments, mortgages, kids' college funds. It's difficult, perhaps impossible, to filter out their noise. A few months back, I made an investment in a wireless company. I talked to one of the engineers, he told me building a transmitter is easy, all the magic's in the receiver."

"I think Nicia has the magic. I wish I had it too." Elena pushed her plate away, resting an elbow on the table. "I understand what you're saying, and to an extent I agree, but what's the point of it all?"

Ben saw danger in replying. He understood it might work against him but couldn't turn back.

"Ah, the why question," he said. "There are two types of people, those who absolutely have to have a meaning and those that don't … and there's no bridging the two. I'm thinking you can't conceive of your existence without there being a reason."

"You're right, one hundred percent right. It's simply a nonstarter for me to think that life has no purpose," she said.

Elena appeared to be enjoying the conversation, Ben thought it safe to continue.

"So that's the great argument of the theologians."

"What is?"

"Science can explain how, but not why."

"Right," she said. "You can't ... it can't."

"There isn't a why ... so no explanation is needed," he continued. "In fact, I'm the exact opposite, I can't conceive of there being a why."

"There has to be a point to it all. That's why I believe in karma."

"But the people that came up with karma and reincarnation were missing ... ah, some key information."

"Like what?"

"Let's say I was born—what, four hundred years ago. I'd possess relatively little understanding of life and the world around me. Take biology, for example, the cell wasn't discovered until the seventeenth century, evolution wouldn't be described for two hundred and fifty years, DNA three hundred and fifty. The concept of molecular biology would be impossible to explain to all but a few geniuses; you'd probably be arrested for trying. Send me back to that time and show me a forest with all its wonder and I wouldn't have a clue how it got there. What could I do; kill a deer, dissect it? I'd be even more baffled by what lay inside. No doubt, I'd happily accept whatever mumbo jumbo any monk in a robe had on offer."

"I never thought like that before," she said.

Ben had tired of philosophy—and it might be his last night with Elena. Nothing he'd said tonight would alter her decision to leave Kefalonia, quite the opposite. Better to change the subject now, before the noose tightened further, and concentrate on enjoying himself.

"Hey, this isn't fair!" he said. "It's our last night together—you asked me to tock, so I tocked. Did I give the correct answer?"

"Yes, I think I understand you better now."

Ben studied Elena for clues, trying to decipher her vague reply. Had she connected with his viewpoint or had he painted a picture of himself as shallow and empty? For the first time, Ben tried to see himself through her eyes, the wealth, the yacht, the lack of a career, his meaningless philosophy. He probably did not compare well to the man waiting for her in Boston.

He needed to figure a way out of his dilemma.

"Did you like my do-it-yourself Zen? Maybe you can create your own flavor; take a pinch of mine, a sprig of karma and voila!"

"That's exactly what I'm going to do." Elena spoke figuratively. Certainly, she would use his aimless rationalism to justify her decision to return home.

Ben gulped down a glass of water, hoping to counter the effects of the wine. The second bottle of Agiorgitiko was half-empty. If only he could clear his head, stick to the original plan and just enjoy the evening. Maybe it was the drink; maybe, now dinner was almost over, the reality of no more Elena had sunk in; maybe it was time to change strategy, to talk her into staying.

"I know you said this is our last night but it doesn't have to be." He spoke with what little confidence he could muster.

The wine made him feel hot and sticky; he looked at Elena, dreading to detect pity in her glance. She did not speak.

"We could stay here; go to Italy, Paris, anywhere."

"Ben, my mind's made up; I'm going home on Wednesday."

There wasn't a trace of doubt in her voice.

"Well just for the record, I want you to stay." He failed to mask his disappointment.

So emphatic was her answer that Ben had no option but to let the matter drop. A twinge of self-doubt stabbed at him for losing out to the unknown boyfriend.

"You're sweet," she said.

Ben didn't want to be sweet; his mind was stuck in a moment in time, a moment when a girl in an olive colored dress stood pondering a mysterious problem near his table at a quayside restaurant, triggering something inside him.

Ben thought about saying goodbye immediately after dinner, forgoing the hotel. The love chemicals were flowing in torrents; what names had Eric given them? If he said goodbye now, damming the stream might be easier.

The delicious shape of Elena consumed him; thoughts of finding a replacement scared him. He dismissed all thoughts of an early night.

"Let's order coffee … and ouzo," he said, resolving to get back on track. Wednesday's three days away, anything can happen.

"I wouldn't mind a cappuccino," said Elena then excused herself and went to the restroom.

Over the course of dinner, she had taken on a new identity, that of a goddess. He watched her glide along the stone tiled floor, legs perfectly revealed in her short white skirt. Ben wallowed in his own obsession.

The restaurant had emptied without him noticing, the chatter of diners replaced by crickets, singing their endless song in the trees behind. Not for the first time the sound of the island captivated him; now its soothing rhythms assuaged the torment of his rejection. By the time Elena returned, Ben was, once again, the man of the Hotel Dionysius.

Catching the waiter's eye, he mimicked signing the check then knocked back his ouzo. "What's going to be your favorite memory of Kefalonia?"

She placed her elbow on the table, resting her chin on her palm. "There's so many, it's hard to say. The festival with my dad … meeting you, the lighthouse, last night in the olive orchard, the yacht…" Elena elected not to include the morning at Dimi's. "How about you?"

"Where to start—meeting you in Fiskardo; the night at the hotel, the owl ... right now."

Elena smiled, satisfied that her impulse to stay on the island had worked out so well.

I wouldn't have missed it for the world, she thought.

"Shall we?" he asked, adding a handsome tip to the bill.

Ben ambled across the stone floor of the now-silent restaurant, a step behind Elena; the empty tables echoed his sadness at their imminent parting; he reminded himself again not to care.

"My room overlooks the harbor; it's really pretty at night," he said.

They walked arm-in-arm back to the Jeep.

"Do you have a view of the bridge?" she asked suddenly.

"Yeah—it's kind of dark though—but there's an obelisk nearby, in the center of the lagoon, it's all lit up at night. Do you want to take a walk? I'd like to see the town from out on the water."

He opened the passenger door, pleased with his suggestion. A late night stroll along the bridge would prolong the dreaded moment of Elena's goodbye; perhaps some magic might occur out in the lagoon.

"I'd like that," she said. "I've seen the bridge in the distance a few times but haven't been there yet. This will be my last chance."

The air, redolent with summer, swirled around the windshield, eddying into their faces. Elena's arm hung out of the window, her hand floating through the night like driftwood on waves. The Jeep streaked back to Argostoli.

Minutes later they reached the outskirts of town and turned right, descending towards the lagoon at the southern end of the harbor. Elena remained quiet until Ben stopped the car by the promenade.

"You okay?" he asked, noticing her silence.

"Yes, I was just thinking how perfect the evening has been. I hardly want to risk speaking and spoil it."

Relaxed and sedated by the wine, Ben agreed. "I know what you mean."

Elena was first out of the Jeep and stood admiring a line of newly planted palms. Spaced a few yards apart, they formed a boundary between the sidewalk and the recently restored promenade. The stems of the young trees didn't reach higher than her midriff. She ran her finger across the angled cuts where last year's leaves had been removed. "I wonder if they're some dwarf variety. If we come back here when we're old, will they be fifty feet high?"

Ben joined her. "I'll be grey-haired way before you, so maybe only thirty or forty feet."

"Do you think I'm too young for you?"

"You're perfect. You know the formula, right?"

"Formula?"

"Yes, a man should look for a girl who is half his age plus seven."

Elena made calculations testing his theory as they stepped on to the old stone bridge. The obelisk stood out like a beacon in the center of the lagoon a quarter of a mile away.

"I wonder why the bridge doesn't follow a straight line," said Ben. "Do you know its history?"

The old structure zigzagged across the inlet, heading first to the obelisk, before changing direction to the opposite shore.

"Sophia told me the British built it in the early nineteenth century, it's called Drapano Bridge … Drapano is the place on the other side—that's where the cemetery is."

Closed to traffic, the old bridge was a peaceful sanctuary at night. Gentle waves lapped against the walls a few feet below. They reached the obelisk without meeting another person.

"Oh what a pity—you can't get to it," said Elena.

The stone edifice wasn't part of the bridge but built on a concrete raft in the bay.

"I think it has more effect, just floating on top of the water."

He reached for his camera. "Come on, model for me."

Elena posed, dreamlike, before the incandescent floating column; the lights of the harbor twinkled behind her. His camera flashed, and flashed again, as Ben shifted angles.

***

The flashes stopped, Elena's eyes adjusted to the night, to the stars above the dark hills of the opposite shore; above the cemetery, above the tomb of Stamos.

"Sit on the wall," he said.

Ben took more pictures, getting down on one knee, moving closer; Elena's toes pointed downwards, barely touching the floor, enhancing the elegant shape of her legs.

"I don't want you to leave," he whispered.

***

The faint light of a bicycle coming towards her from the Drapano side distracted Elena, she thought of Dimi, how he might paint her.

"Shall we go," she said.

37

An insistent, heavy knock rapped on the hotel room door. The sound barely carried through the spacious suite and onto the balcony outside. The knock repeated, louder this time.

"That'll be room service," said Elena.

She leant against the balcony rail, overlooking the lagoon. Ben walked across the bedroom, switched on the lights, and opened the door. A waiter, in formal white dress, entered carrying two cocktails on a silver tray.

"Just put it down there." Ben tipped the man with a five Euro bill.

The waiter nodded and left. Ben turned off the main lights, returning the room to a faint orange glow.

"One last cocktail … a perfect end to a perfect evening," He handed a drink to Elena; their glasses chinked.

She skimmed the surface with her lips, letting the clear liquid run over her tongue. Such a fiery taste was at odds with the cold frosted-feel of the martini glass. This notion always delighted her.

Across the lagoon, a thousand stars shone above the mountains of Kefalonia.

"You're right, it's a pretty view." Elena watched the car headlights following the bends along the road to Fiskardo.

"Unforgettable..." Ben waved his hand in the direction of Drapano Bridge. "The obelisk looks like a candle, floating on the dark lagoon."

The twinkling panorama was a picture postcard memory for Elena, a fitting souvenir of their ephemeral passion. What an excellent decision she had made, extending her stay on the island; so many secrets stored for the future. Things had worked out well.

Stepping into the room, she placed her martini on the table next to the bed. Ben stood outside and watched her turn towards him, holding out her hand in the dim light.

He stepped inside and reached for her; Elena unhooked the fastener of her halter-top, clutching the two ends with her right hand. They held each other, in the darkness, their eyes inches apart, delighting in the moment.

"Thank you for everything," she whispered.

A single teardrop formed in the outer corner of her right eye, she could feel it growing larger, ready to fall. Elena tilted her head back, but it was too late, the tear slowly made its glistening way down her cheek. Ben traced its arc until it dissolved into her skin, its tracks forever etched into his heart.

Funny how he'd woke this morning, restless and troubled, thinking about Elena; tomorrow would be the same, and the day after. For a moment, he imagined the love chemicals gushing like geysers inside his brain, raging beyond his control. Even if he possessed the will, it was too late to close the floodgates. Ben vowed to find a way, any way, to make her stay.

38

Ioannis sat outside at a large oak table under the shade of a cluster of pines. Far out to sea, the early evening sun cast its still powerful glare over the land. Through the branches, smoldering red sunlight created patterns on the table. Beyond the pines, an olive grove sloped down towards the phosphorescent bay of Argostoli.

"Where did everybody go?" asked Nicia.

"They took the kids to Makris Gialos Beach. I don't know when they'll be back," replied Elena. She closed her eyes, tired from the day's events, the festival of Saint Gerasimos, the visit to Drapano Cemetery. "I'll call Mom if you like."

"Don't bother them," said Andreas. "They'll come back when they're ready."

With an eternal persistence, the cicadas' rasping calls permeated the air; loud and vociferous from the pine branches above, softer, more melodic from the distant orchard beyond.

Ioannis sipped a cold beer, his second. "When I saw the inscription on the tomb, I thought only of myself," he said.

"What do you mean?" asked Nicia.

"For the brother that we had," said Ioannis, repeating the epitaph. "I didn't think about you, but Stamos was your brother too, and yours, Andreas. You were always like a brother to me—now you are a true brother through marriage."

Elena looked at Nicia; she'd never heard her father mention Stamos by name.

"What I said was true," Ioannis continued. "I remember everything about that day; the sound of the insects in the garden, Stamos calling me to play, the wooden water barrel. It wasn't my fault."

"Of course it wasn't," said Nicia. "How can you think that?"

"I betrayed Stamos," said Ioannis.

"Dad," said Elena; she could tell he was close to tears.

"If only I had prayed for him like I prayed for myself. Saint Gerasimos might have intervened and spared him. I've never been able to forgive myself. I was selfish, concerned only for my own safety."

"Nobody blames you," said his sister.

Elena had never heard her father open up like this before; she doubted whether anyone had.

"I waited for what seemed like an eternity until the rescue party arrived. Saint Gerasimos was by my side, talking with me— he told me stories from his childhood; his icon was on the floor a few feet from my face. Finally, men appeared, they asked me who was in the house. I told them—Grandma's right here and Stamos outside. Only then did I realize Stamos wasn't there, that he hadn't come to help me." Ioannis paused, choked up by the memory, "I heard the men in the garden—I heard a man shouting, 'The boy is dead'."

Nicia poured herself another coffee, "Father told us they took you to a temporary hospital."

"They carried me across the street. I remember hearing Father's voice—he stood over me but I daren't tell him what I'd done."

"Why did you never tell us what you were going through?" Nicia asked.

Ioannis took another sip of beer.

"After I woke the next morning, I thought I'd die from grief. I couldn't think of anything but my shame. The day after was the same; losing Stamos was just too much to bear," he paused, bracing himself to continue. "I suppose there's some kind of safety mechanism built into all of us, especially the very young.

One morning, at the farm, two or three days after the earthquake, I remember waking up to the dawn. I sneaked out of the tent and climbed up into the oak tree; the climb was difficult, my leg hurt. I finally made it to the branch where I'd watched the sunrise the day before the big quake. The roosters were still there to greet the sun, the crows too."

He stopped again, seeking the right words. "I don't know—something snapped inside, the pain must have been intolerable. I … I buried Stamos again, in some vault, deep in within. Just as though I'd flicked a switch, the misery melted away at that moment, at sunrise, in Father's tree, replaced by emptiness, emptiness free from pain. I've been keeping Stamos locked away ever since."

Nicia put her hand on her brother's arm, "Little Yanni."

Ioannis smiled at his sister.

A pale scrawny cat stretched out on the steps underneath the courtyard gate, sparking a memory in Ioannis. "Yanni, the cat scratched me; I just wanted to help it. Do you remember, Nicia?"

"Like it was yesterday," replied Nicia.

"Andreas, I don't know how to thank you enough for everything. The memorials at the cemetery are truly special. I'll go back to the States tomorrow with a happy heart."

"There's no need to thank me, we're family."

Elena thought of the photographs she had taken of the tombs, of the strength of the family around her.

"Why did you decide to finally come home?" Andreas asked.

"I started to have flashbacks of the earthquake," said Ioannis, "and dreams…"

Elena was surprised at her father's newfound openness.

"About three months ago, I started having sickening dreams. One night, I woke up in a sweat from the most terrible nightmare."

"About the earthquake?" asked Nicia.

Ioannis didn't reply to the question; he continued to recall his dream, speaking as if in a trance.

"I was in an abandoned factory or maybe a warehouse. It was daytime, yet quite dark; the windows small and far away. I stood looking down into a pit, the kind they use to inspect cars, only it wasn't so deep—like the distance from a train platform to the tracks. A young boy, a child, knelt in the pit, partially buried in sand, his hands tied behind his back."

The recitation of the dream disturbed Elena; she didn't want to hear anymore.

"Somehow, I was both the man above and the boy below. I could experience both their feelings. The dream was very real. I started to shovel sand from a large pile into the pit, on top of the bound figure. The boy began pleading for his life. He had trusted me; I felt his shock, his sense of injustice as though I were he. To silence his cries, or hide my shame, I pulled a…" Ioannis stumbled for words, "some … thing from my coat pocket and jumped into the pit, next to the boy."

Everyone looked on speechless.

"Like an executioner, I placed this … thing over his head, blindfolding and muzzling him. Even though silenced, I could still hear his pleas. The dream was so real, so clear…"

The people around the table remained silent; Ioannis held his head in his hands.

The silence became uncomfortable. Somewhere in the olive orchard, a crow called out, breaking the spell; Andreas finally spoke.

"Do you think the boy in the dream represented Stamos?"

"No," replied Ioannis, "I think the dreams were a reminder, a reminder that I'm getting old," he paused. "Shutting out the memory of Stamos was always going to come back and haunt me … the dreams told me it's time to face up to the past."

"What happened at the festival? You hardly said a word," said Nicia.

"What is there to say after more than fifty years," said Ioannis. "I'm not an eloquent man, all I can say is that thanks to your love—all your love, and the love of the Saint, I go home tomorrow with my heart at peace."

"That's all that matters," said Nicia.

"For the second time in my life, the Saint talked to me," said Ioannis. "Remember the sermon—at the plane tree? The Metropolitan said… We aren't carrying Gerasimos out; he comes forth, lighting up the valley with his presence… At the plane tree, I could feel his spirit in the leaves of the trees; the call of the insects, the song of the birds. I could feel him in the vines, growing in the fields over the monastery wall. He gave back my childhood.

That was what he said to me."